What _____ Are Saying about Laura V. Hilton and
Surrendered Love…

Laura's Amish fiction stands above the crowd, offering far
more than romance without any cookie-cutter characters.
Surrendered Love deftly explores the painful consequences of
self-loathing, the freedom in forgiveness, and the sometimes
sacrificial cost of love. You will not be disappointed.

—*Carole Towriss*
Author, *In the Shadow of Sinai*

No one can write a story that keeps me guessing like Laura
Hilton. Romance, choices, forgiveness—*Surrendered Love*
has it all.

—*Tanya Eavenson*
Author, *Unconditional*

Surrendered Love takes a novel's sojourn to observe emotional
and intellectual struggles of an Amish girl and an ex-Amish
cop who must come to a decision regarding steadfastness
to the Ordnung. Laura V. Hilton writes with the Amish
romantic sweetness of apple butter daubed on a baking-soda
biscuit.

Columnist, Angelkeep Jo_____ *y*
Author, *Th_____l*

Laura Hilton has done it once more! When you think the tale
never changes, she brings a story that is different from any
other Amish romance you will ever read. *Surrendered Love* is
a beautiful story that shows God's forgiveness and mercy are
always there, even when we choose to run away from Him.

—*Cindy Loven*
Book reviewer, cindylovenreviews.blogspot.com

With deep characterizations, sweet romance, enough mystery to keep you flipping the pages, and secondary characters who truly make you care, *Surrendered Love* propelled me forward, captivating me to the end.

—Miralee Ferrell
Author, *Love Finds You in Sundance, Wyoming*

Laura Hilton drew me in from the first sentence of *Surrendered Love*. She creates living, breathing characters you can't help but care about, throws them into suspense-filled dilemmas that keep you reading to see how they can possibly work it all out, and seasons it all with just the right touch of gentle humor. Troy and Janna's story made me rethink my opinion of Amish fiction.

—Laura McClellan
Speaker and author, www.laura-mcclellan.com

I fell in love with Janna and Troy's story. They have a struggle that seems impossible to surpass. A terrible secret, a troubled teenager, and the possibility of a shunning make this Amish tale a heartfelt read.

—Diana Lesire Brandmeyer
Author, *Mind of Her Own* and *A Bride's Dilemma in Friendship, Tennessee*

Breathtaking, remarkable, and unpredictable Amish fiction! Laura V. Hilton creates a poignant Amish tale of forbidden love, tragedy, and shocking revelations in this heart-throbbing Christian narrative. *Surrendered Love* reveals a previously unspoken attraction between the bishop's daughter and a young, formerly Amish, policeman that threatens verboden passion as they seek God's leading in love and through disaster.

—Nancee Marchinowski
Book reviewer

Surrendered Love

Surrendered Love

The Amish of
Webster County

LAURA V.
HILTON

w

WHITAKER
HOUSE

Publisher's Note:
This novel is a work of fiction. References to real events, organizations, or places are used in a fictional context. Any resemblances to actual persons, living or dead, are entirely coincidental.

All Scripture quotations are taken from the King James Version of the Holy Bible.

SURRENDERED LOVE
The Amish of Webster County ~ Book Two

Laura V. Hilton
http://lighthouse-academy.blogspot.com/

ISBN: 978-1-60374-507-9
eBook ISBN: 978-1-60374-731-8
Printed in the United States of America
© 2013 by Laura V. Hilton

Whitaker House
1030 Hunt Valley Circle
New Kensington, PA 15068
www.whitakerhouse.com

Library of Congress Cataloging-in-Publication Data (Pending)

1 2 3 4 5 6 7 8 9 10 11 **UJ** 20 19 18 17 16 15 14 13

Dedication

In memory of my parents, Allan and Janice; my uncle Loundy; and my grandmother Mertie, who talked about their Pennsylvania Amish heritage.

Acknowledgments

I'd like to offer my heartfelt thanks to the following:

The residents of Seymour, Missouri, for answering my questions and pointing me in the right directions.

Jim Hinson, retired police officer, for answering general police questions and giving me quotes, as well as the Chief of Police in Seymour, Missouri, for answering questions related to the bear and the horse running into a vehicle and tipping over—two events that really happened, but with the horse, some creative license was applied as to the characters and the type of vehicle it hit.

Aunt Jean, for keeping me up-to-date with events in Seymour.

Andrew and Mihir, for providing physical therapy advice. And Mom, whom I watched and learned from when she was undergoing her own physical therapy.

Stephanie Whitson, for information regarding gunshot wounds.

Steve, for medical help required.

The amazing team at Whitaker House—Christine, Courtney, and Cathy. You are wonderful.

Tamela, my agent, for believing in me all these years.

My critique group—you know who you are. You are amazing and knew how to ask the right questions when more detail was needed. Also thanks for the encouragement.

Candee and Therese, thanks for reading large amounts in a short time and offering wise suggestions.

My husband, Steve, for being a tireless proofreader and cheering section.

My sons, Michael and Loundy, for taking over kitchen duties when I was deep in the story, and Kristin, for help with household chores.

To God be the glory.

Glossary of Amish Terms and Phrases

ach	oh
aent(i)	aunt(ie)
"Ain't so?"	a phrase commonly used at the end of a sentence to invite agreement
banns	public announcement in church of a proposed marriage
boppli	baby or babies
bu	boy
buwe	boys
daed	dad
danki	thank you
dawdi-haus	a home built for grandparents to live in once they retire
dochter	daughter
dummchen	a ninny; a silly person
ehemann	husband
Englisch	non-Amish
Englischer	a non-Amish person
frau	wife
großeltern	grandparents
grossdaedi	grandfather
grossmammi	grandmother
gut	good
"Gut morgen"	"Good morning"
"Gut nacht"	"Good night"
haus	house
hinnersich	backward
"Ich liebe dich"	"I love you"

jah	yes
kapp	prayer covering or cap
kinner	children
kum	come
maidal	an unmarried woman
mamm	mom
maud	maid/housekeeper
nein	no
naerfich	nervous
onkel	uncle
Ordnung	the rules by which an Amish community lives
Pennsylvania Deitsch	Pennsylvania Dutch/Pennsylvania German, the language used most commonly by the Amish
rumschpringe	"running around time," a period of adolescence after which Amish teens choose either to be baptized in the Amish church or to leave the community
ser gut	very good
sohn	son
verboden	forbidden
"Was ist letz?"	"What is it?"
welkum	welcome

Chapter 1

The police officer sorting though the Gala apples reminded Janna Kauffman of Hiram Troyer, but this Englischer couldn't be her teenage crush. With a sigh, she focused again on the display in front of her. Cabbage. She picked up a head. Homemade coleslaw would go well with the hamburgers and baked beans she had planned for supper. As she set the cabbage in her cart, she couldn't help stealing another peek at the handsome officer. Dark blond hair, cut in a fancy hairstyle; trim build…ach, she shouldn't be noticing such things about an Englischer.

Janna looked away, but not before he glanced back at her. She did a double take. She thought his eyes were blue, like Hiram's, but she couldn't be sure; he turned around and walked away. Probably headed for the doughnuts. She smiled and turned her attention to her shopping list.

10 bags carrots (5 lbs. ea.)

When she placed the carrots in her cart, the hair on the back of her neck stood up with a tingling sensation, as if someone were watching her. She turned and caught the policeman's glance just before it slid away. A thrill shot through her to think that an Englischer might be attracted to her, an Amish woman, but she stifled it. His interest was a moot point. Of course, he might have just been curious about why she'd loaded her cart with so many carrots.

He disappeared around a corner and down an aisle. She picked up her list again.

10 oranges (Emma Brunstettler)

Emma believed that an orange a day kept all sickness away. And it seemed to work for her. Janna selected ten ripe ones and loaded them into Emma's mesh bag. The hair on the back of her neck rose again, as did her pulse. Her breath hitched.

She wouldn't look. Instead, she lowered the bag of oranges into the cart. Somehow she missed, though. They tumbled out and went rolling across the floor.

"Klutz." A woman carrying a plastic basket stepped over the fallen fruit and hurried away.

As Janna bent to pick up the first of the escaped oranges, she noticed a pair of legs wearing blue pants approaching. It might be a store manager, coming to yell at her. Hopefully not. Worse, it might be the police officer. Had he witnessed her clumsy humiliation? She didn't know which she dreaded more. She risked a glimpse as he crouched and started gathering up the oranges. The police officer. He grinned as he reached out to hand them to her. She tried to keep her burning face averted as she stretched out a quivering hand to accept the fruit and then stuffed each piece back inside the bag.

His smile would have made her weak in the knees, if she weren't already squatting. Even so, she put one hand on the floor to keep her balance.

He stood, picked up his few grocery items from the edge of a display, and turned to go.

She found her voice. "Danki."

He glanced back at her and winked, causing her heart rate to accelerate even more. "Careful with those oranges. They'll get you every time." He strode toward the checkout lines. She smiled when she noticed the box of doughnuts and canister of coffee he had tucked under one elbow. In his other hand was a bag of apples.

Janna gripped the bag of oranges in one hand and slowly stood, watching him as he moved through the checkout line, even as she gave herself a silent yet stern lecture for ogling him the whole time.

An hour later, she pushed the cart, piled full with her bagged purchases, outside and across the parking lot to her buggy, her thoughts still on the handsome police officer.

She started sorting through the bags, searching for the Yoder family's groceries to load first, since their home was the last stop she would make along her delivery route.

"Janna Kauffman?" An Englisch man's voice shattered her concentration.

Janna's heart stuttered. Was it *him*? She stopped rifling through the plastic bags in her cart and looked up. A policeman approached, but he wasn't the one from the store. This man had dark hair, and sunglasses covered his eyes. Her heart crash-landed somewhere in the vicinity of her toes.

"I'm Officer Pete O'Dell."

Janna summoned a smile. "Is there a problem, Officer?"

He didn't grin back. His lips didn't even twitch. She stiffened, trying to prepare herself for the bad news she felt sure she was about to hear. She searched her mind for possibilities. She knew she hadn't double-parked, and dropping oranges wasn't against the law. Maybe there'd been an accident.

Just then, the passenger door of the police cruiser parked behind him opened. Her rush of thoughts stopped as the blond officer from the store climbed out and approached her, sliding his sunglasses down from the top of his head to cover his eyes.

Her face heated again in shame for having stared at him in the store. He looked at her buggy, and the stacks of coolers labeled with the full names of Amish men. "Where'd you get all these?" He opened up the lid of a red cooler labeled "Elam Troyer"—the father of her childhood crush. That seemed like a slap in the face. The cooler would be empty, except for an ice pack.

Janna sucked in a breath. The officers probably thought she'd stolen the coolers. "It isn't what you think." She waved a hand toward her cart, still piled with plastic bags. "I do their grocery shopping." Embarrassed at being caught in yet another humiliating situation by the cute cop, she pulled her shopping list out of her pocket and shoved it toward him.

He took it and began scanning it.

Officer O'Dell shifted his weight. "Are you the guardian of a Meghan Forrest?"

Renewed panic filled Janna. She pushed down her fears and nodded. "She's my niece."

"Has she contacted you today?"

"No, but she can't; she's in school." At least, that's where she was supposed to be. But if he was asking, then maybe it was Meghan who was about to receive bad news. "Is it her mom?" She froze, dreading the answer. If anything had happened to her sister Sharon, she didn't know what she'd do.

"Your niece was just picked up for shoplifting," said Officer O'Dell, matter-of-factly. "We need you, as her guardian, to come to the police station."

"Excuse me?" Janna shook her head. This couldn't be happening. "I think you must have the wrong person. Meghan is still in class." She glanced at the position of the sun, then looked for a watch. She found one, conveniently located on the arm of the handsome officer. Almost noon.

The other officer still studied her shopping list, not contributing anything to the conversation.

"Well, apparently she decided to skip school today. Will you come with us to the station, Ms. Kauffman?" Officer O'Dell's question sounded more like an order, as if she had no choice.

A knot formed in her stomach. "I'll be there as soon as I can." But she stood there, staring at the plastic bags in the cart. Plastic bags full of perishables. She needed to deliver the food first. Or sort it, at the very least, load it into the coolers, and pray that it would still be cool enough after she'd handled the situation with Meghan. Otherwise, she'd have to pay out of her own pocket to replace the spoiled food. Besides, late or incomplete orders wouldn't help her business any. And here, she'd been marveling at how well her day had been going.

"Now would be a good time, Ms. Kauffman." Officer O'Dell grabbed a plastic bag from her cart and tossed it into the buggy.

Janna reached for the bag and pulled it back out. "I'll be there as soon as I can," she said again. Maybe he hadn't heard her the first time. "I have to get these bags sorted and put the food in the coolers so it won't spoil."

"Go on, O'Dell. I'll help her." The blond policeman handed her back her list. He ran his fingertip over Elam Troyer's name written in black permanent marker, then turned his dark sunglasses in her direction. "What can I do?"

Officer O'Dell scowled and strode back to his cruiser.

Janna swallowed. She wasn't Meghan's parent—just one of her temporary guardians, until Sharon felt ready to welcome Meghan back home. She sighed. Since the police probably wouldn't ask a parent to fly in, she would have to deal with it. Unless Daed could do it. For a second, her hopes flared. Then died. Nein, Daed and Mamm were in Springfield, visiting someone in the hospital. Their driver wouldn't bring them home again until this evening. She was it.

"I don't know if you can help," Janna said. "I need to pack the items on my list in the proper coolers. I tried to keep the orders separate in the store, but the bagger sort of packed them into the cart at random, so I still need to figure out who gets what." Normally, she was better organized, but this time, the police officer had taken her rational capacities prisoner.

"Then, you tell me which cooler it goes into and I'll put it in."

She watched his eyebrows rise above his dark glasses. He really did seem familiar…

"So, why do you do their grocery shopping?" He tapped his fingertips on the lid of Elam Troyer's red cooler.

She shrugged and decided to answer generally. The Troyers' reasons were personal and certainly none of his concern. "Oh, various reasons. Some are too sick or old or physically unable; some are mamms with newborns at home. Others are widowers with no interest in shopping." She looked through the contents of one bag, consulted her list, then handed it to the officer. "This goes to Elam Troyer."

A muscle flickered in his jaw. She wondered if the name meant something to him.

But it was probably her overactive imagination.

He should be shot for neglecting his parents like he did. Hiram Troyer, better known as Troy, removed his hand from the top of the cooler, lifted the lid, and lowered the plastic bag inside. He'd run by their house on the way home and check on them. If they were paying someone else to do their grocery shopping, then something must have happened.

He held up another bag. "Same family?"

She nodded distractedly as she sorted through another bag.

He dropped it in the cooler, keeping his gaze on her. *Janna Kauffman. I'd figured she would have gotten married by now. She always stood out at the singings and frolics, back when—* No point going there. That was a lifetime ago. Still, when he'd seen her eyes for the first time in years, it had felt like an earthquake, rocking his heart and rearranging his mind. The aftershocks still rumbled through him.

But his thoughts were no longer scrambled; they were crystal clear—and he knew exactly what he wanted to do. He just didn't know how he was going to do it.

Janna handed him several more bags. "These are the last of Elam Troyer's."

He was glad his sunglasses hid his eyes as his gaze slid down her curvy body beneath the usual cape dress, hers lavender. She was still as attractive as ever, with light brown hair and hazel eyes. She'd skipped the black bonnet the women usually wore over their prayer kapps when they went out—but he'd seen other women do that, especially as the days got warmer. And they'd been reaching 80 degrees almost daily for almost a week now. Eighty-two, he thought he read on the digital sign in front of the bank. He could have been mistaken, though, because gazing into Janna's eyes left him reeling. He looked away.

He'd left Meghan locked up in custody in the otherwise empty police station. He slid his glance back to Janna, then away. "Hurry and finish."

Okay, that was a bit abrupt, but he needed to get back to the station before the manager of the store Meghan had allegedly robbed showed up to give a statement. She'd been running the cash register and needed to find someone to cover for her.

Troy glanced in the direction of the police station. Maybe O'Dell had gone straight back there. Troy had told him he'd talk to Janna, but, as usual, O'Dell hadn't listened. Probably because a hint of action beat the dispatcher job O'Dell was supposed to be doing today.

Come down to it, Troy needed to do his job, instead of standing there staring at this woman. He needed to get away from Janna and the feelings she awakened in him.

Years of striving to be the model bishop's daughter, and here she was, on her way to the police station. At least she wasn't the one in trouble. She hoped shoplifting wasn't punishable with jail time. Sharon would never forgive her if Meghan ended up with a sentence to serve. Maybe she could talk the nice blond policeman into going easy on her niece. And somehow keep the news from her older sister.

As Janna maneuvered her buggy into the parking lot of the police station, she began to regret the samples of meat and cheese she'd succumbed to while shopping. They weighed heavy in her stomach.

She climbed out of the buggy, tied the reins to a telephone pole, and went inside the station, wishing again that she didn't have to handle this. Wishing the problem would just disappear. If only the blond policeman had waited for her. But he'd disappeared before she could talk her horse, Tulip, into leaving the grocery store parking lot.

Officer O'Dell sat at the reception desk with his feet propped up in front of him, a full mug of koffee in one hand, what appeared to be a McDonald's burger in the other. The room smelled like fresh-brewed koffee. A glance around showed an almost full pot on a file cabinet.

"Ms. Kauffman," he said around a mouthful of food. "Go on in." He pointed abruptly over his shoulder at a partially closed door.

Janna inclined her head to acknowledge his directions and then stepped over to the door. She knocked once, then pushed it open.

The blond officer sat behind a big desk, talking on the phone. King of the office, apparently. He cast a quick glance in her direction but made no visible acknowledgment of her presence. He was attractive, but instead of the friendliness she'd seen earlier, now his expression was stern. She probably didn't know him. Maybe she'd just seen him around town a time or two.

Meghan sat hunched over in a far chair. She didn't look over at all. Not gut.

A woman wearing tight black pants and a low-cut hot pink shirt stood against the wall on the other side of the desk. She, too, kept her eyes down, as she played with the bangles on her wrist.

Janna inhaled as deeply as she could, given the knot in her stomach. She pressed a hand to her abdomen, hoping to keep her snacks down.

The officer finally set the phone in its cradle and looked up at Janna. His blue-eyed gaze pierced her. He was handsome but scary—not someone she'd want to tangle with on a dark dirt road. Or even in a brightly lit office.

He nodded at the empty chair facing his desk. "Please, have a seat."

She thought she'd rather stand, like the woman with the bangle bracelets. Position herself right there by the garbage can, in case her food decided not to stay put. But obediently, she dropped compliantly into the chair. Again she glanced over at Meghan, who studied the floor as if fascinated by the pattern in the linoleum tiles.

Janna cleared her throat. "I'm sure this is just a simple misunderstanding."

The officer slid three cards, each one bearing a pair of earrings, across the desk. All of them were dangly and sparkly. Definitely Meghan's style. "We found these in your niece's possession." His voice was stern. "Would you like to see the surveillance video?"

Not really.

He went ahead and pushed a button of the remote control on his desk. On the monitor behind him, a rather grainy picture appeared of Meghan and someone Janna didn't know. She must have gotten away, or maybe they'd put her in another room. Despite the poor quality of the film, it was clear enough to see both girls slip some merchandise into their pockets.

He pushed another button, and the screen went blank. His cold eyes speared Janna again before he shifted his gaze to Meghan. "Shoplifting is a serious crime, and it usually lands you in jail for up to a few months. But, since this is your first offense, we're willing to work with you." He gestured to the woman with the bracelets. "Ms. Taft, the manager of Dollar General, has said she won't press charges if you agree to six weeks of community service. I just talked to the district attorney to make sure this was agreeable. He said you could begin Monday after school. You'll report to the county courthouse. And you will not enter that store again. If you do, the management won't hesitate to report you for trespassing."

Janna nodded. "I'm sure it won't happen again." *I hope.* She glanced at Meghan to look for any indication that she felt the same way, but her niece's face was impassive.

He tapped the cards holding the earrings. "The DA also expects you to pay for the merchandise you stole. Three times the retail value."

Janna glanced at Meghan. "How much did they cost?"

"Twenty-nine ninety-five," said the woman standing there. Her tone was less than friendly.

Janna couldn't hold back her gasp. "And you want her to pay three times that much?" Acid burned in the back of her throat. She stood and moved to the trashcan.

"Take a seat, Ms. Kauffman." This officer meant business. She wondered what had become of the kind gentleman who'd help her gather her fallen orange and later load her buggy with groceries. This man looked the same, but his attitude and bearing were completely different.

Janna cast him a frantic look, then lost the contents of her stomach—and what was left of her pride.

Ms. Taft gagged.

"Eww, Aunt Janna. Gross!"

At least Meghan had generated a reply.

Blinking back tears, Janna wiped her mouth with her sleeve.

The officer stood, opened a miniature refrigerator, and produced a bottle of water. Her throat burned.

"Thank you." She reached to accept the water from him.

When their hands touched, fire shot through her fingertips, and she glanced quickly at him. His blue eyes widened as they met hers, but his expression remained sympathetic. Maybe he was friendly after all, and not so scary. She set the garbage can outside the door and then approached his desk again.

"Now. Back to business." The officer's voice hardened, and he sat down, all traces of kindness gone. "As I was saying…." He repeated himself, with enough force to make Janna's stomach churn again. No matter the punishment Daed would kum up with for Meghan, it couldn't be harsh enough for forcing Janna through this torture.

Something the policeman said must have penetrated Meghan's indifference. She flung a wad of cash on the desk. Her hands didn't even shake.

Janna stared in disbelief at the bills. Sharon sent Meghan a monthly allowance, but with the way Meghan spent money, Janna hadn't thought she'd have any money left.

The manager reached for the stack and flipped through it. Apparently satisfied with the amount, she slid it into her pocket. "Thank you, Officer," she almost purred. Then she turned to Janna and hissed, "If that thieving brat ever sets foot in my store again, you can be sure I'll have her arrested." She flipped her hair, spun on her heel, and stomped out of the office.

"Thank you for coming in, Ms. Kauffman." The uniformed man rose to his feet. "You can go now. I'll escort your niece back to school."

Janna didn't even try to force a smile. "Thank you, sir." She turned to Meghan. "I expect you to kum straight home after school. We are going to have a talk."

"What. Ever." Meghan punctuated the words with a sneer. "You aren't my mom."

Her comment struck like a fist, knocking the air from Janna's lungs. No, she wasn't Meghan's mom. But she had once been her favorite aunt. They'd been more like sisters, really, since they were only five years apart.

Janna glanced at the police officer on her way out. In light of the humiliation she had just suffered, she decided that if she never saw him again, it would be way too soon.

She also decided that, whatever Sharon's reasons for sending Meghan to Seymour to live with her Amish relatives, they weren't gut enough.

Chapter 2

*T*roy pulled the police cruiser into the gravel drive between his family's barn and their big gray house. A buggy was parked outside, the horse tethered to the ground. There was a cooler in back. Janna's. His heart rate increased. No sooner had he cut the engine than the door of the house opened and his young nieces and nephews spilled out, surrounding the car. "Onkel Troy! Onkel Troy!" they chanted. "Can you make the siren go?"

To humor them, Troy pushed the button for the siren and flashed the lights, keeping an eye on Janna's horse to make sure it didn't spook. Other than a small step forward and a toss of the head, the mare didn't pay the commotion any mind.

The door of the house opened again, and Mamm stepped out, wiping her hands on a dish towel. She smiled. "What brings you by?" she called, as he got out of the car.

"Just checking on everyone." Troy climbed the porch steps, the four children on his heels. "I saw Janna Kauffman at the grocery store today, with a couple of Daed's coolers. Didn't realize she'd been doing your grocery shopping."

Mamm's smile broadened. "Nothing's wrong. Your grossmammi is just trying to get a quilt finished for the fund-raising auction next month. And your sister's on bed rest until the boppli comes, or she would do it. She needs a babysitter, ain't so?"

"But hiring someone to buy your groceries...." He kept his voice low, not wanting Janna to overhear. "You could've called me." He would've been glad to help them out that way.

"Ach, don't worry so much. Besides, you're busy. Janna only charges us for the groceries and a little extra for her time. A trip to town and back takes a gut portion of the day, time I'd rather spend doing other things. The service is worth the cost, believe me. She's such a sweet girl, and so helpful. She even insists on putting the food away when she makes a delivery." Mamm turned back toward the house. "Do you have time to kum in for a cup of koffee and a slice of pie?"

With Janna's inside? Definitely. Troy grinned. "Where are Daed and Paul?" He glanced around.

"They've been hired out for some construction work." Mamm fluttered her hand in the direction of the road. "Someone came by in a van this morning and picked them up. And Grossdaedi is taking a nap."

"I can stay for a few minutes." Troy followed Mamm inside. "I'll say a quick word to Elisabeth, if she's awake." He went upstairs and to the end of the hallway, to the room his sister shared with her husband, Paul, and peeked in the open door. He hoped Janna wouldn't leave while he was upstairs. "Hey."

Elisabeth smiled. "Hiram." She closed the cooking magazine that rested on her lap.

"I go by Troy now." He wasn't sure why he bothered to say that anymore. For years, she'd refused to call him by the name he preferred.

She shrugged. "What brings you by?"

"Just checking on things." He wasn't about to tell her he'd seen Janna in town and had hoped to find her here. Elisabeth would remember his infatuation with her, way back when.

"Pie's on the table." Mamm appeared in the doorway. "Elisabeth, would you like a slice?"

She shook her head. "Nein, danki. I'm large enough without it." She grinned and reached for a skein of blue yarn. "I need to do something productive." She glanced at Troy. "I'm making some bootees."

"A bu, jah?" Troy smiled at her as Mamm retreated down the hall.

"I think so." Elisabeth shifted. "You need to get married so you can start having kinner of your own."

Janna's face flashed in his mind. Troy shook his head and stepped backward. "Nice to see you, Elisabeth. I'll stop in again soon."

After he ate the pie Mamm set out for him, maybe he'd stop by the Kauffmans' and have a talk with them about Janna. Make that Meghan. He sighed. Why did Janna consume his thoughts as she did?

Downstairs again, he followed the sound of soft voices coming from the kitchen. Grossmammi and Mamm watched as Janna hoisted a cooler of food onto the counter. Another cooler sat by her feet, the lid propped open. He sucked in a breath at the sight of her hem swaying above her ankles and feet, bare except for her flip-flops.

Funny how he still found modestly dressed women more attractive than those who showed off their assets.

Okay, he had it bad. Already. Or maybe it had just built up over the years, undetected, under the radar. And only now did he acknowledge it.

Janna glanced up, and the color fled her face. "You…? I thought…I wasn't sure…." She swallowed hard.

"Yeah. I mean, *jah*. It's me, Hiram. I go by Troy now."

She didn't appear thrilled to see him. Given what had transpired that afternoon, he supposed she shouldn't be. The situation with Meghan, and the unpleasant episode with Janna and the garbage can, had completely destroyed the flirting they'd done in the grocery store—if she even would have acknowledged it as such. He'd noticed her checking him out while he paid, though, and they had definitely flirted.

Troy shook his head. He was Englisch now. Nothing would change that. Not even a beautiful Amish woman from his past. And his attraction to Janna Kauffman *was* a thing of the past. He needed to remember that.

But he still couldn't keep from stealing glances at her.

Janna watched Rosie Troyer bustle about the kitchen—and tried to ignore the almost tangible gaze of her son. She wasn't sure she wanted to stick around and eat pie with Hiram—Troy—whatever he answered to these days. He hadn't joined the church prior to leaving the Amish, so he wasn't shunned; he'd just disappeared from her life.

She really couldn't take that personally. After all, she'd only had a crush on him. Only wished he would ask to take her home from singings and frolics. But, other than flirting, he'd done nothing to indicate he'd been interested in her in *that* way.

Since he'd joined the Englisch world, she supposed he found most Amish women frumpy compared to their fancy counterparts. He probably preferred the revealing attire of Englisch women. She didn't stand a chance.

Not that she ever had. And not that it mattered. It shouldn't.

Still, her best friend, Kristi, had fallen in love with an Englisch man—and gotten herself shunned in the process. She wished she could talk to Kristi right now.

Rosie Troyer cut a slice of blueberry pie, poured a glass of iced tea, and set them both on the table with a fork and napkin. "There you go, Janna. Please, sit and eat. You don't need to leave right away."

She set the now-empty cooler on the floor beside the other one. She would have offered to put them away, as she usually did, but she thought Hiram/Troy would probably insist on doing it. "Danki, but I shouldn't stay long. There was bit of trouble with my niece this afternoon, and I told her to kum straight home after school, so I need to make sure she did. Daed and Mamm went into Springfield for the day."

Apparently Rosie Troyer was not about to let her leave. She grasped Janna's arm, gently yet firmly, led her to the table, and pulled out a chair. "Sit." She waited until Janna obeyed, then sat down next to her, taking Janna's hands in hers. "What happened with your niece today, that poor dear?"

Janna glanced across the table at Hiram/Troy. He met her eyes with a steady gaze, and he didn't look away.

She lowered her eyes as her face heated. "I'm not so sure she's a 'poor dear.' She...." She shook her head and pushed the pie away. "I can't say. I need to go." She swallowed hard and bolted from the chair. In the doorway, she turned around and added, "*He* can tell you, if he wants to."

She hurried to her buggy. Not that she was in a big rush to go home. The situation with Meghan was only bound to get worse.

❧

"What did you do to her?" Mamm swiveled in her chair to face him.

"Me? I didn't do anything to her." Troy got up and walked to the window. He watched Janna drive away, ignoring the gaze of disapproval Mamm's eyes were surely boring into his back. His lips twitched. "You know I can't tell you what

happened. But I'm sure you'll hear it through the grapevine."
He turned around and grinned. "Probably by nightfall."

"Ach, you." Mamm came over and swatted his arm playfully.
"I saw the way you watched her. You like her, ain't so?"

He heard a hopeful note in her voice. "I can't tell you that,
either." He headed back to the table and the waiting piece of
pie. Hopefully, the teasing remark had been enough to dispel
any expectation that he would fall in love with an Amish
woman and return to the faith.

"I suppose I'll know that by nightfall, too, ain't so?"
Mamm planted her fists on her hips. "It'd be nice to get
information from my own son for a change."

He shrugged. "Whenever there's anything to tell." He
lifted a forkful of pie to his mouth. "As soon as I finish this, I
need to run. There's another stop I need to make."

Mamm's eyes widened, and he shook his head. "Official
business." Sort of.

Forty-five minutes later, he maneuvered the police cruiser
down the Kauffmans' driveway. He didn't see any sign of the
buggy, but he assumed Janna had gone straight home. No one
came out to greet him, though.

He parked the vehicle, climbed out, and mounted the
steps to the back door. Then, he hesitated. If he were Amish,
he would follow custom by simply opening the door and
hollering hello. But he was an outsider now.

He pulled in a breath and knocked. Then, feeling a bit
insecure, he lowered his sunglasses over his eyes.

She opened the door a moment later. Barefoot. She held
a pitcher of lemonade in one hand. Her eyes widened. "Are
you stalking me?" She didn't smile. A millisecond later she
gasped and then covered her mouth with her free hand. A
pretty blush colored her cheeks. "Ach, my manners! I'm sorry,
Officer. Please, have a seat." She gestured toward a porch
chair. "I'll be right out."

Officer. Not his name. Either of them. Troy sighed and headed for the chair she'd indicated. He paused beside it, then bypassed it for the porch swing, which looked more inviting. Sitting there might put her more at ease. It would communicate that he wasn't here on official business. He just wanted to lean close to her, engage in casual conversation, and confirm that he hadn't merely imagined the sparks he'd felt when their fingers had touched.

Okay, maybe it was official business. He needed to talk to Janna's father—Meghan's grandfather. But only after he'd made some friendly conversation with Janna. Renewed their relationship a little, so she wouldn't feel uncomfortable around him. He swallowed and then lowered himself onto the chair. Not the swing.

A few minutes later, Janna came back outside, carrying two full glasses of lemonade. She handed him one, then took a seat on the swing, tucking her legs under the skirt of her dress. "What'd Meghan do now?"

So much for getting to know each other again. She cut right to the chase.

"Didn't she come home?"

Janna sighed. "She's upstairs, in her room. With the door shut."

Good. He didn't need to go looking for her, then. He pulled in a breath. "Is your dad home?"

"I'm expecting my parents any moment." She glanced toward the road.

Troy frowned. "Meghan told me that her mother designated you and your family as her legal guardians. May I ask why?"

Janna hesitated a moment, as if weighing what she should say. Then she looked at her feet. "The home for troubled girls wouldn't take her. They said she wasn't ready."

Chapter 3

Janna waited for him to say something. After almost a minute of silence, she dared to look up. She wished he'd remove his sunglasses. Why did he feel the need to hide behind them, anyway?

A muscle flexed in his jaw. "And the Amish community *is* ready for her?"

Janna couldn't answer. *She* wasn't ready for Meghan, but she was already there. To stay.

"How long has she been here?"

"It will be a week on Friday. Sharon flew in with her and enrolled her at the local school. She wants her with the fancy kids, not ours." It'd taken Meghan only two days at the new school to get involved with the wrong crowd.

"She's older than fourteen." He studied her. "Do you have counselors lined up?"

Janna shook her head. "You know that's not our way." She glanced toward the road as a white van drove in. "Daed and Mamm are home."

Officer Troyer stood. He moved a step closer to her and touched her shoulder. She jumped at the unexpected physical contact—and the sparks that rocketed through her.

"I'll keep your family in my prayers," he said quietly. Then, he released her and turned away.

Daed opened the passenger door, handed some money to the driver, and climbed out. He opened the back of the van for Mamm and waited for her before approaching the porch.

His gaze met Janna's, then he raised his eyebrows and glanced at the man standing near her. He marched up the steps and looked at the name tag pinned to his chest. "Troy Troyer?" Daed frowned as if he were trying to place the name.

"Used to be Hiram. Generally go by Troy now, Bishop Dave." He nodded at Mamm. "Mrs. Kauffman."

Mamm patted his arm. "You know I answer to Abbie. It's gut to see you. You must kum in and rest awhile. After you finish the business that brought you here." She moved past them and went inside.

"Troy." Daed nodded. "It suits you. What brings you by?" His glance darted to Janna for a second and then back again.

Janna shifted. Daed probably thought Officer Troyer had kum courting. Nothing could be further from the truth.

"Had a bit of trouble in town today." Troy inclined his head. "Janna was caught shoplifting."

"Janna?" Daed's gaze shot back to her.

She sucked in a sharp breath and nearly choked on it. After a moment, she glared at Troy. "Meghan. Not me."

He started, red creeping up his neck. "Sorry. I meant Meghan. My partner and I, we found Janna in town and called her in to the station, since she's listed as Meghan's guardian, as well as you and your wife. Given your title as bishop, I thought I best come speak to you about the matter."

Daed frowned, his lips thinning, his eyes narrowed. After a moment, he reached up and removed Troy's sunglasses.

Troy reared back, his eyes wide. Janna wished she'd had the nerve to do it. Daed folded the glasses and held them loosely in his hand. "And Janna has nothing to do with it?"

Troy shifted. He glanced at Janna, but his eyes didn't quite meet hers. He looked back at Daed, his expression schooled.

Her cheeks heated. Ach, why did Daed have to go that direction with his thoughts? And Troy's lack of a response—she wasn't sure what to think of it herself. Though, probably he hesitated to answer in her presence. And he wouldn't want to state bluntly that she wasn't any interest to him. "I...I need to check on dinner." She unfolded her legs from under her, sprang up from the swing, and slipped inside.

"Bishop Dave, would you have time to take a brief walk?" Troy nodded toward the road. "I need to talk to you about Ja—Meghan."

"Both of them, I'm thinking," Daed said. "And maybe your eventual return to the church, jah?"

Janna opened the door and went inside, shaking her head. Troy would be glad to see the last of them.

Troy turned and watched Janna go. There had definitely been sparks—at least on his end. He'd give a lot to know if she'd felt them, too. But he could hardly follow her inside and ask. He led the way back down the steps, wishing he had simply let things go. Janna could have told her dad about Meghan, and then Troy wouldn't be facing a man who saw entirely too much—a man who was the father of the girl he was attracted to, not to mention a girl he couldn't be more unworthy of. As for the church....

Bishop Dave fell in step beside him. "So, you like being a police officer, Hiram Troyer?"

"Troy," he corrected him automatically. "Yes sir, I do. Usually."

Thankfully, the bishop didn't address Troy's blatant gawking at Janna. Yet.

"So, Meghan caused you some trouble today. Are you here for official business?"

"No." Oops. He hadn't meant to admit he'd come for reasons other than Meghan. He cleared his throat. "I understand she's been here only a week or so."

Bishop Dave looked away. "There's a lot unsaid. I think it'll take awhile to uncover some of her underlying issues. But jah. Not two weeks yet. She's still struggling with the early bedtime and early rising. And the chores…." He shook his head. "But you didn't kum to hear about my trials. Tell me what you have decided her punishment will be. Or should I ask Janna about that later, so you can get straight to the main purpose of your visit?" A slight smile flashed.

Troy's face heated at the insinuation. "Meghan is no longer permitted to go shopping unless accompanied by a guardian. And she must perform six weeks of community service. I'll get in contact with some local organizations and set it up. There are probably some serving opportunities within the Amish community, as well."

"To be sure. The schoolhaus could use some cosmetic work."

Troy smiled. "I'll be in touch. Sorry to have come by with such news."

Bishop Dave shook his head. He stopped walking and turned to face Troy. "That isn't the reason you came by. Never lie to yourself, sohn. You came because a certain young woman caught your attention today."

So, it wouldn't go unaddressed. Troy looked away and ran his hand over his chin. Yes, but there was no way he'd admit that to her father—even if the father already knew. Because admitting his attraction would mean talking about issues he couldn't face and traveling a road he wasn't prepared to go down.

After a long pause, Bishop Dave sighed and handed him back his sunglasses.

Troy took them and slid them into his pocket. "I should probably go." He turned back.

"They will have set a place for you for dinner. I hope you aren't planning on declining."

Troy chuckled. "I know better than to eat dinner with a girl I just arrested."

Bishop Dave sighed again. "Jah. Gut point. But her attitude needs an adjustment, with your presence or without it. We would like you to stay."

❧

Janna had just arranged the drinking glasses she'd filled with ice around the table when Mamm entered the room. She stopped and surveyed the settings. "You forgot a place for Troy."

Janna frowned. "You aren't expecting him to stay, are you?"

"I'm expecting that your daed invited him, and he'll want to see a place set, even if Troy doesn't stay."

Janna nodded. She set another place and was filling the glass with ice when the door opened. Daed and Troy both came in. Her breath hitched, her face flushed. "I'll go get Meghan." So much for her appetite. She hadn't eaten since her episode at the police station, and she'd been starting to get hungry. Not anymore.

"I'll get Meghan," Daed said, sending Janna a look of confusion. "You stay and help get dinner on the table. Troy, you may wash up in the bathroom down the hall."

It was a relief when both Daed and Troy left the kitchen. Janna grabbed a potholder and carried the pot of baked beans from the stove to the table, where she set it beside the platter of hamburgers. Mamm hurried to the refrigerator to get the potato salad and coleslaw Janna had fixed earlier. A peach cobbler warmed in the oven.

Janna was filling the glasses with lemonade when Troy came back into the kitchen. Her hand trembled, and some of the liquid spilled on the table.

Troy hadn't noticed, apparently. "Smells gut in here." He smiled at Mamm. "Danki for having me."

Mamm flicked her hand. "You're always welkum. You can sit here." She pointed to a chair.

Mamm's arrangement would put Janna and Meghan next to each other—and across from Troy. Within close proximity, too, since all of the leaves had been taken out of the table, put back only when Janna's siblings came home to visit. Janna wasn't sure the arrangement was such a gut idea. She supposed it was better than being next to him, though.

She went across the room to get some bread, baked fresh that morgen, and some grape jelly, made from the wild grapes that grew on their property. She turned to carry them back to the table and plowed right into something hard. Hands came up to grasp her upper arms. Sparks flared to life. She breathed in a masculine scent mixed with soap.

"Steady there."

Troy's breath stirred the loose hair on the top of her head and whispered across her kapp. She shivered. His hands tightened momentarily on her arms, then abruptly, he released her and stepped back.

Her face blazed. She didn't dare look at him. "Excuse me." She skittered around him to the table, almost running into Daed. "Sorry." She put the slightly squished loaf of bread and the can of jelly on the table, then dropped into her seat, bowing her head.

Meghan pulled out the chair next to her. "Sheesh, Aunt Janna. It's like you have a crush on him or something. But you can't have a crush on a cop." Her words were punctuated with a sneer. "Especially *that* cop."

Chapter 4

*T*roy wasn't surprised when Janna made a strangled noise, rose from her seat, and bolted from the room. He didn't know what to do or say at that point, either. His own breath was stuck in his throat, heat rising on his neck.

Moisture coated his palms. There was a chance Janna might feel the same way. Or, maybe he dreamed this whole crazy scenario.

Bishop Dave sat there with a facial expression that was half frown, half smirk. He looked as if he wasn't sure whether to send Meghan to her room or to laugh at the whole string of events. Not that there was anything humorous about the situation. Not with Meghan's glare fixed on him, and Janna's mamm sitting there looking somewhat stunned.

Come right down to it, laughing should be the last thing on the bishop's mind, considering he'd come into the room to find Janna in Troy's arms. Almost. Troy nearly squirmed, remembering how alive she'd felt as he held her—how right. How tempted he'd been to pull her even closer, to wrap his arms around her.

No. He shook his head, a lump forming in his throat. He wouldn't go there.

Bishop Dave pulled on his beard, his expression sobering. Becoming stern. "Meghan, we'll discuss your attitude after dinner. But first, you need to apologize to our guest for disrespecting him and his position."

Her lips twisted. "Sorry."

Right. Troy swallowed. He glanced at the platters of food on the table. Agreeing to join them had been a bad idea. He started to slide his chair back. "Maybe I should leave."

Bishop Dave bowed his head and closed his eyes. It would be rude to get up and leave in the middle of silent prayer, so Troy lowered his head, as well. *Lord, bless this family. Bind the hands of Satan that seem intent on destroying it. Minister to them as only You can. Help them to know how to handle Meghan.*

He heard a slight noise and peeked up. Janna slipped into the chair across the table from him. Her face was still flushed, but at least she was there. He smiled and closed his eyes again. *Ach, Janna. Lord, I don't understand this overwhelming attraction to a woman from my past—a past I left for reasons You know. I won't go into them now.* He pulled in a breath. *Bless the hands that prepared this food. Amen.*

He raised his head and met Bishop Dave's expectant gaze. "So, Troy. Tell us what you've been up to since you left."

❦

When supper was over, Janna rose from the table and started collecting the dirty plates. Daed held up a hand to stop her. "Meghan, please clear the table and wash the dishes. Your grossmammi will dry them and puts them away. We'll talk when you finish."

Meghan stood with a scowl. Really, it was amazing how quickly she obeyed Daed. Maybe Sharon had made a wise call, sending her to live with them. Or maybe not. That remained to be seen.

Troy rose to his feet. "Danki again for having me. It was delicious, Mrs. Kauffman."

Mamm beamed. "Janna fixed it all."

Troy nodded and turned to Janna. "It was ser gut. Will you see me out?"

Janna gulped. She didn't want to. She didn't understand the feelings he evoked in her. But it would be rude to refuse. She led the way to the door.

Daed followed them outside. When they reached the police car, he clapped Troy on the shoulder. "Don't be a stranger around here, sohn. You're welkum anytime."

Jah, kum by! was chased away by *Nein, don't.* He'd get her hopes up, and for naught. Nothing could ever kum of them. She didn't want to get shunned.

"And remember, I'm available whenever you need to talk." Daed gave Troy a look that Janna couldn't decipher.

Janna raised an eyebrow.

Troy nodded. Daed gave him another penetrating look before turning and heading for the barn.

Janna hesitated by the car, unsure of Troy's reasons for asking her to walk him out, and even less sure of what Daed had been referring to when he'd invited Troy to talk to him anytime. Maybe he wanted to discuss whatever it was that had drawn him away from the faith and into the world.

Janna would be interested to find out. But she'd never been privy to Troy's thoughts as a teenager, though she'd desperately wanted to be noticed by him. Wanted to spend time with him. Wanted to get to know everything about him.

She'd had more interaction with him today than in the entirety of their rumschpringe—considering he'd left when he was seventeen, and her infatuation with him had never really progressed beyond that stage.

Troy leaned against the door, hands loose at his sides. "So, Janna…what are you doing Saturday?"

Janna felt a glimmer of hope. He wanted to know her plans? But the expectancy was snuffed out when she realized what he was likely to have in mind—a community service project for Meghan. If he thought she was going to oversee it, he was sorely mistaken. Gut thing she already had a long list of items to accomplish. She smiled in relief. "I'm going into Springfield, as I have a lot of shopping to do for my clients. There's a big order of fabric to fill, and…well, I guess that doesn't matter to you. But you'll need to talk to Daed about Meghan's community service. He's more her guardian than I am."

Something in his expression faded. "You and your parents are listed as sharing the role equally." He hesitated a long moment, observing her. "Do you have a ride lined up for Saturday?"

"Nein, not yet. But I'm sure our usual driver will take me. Or his frau, since I'm going shopping, and you know how men are." She flashed a grin, remembering the panicked look of the male driver during her last big shopping trip.

He frowned. Then, softly, he said, "I'll take you."

"What?" Janna blinked. She hadn't expected that.

His hand made a move toward her, then dropped. "What time do you want to leave?"

"Ach, nein. I couldn't ask you to take me shopping." Janna shook her head.

"You didn't ask. I offered."

She nodded. "I should leave around eight." Really, she'd love to know what had possessed him to volunteer for a shopping trip. Probably so he'd have a captive audience while he talked about Meghan's community service. She'd have to make sure she had a driver's number with her, in case Troy left her stranded when he realized she'd been serious when she'd said she had a lot of shopping to do. "I'll pay you, of course."

Troy smiled, straightened, and opened the car door. "I'll see you Saturday, then. If not before." He glanced toward the house. "Do you want me to pick you up here in the drive? Or down the road apiece, so no one will see?"

Janna blinked. "Why? It's a shopping trip. I don't imagine you'll be allowed to take a police car on a personal errand like that."

"Who said anything about a police car? I'm bringing my motorcycle." He gave her a wicked grin.

Her face heated as she imagined her arms wrapped tightly around his chest, her body pressed against his back, just like the Englisch couples she'd seen on the highway. Was it wrong for her to want to experience that? She took a step back. "Ach, nein, I…. Nein."

He got into the car. "I'm kidding."

Troy knew he shouldn't mislead Janna and turn their shopping trip into a date. But he couldn't help himself. He didn't know if she was being courted by an Amish suitor. He wanted to ask her if anyone took her home from singings or on buggy rides in the evenings, but she probably wouldn't tell him, things being as they were in the Amish community.

If she were seeing someone, she wasn't in love with him. Because, if she were, she wouldn't have interest in anyone else. And he sure saw interest when she looked at him.

That was a small consolation, though he didn't know why it mattered. He'd left the Amish and wasn't about to return. Not even for a girl. He reached out to close his door.

She held up her hand. "Wait."

He raised his eyebrows.

"If this is so you can have someone to talk to about making arrangements for Meghan's community service, then—"

"It's not." He grinned. He hoped he appeared confident. Self-assured. Maybe even a bit cocky. "I'm taking you on a date."

Her mouth dropped open.

Troy shut the car door before she had a chance to voice her objections. He knew them all, anyway. *One: You jumped the fence.*

He turned the key in the ignition as he continued his mental list of objections. *Two: You became Englisch.*

He raised his hand and waved.

Three: You have no plans to return to your roots.

Four: You are a cop. The cop who arrested my niece.

He backed the car out of the driveway. She stood there, watching him go. *Yep, definitely interested.* He grinned.

He couldn't wait for Saturday.

Chapter 5

*J*anna watched until the police car disappeared around a curve. Then, she turned to go inside the haus. She climbed up the porch stairs and jumped when the door slammed open and banged against the haus. Meghan stomped outside, down the steps, and around to the back of the barn.

Janna raised her eyebrows. After a moment's hesitation, she opened the swinging door and went inside, quietly shutting it behind her. Mamm put away a dish and turned. The wary look in her eyes faded when she saw her daughter.

"Was ist letz?" Janna held up her hands.

Mamm shrugged. "Who can tell with that girl?" She picked up another dish and wiped it dry. "She looked out the window, and when she saw you and Troy standing there talking, she muttered a comment I couldn't make out and then stormed out of here. Probably a gut thing he drove off when he did. Who knows what she would have done?" She put the dish away. "I hope she went to find your daed. He said to send her out to the barn to talk when she was done in here."

"I don't know where she went." Janna glanced outside, then looked back at Mamm. "Around the back of the barn, for sure."

Mamm nodded. Then, an odd look filled her eyes. "He's a nice young man."

"He jumped the fence," Janna said, slowly.

Mamm shrugged. "He's in his rumschpringe. He'll return. Eventually."

Janna wished she shared Mamm's confidence. It'd be so nice if he did return, and noticed her, and….

Apparently he had noticed her. He'd asked her on a date.

Well, he hadn't exactly asked. More like *commanded*. *Decreed. "I'm taking you on a date."*

Funny how that still excited her.

It shouldn't.

She dipped her head as shame washed over her. She couldn't feel this way about an Englisch man. She'd given her friend Kristi countless lectures before she utterly succumbed to the charms of the Englisch vet she married, and here she was, falling for an English police officer.

Mamm started to say something, but it didn't register. Janna was already darting out of the room and up the stairs. She shut herself in her bedroom.

She needed to get out. Needed to find a friend and talk. Maybe not talk. How could she admit to something like this?

A door slammed downstairs. "It's not fair!" came the now-familiar complaint. Seconds later, Meghan pounded her way upstairs. Her bedroom door slammed shut.

Janna sighed and then tiptoed downstairs. She needed to find a quiet place to pray.

Troy drove his two-toned green and white pickup down the narrow dirt road leading to the creek. It had a name, he supposed, but it had been called just "the creek" for as long as he could remember. He wanted some time alone to pray, to talk to God, to release his stress. The atmosphere of the small house he shared with his roommate, Joey, was anything but conducive to prayer. The TV was usually blaring. Time alone with God in nature, with fish his only company, was just what he needed.

He cut the engine, grabbed his McCafé mocha, and climbed out before he noticed the buggy parked close to the tree line. The horse stood on the bank, drinking from the creek. He didn't see a driver anywhere, but that was okay. As likely as not, the Amish man would be a few feet from his horse, his line in the water. The two men would nod at each other, exchange a few words about the forecast and whether or not the fish were biting, and then ignore each other.

Troy pulled his rod and tackle box out of the back of the pickup and headed down to the water. No sign of an Amish man in the vicinity.

But there was a woman, dressed in lavender and a prayer kapp sat on a boulder a few yards down, her flip-flops beside her.

She looked up and blanched at the same time he recognized her. Maybe he shouldn't have been so cocky when he'd announced his intentions for Saturday. "Janna?"

"I needed to pray." Her voice was flat, lacking its usual lilt. Had something happened at her house after he'd left? That had been under an hour ago.

Funny. The same thing he needed. And they preferred the same spot?

"Everything okay at home?" He shouldn't have asked— that was delving into personal territory. Her reasons for coming here were private, as were his. "Never mind. That's none of my business."

"Actually, it is, somewhat. Daed told Meghan she has to clean and paint the schoolhaus for her community service. She didn't take it well." Janna fingered the open book in her hands. A prayer book? Or maybe the Bible. Most likely the latter, as it was thick.

"Gut your daed is taking charge." He sat down next to her. A hand's breadth away. He put his fishing gear on the ground beside him.

Sitting there had probably been a presumptuous move, he realized when she stiffened. But she didn't scoot further away.

"I didn't know you were here. I'm really not stalking you, as you suspected earlier, though I'm sure it appears that way." Her smile was weak. "I shouldn't have said that."

"It's okay." He took a sip of his coffee and then set the cup beside him on a level part of the boulder.

"Meghan stormed inside, screaming, 'It's not fair,' and started throwing stuff in her room. I'm getting tired of this. I mean, even when all my brothers and sisters lived at home, it was never this…volatile."

Troy nodded. "My home was pretty peaceful, too, with just my brother and sister, and…." He swallowed. Hard. And looked away. His eyes burned.

After a moment, her hand rested on his. Squeezed. A bold move for an Amish girl. He glanced at her, the moisture in his eyes blurring her image.

She started to pull away, but he stopped her with his other hand. "Danki."

"Do you want to talk about it?"

He shook his head. What was there to say? Just that demons from the past reared their ugly heads from time to time. Demons he couldn't seem to eradicate.

He didn't know if he'd ever be able to.

And those demons were what would make a lasting relationship with Janna impossible.

❧

Janna held her breath, and she didn't dare pull her hand away, lest she break the spell of the moment. She'd waited so long for this man to notice her. She remembered whispering to Kristi about him—how cute he was, and how she wished he would ask to take her on a buggy ride. She remembered Kristi consoling her when he left alone or with another girl. Kristi promising that he'd notice her someday.

It seemed that he finally had, in a huge way. But the timing was all wrong.

He was all wrong.

Maybe that was why God had never answered the fervent prayers of her teenage heart that Hiram Troyer would court her. Love her.

Because He, being almighty and omnipotent, knew that Hiram would become Englisch and, as a result, would virtually cease to exist. In fact, Hiram Troyer didn't exist. He answered to Troy now—a derivation of his last name. Troy Troyer. Nein mamm would have saddled her sohn with a name like that.

But Janna rather liked it. Maybe too much.

Perhaps it was because Troy seemed to fit this Englisch man sitting beside her better than Hiram ever had.

With her free hand, she gently flipped her Bible shut and set it on the boulder beside her.

His finger grazed the top of her hand, leaving flames in its wake.

She froze, her eyes fixed on their clasped hands. Then, slowly, she raised her head to look at him.

A muscle jumped in his neck as he gazed at the opposite bank. She glanced that way, too, but saw nothing of note. Nothing, except possibly some distant memories that he alone could see.

She must have moved or made a sound because he shook his head, smiled at her, and picked up his koffee. He released her hand. "Danki, again. I needed that."

She looked down. "About Saturday…."

"Please don't cancel."

How had he known she planned to? Needed to? "I…I can't. I…you…." She swallowed.

He reached for her hand again but stopped short of taking it. "I know all the reasons. And I understand."

Still, pain filled his eyes. She hated that she was the reason.

"I'm sorry." She looked down.

"I'm still willing to drive you. I'm off that day. I'd be interested to see the types of purchases Amish women request of their personal shopper in the big city."

She laughed. "You'd be surprised."

"So, you'll let me take you?"

"As a driver, jah. As a date, nein."

"Maybe as a friend?"

She hesitated.

"You can never have too many friends. Besides, you might need me in your corner."

"I'm not sure I can be friends with you." She looked at him.

For a second, he stared at her, hurt reflected in his gaze. Then, he flashed a smile. "Careful, Janna. I might get the misguided impression that you like me."

She stood and picked up her Bible. "How do you know it'd be misguided?" That was too bold. Too flirty. She didn't dare look at him. Instead, she gathered Tulip's reins and led her toward the parking lot.

He laughed. "So, you do like me?"

She had no intention of answering.

A few seconds later, Troy fell into step beside her. "I'll hitch your horse for you."

"I still won't answer." She heard a teasing note in her voice. Wondered if he'd picked up on it.

"You don't have to. I'm a police officer. I can read body language." He chuckled. "Your silence speaks volumes."

Her heart rate accelerated. Troy knew how she felt. Or at least had the right idea.

He took the reins of the horse from her, leading Tulip over to the buggy. He had her hooked up in no time. Quicker than she could do it.

She placed her Bible on the buggy seat, climbed in, and looked down at him. "Danki. I guess I'll see you Saturday, unless we run into each other earlier."

He nodded.

She prepared to click at Tulip, but she stopped herself. "I don't want to go home." The admission was whispered, or so she'd wanted it to be. She winced at having blurted it out like that. Blushed at having as good as admitted—out loud—that she had a crush on Troy.

She glanced over to catch his reaction to her statement.

He opened his mouth, then shut it without making a sound.

She had no choice, really. Even if he offered to take her someplace else, she'd have to refuse. Even if she wanted to stay and watch him fish, she'd already been here long enough, and if anyone saw them, tongues would wag.

Troy stepped back. "I'll be praying. For you, for Meghan, and…." He winked. "I hope we do meet again. Maybe tomorrow. Same time, same place. I'll bring you a koffee."

Chapter 6

*T*roy waited beside the creek, his fishing line dangling in the water. He'd set his coffee, and one extra, on the boulder. *Their* boulder. At the same time, he felt like a fool for even hoping she'd show up. For believing they'd arranged a meeting—a date, of sorts. He'd been there for over an hour, and still no horse clip-clopped down the road; no buggy wheels crunched on the gravel. And now, no steam rose from the top of their coffees. The dollops of whipped cream would have dissipated.

She wasn't coming.

His heart hurt with the finality of that thought.

She'd stood him up.

Well, no. Not exactly. After all, she hadn't said she'd be there for sure. Hadn't even made a token promise.

All she'd given him was a smile. A sweet smile that had made his heart flip somersaults and turned his knees to mush. And then she'd clicked at her horse and left.

Leaving him with the hope of seeing her again. Waiting for her, with two ruined coffees. Should he order one for her on Saturday?

At least he still had Saturday to look forward to, even if it wasn't a date. Even if he'd been demoted to the position of being her "driver." At least he'd be with her.

He reeled in his line and carried his gear back out to his truck. As he loaded it in back, he glanced down the road again, to see if she was on her way. Better late than never.

It appeared to be never.

He dropped the tackle box into the bed of the truck, satisfied by the loud thump it made. *Oh, Janna.*

After another long glance down the road, he went back to the boulder and collected the two coffees. His and hers. He downed the cooled contents of his cup, then tossed it into the plastic shopping bag he'd hung from the latch on his glove box.

Then he held hers for a long moment, debating what to do with it. Drink it? Toss it? Or maybe drive by her house and see where she'd been? Remind her that they'd had a date, and she'd stood him up?

How pathetic that would be.

He set the full cup in the beverage holder and started the engine. He'd go home, warm up a TV dinner, and watch whatever lame show his roommate had on. Unless Joey actually had found a life, and was out doing what Troy had spent the night dreaming about. Spending time with a pretty girl, talking, developing a relationship. A friendship.

Maybe something more.

The truck seemed to have a mind of its own, because Troy found himself cruising the dirt road outside of town—slowly, since he didn't want to attract too much attention from the Amish—and then turning into the Kauffmans' driveway.

He cut the engine and stepped out of the truck, the cold coffee in hand. He'd taken two steps toward the house when the door opened. Janna appeared, looking as fresh as springtime in her green dress.

"Troy?" Her brow furrowed. She tilted her head slightly to the side.

Did she have to look so confused?

"I…." He pulled in a breath. "I thought we'd agreed to…,"

"Ach." Her eyes widened. "*Ach.*"

Right. He'd been sitting there waiting for over an hour, and she'd forgotten. She had a not-so-wonderful ability to cut a man down to size.

He was pathetic. All he could think to do was to hold out the McCafé cup. "It's cold by now." *Brilliant conversation opener. Surely, you could have done better than that.*

She took it. "Danki, Troy. Do you want to kum in?"

Not really. He wanted to walk hand in hand in the pasture behind the barn, alone with her, talking. Whispering. Obviously, he'd read more into their chance meeting yesterday than he should have.

"Nein, I just wanted to bring you your koffee." *And see why you stood me up.*

"Mamm asked me to teach Meghan how to make jam. I'd gathered some wild strawberries this morning, so we've been putting it up."

Jam, or maybe Meghan, had taken his place.

"I'd be glad to give you some to take home."

"Would Meghan have a problem with my coming in? I mean, I get the impression it's going okay with her right now." At least, Janna didn't appear stressed.

She glanced back at the house, then looked again at him. "I'll take my chances." She peeked over his shoulder, toward the barn. "Besides, Daed's coming. It'd be rude to send you away now."

Troy spun around and saw Bishop Dave striding toward him, a big smile on his face. "Troy Troyer. What brings you by again today?"

Troy waited for a reaction. Sure enough, Bishop Dave's gaze slipped ever so briefly to Janna, then back. The twinkle in his eyes stated that he knew the answer. That he might even approve. Yet Troy knew that if the situation was reversed— if he were an Amish bishop, and a "black sheep" had come to court his daughter—he wouldn't be quite so calm and welcoming.

Especially considering the bishop had already lost one daughter to the world—Meghan's mother.

"I'll go warm this," Janna said. He heard a soft click as the door shut behind her.

"I promised Janna a coffee." Troy cringed when he realized just how pitiful he sounded.

"Gut thing, because we're almost out. Seems my dochter forgot to shop for her own family on her last trip to the store." Bishop Dave chuckled. "Let's go inside. I've always wanted to taste that fancy koffee, anyway. See what the craze is among some of our young people."

❦

"Where'd you get that, Aunt Janna?" Meghan eyed the brown McCafé cup with something akin to lust in her eyes.

"Troy brought it by."

Meghan scowled and turned her attention back to spooning strawberries into jars. Janna was having trouble adjusting to Meghan's new hair color, which matched the berries perfectly, kum to think of it. Last nacht, she'd been bleach-blonde.

Janna poured the fancy koffee into a kettle and set it on the stove to warm. It smelled wunderbaar, she'd give it that. Rich and chocolaty. She'd been surprised to see the foamy remnants of whipped cream floating on top.

The door opened, and Daed and Troy came in.

"Have a seat, sohn." Daed glanced at Janna. "Do we have any pie left?"

"Nein, we finished that off last nacht. But I made some mint whoopee pies today." She went over to the counter and returned with a small plate piled with the tasty, cream-filled cookies.

"Ah. You'll make a fine frau someday." Daed winked at her.

Her face heated. It couldn't be any more obvious Daed approved of a match between her and Troy, though he probably banked on the belief that Troy would return to the Amish. He wouldn't be so hospitable if the possibility of Janna joining the fancy world crossed his mind.

But she and Troy were hardly in a position to think about a relationship. They hadn't even scratched the surface of being "just friends" yet. And that step came first. At least, it should, in Janna's opinion.

She dipped a spoon in the koffee and tested the temperature. It seemed warm enough. She filled a mug and held it out to Meghan. "Want some?"

"No." Meghan tossed her shocking hair.

"I'd love some." Daed reached for the mug as Janna turned toward the table.

"Would you like some, too?" Janna filled another mug and started to slide it toward Troy.

"Nein, that's yours."

The note of steel in his voice reminded her of the scary officer she'd faced in the police station yesterday morning. Meghan picked up on it, too, judging by the way her back stiffened. She kept spooning sugar into a measuring cup for use in the jam.

"I'd be glad for some iced tea." He nodded toward the pitcher on the counter.

Janna dropped a couple of ice cubes into a tumbler, filled it with the freshly steeped tea, and set it in front of him on the table.

"Would you like some sugar?" Meghan spoke. "Aunt Janna doesn't sweeten it."

Wow. Meghan *could* be nice.

Janna turned around to give her niece an appreciative smile—just in time to see Meghan pour the entire cup of sugar on Troy's head.

~~~

Troy rose to his feet, sugar falling in sheets from his head to his shoulders and down to the floor. Sticky granules snuck under his shirt collar, tickling his chest and back, and he was sure he'd even find some under his belt.

Good thing he noticed Meghan's smirk before he succumbed to the instinct to vent his anger. She was waiting for an extreme reaction. But he wouldn't give her the pleasure. His foot shifted, grinding the powdered substance into the floor, as he lowered himself back into the chair. He'd left a big mess. "Danki, Meghan. I've never been sweet enough."

Bishop Dave and Janna stood there, mouths open, staring in shock at Meghan.

Bishop Dave recovered first. He bolted from his seat, leaving the chair wobbling from the force of it, skirted around the table, and grabbed his granddaughter by the arm. Then he propelled her out of the house.

Janna let out her breath in a huff. She turned to Troy. "I am so sorry. I don't know where she comes up with this stuff." She picked up a dishcloth, dampened it at the sink, and wrung it out before handing it to him. "You remember where the bathroom is, if you want—"

"I'll trail sugar all over the haus. I don't want to make more work for you."

"My guess is that Meghan will be handed a broom when she gets back inside." Janna's tone was laced with iciness.

Troy nodded, and more sugar rained from his head. He put the dishcloth on the table, leaned forward, and tried to brush it out of his hair.

"Looks like you got most of it," Janna said. "But you'll want to wash it, for sure. If you want to go back and take a shower, I could find some clothes for you to change in to."

Homespun pants, a cotton shirt, and suspenders, no doubt. Troy shook his head. "I'll be fine. I'll wait until I get home."

"But you can't be comfortable. You have sugar in your eyebrows, and…." She picked up the dishcloth. "Hold still." The warm fabric touched his right cheek, while her hand gently gripped his chin, like he was a two-year-old with spaghetti sauce smeared all over his face.

He didn't want to feel like a toddler around her. Or to be viewed as one. He gripped her wrist and pried her gentle fingers off of his face. "I'll do it."

He must have sounded gruffer than intended, because her eyes widened. Color flooded her face. "I'm sorry."

Or maybe she'd just realized she'd touched him inappropriately. But he didn't want to release her, not even when she gave a light tug of her hand, trying to free herself from his grasp.

No, he wanted to pull her closer.

Instead, he let her go.

Janna moved over to the stove and stirred the pot of simmering jam, just as the door opened.

Meghan shuffled back inside, followed by Bishop Dave.

"Sorry," Meghan muttered, but she didn't look at Troy.

Right. He believed this apology just as much as he did the last one.

She spun around and opened the closet door, vanished briefly into the darkness, and then reappeared holding a broom and dustpan.

Did she intend to work around him? Or maybe sweep him up along with the sugar? Neither option sounded appealing. Troy stood. "Let me get out of your way."

She glared at him.

He refused to feel guilty. He wasn't the bad guy in the situation, anyway. Meghan was the one who had broken the law, and his "crime" was having been the officer on duty when the store manager had called to report a shoplifter.

No wonder Janna had escaped to the creek in her reluctance to return home yesterday.

Chapter 7

Janna fumed over Meghan's treatment of Troy. Even if Meghan had been raised in a less-than-ideal home environment, she should have learned some basic manners. Universal rules of behavior. Such as, "One should not overturn a cup of sugar on the head of a guest."

It wouldn't surprise her if Troy never darkened the doorway of their haus again.

Odd how much that bothered her.

And what about Saturday? They never finalized their plans. He probably wouldn't kum to pick her up that morgen. After the meal, nothing was said about it, not even when his blue eyes settled on her briefly before he turned and hurried out the door. He was in such a rush, he forgot the jar of jam she'd given him. He left it abandoned on the table, looking as forlorn as she felt.

Daed walked Troy to his car, where they stood and talked for a few minutes before the cruiser backed down the driveway. When the dust settled, Daed went into the barn, leaving Janna in the haus alone with Meghan, wondering when her next eruption would occur. Mamm was still away at a quilting frolic, and Janna had every intention of disappearing when she came home. She didn't know where she'd go, though. Maybe to a friend's haus.

Janna had just placed the jam jars in a hot water bath when Mamm burst in, the picture of cheerfulness. "We finished the quilt for the mud auction," she announced as she dropped her sewing supplies on the table. "I wish you could have kum, Janna, but I'm glad you started the strawberry jam." She paused, then looked at Janna. "Did I miss anything interesting here?"

Janna gave her a long look, nodded at Meghan, sulking in the corner, and then tilted her head toward the door. She waited for Mamm to work through the nonverbal communication.

Finally, Mamm shrugged in a way that said, "Go. Now. Before I change my mind."

Janna grinned, grabbed her flip-flops, and hurried outside. She still didn't have any idea where she'd go. Before she got to the barn, a blue Jeep pulled into the driveway. She didn't recognize the man behind the wheel, but when her gaze shifted to the woman in the passenger seat, she bit her tongue to keep from squealing. *Kristi!*

She peeked back at the barn but saw no sign of Daed. When the vehicle stopped, she raced over and gathered her best friend in a bear hug. "It's been forever since I've seen you!"

When they separated, Kristi's face was damp with tears. "Jah, but..."—she grinned, blushing, at the man coming around the front of the Jeep—"it's been worth it."

Janna smiled. "Don't let my daed hear you say that." She stepped back. "But marriage agrees with you." Even if it was marriage to an Englischer—a union that had gotten her shunned.

"Bishop Dave," the man spoke, nodding.

Janna turned and saw Daed on the approach. Caught.

He gave her a look that said he'd seen her hug the friend she was supposed to be shunning, but he didn't say anything to her. That would probably kum later. A tiny wave of regret over her impulsiveness washed over her. But then, maybe Daed didn't understand how strong her bond of friendship was with Kristi.

"Shane Zimmerman." Daed joined them. "What can I do for you?"

"We're ready to talk," Shane said, nodding toward Kristi.

Janna tilted her head, curious. Talk about what? Maybe they wanted to repent and join the church. She drew in a sharp breath.

But they'd kum in a Jeep. So, probably not.

Shane made the bold move of taking Kristi's hand, even though they were married.

Janna's eyes widened. She'd love to have Troy take her hand that way—again. That time at the creek had been way too brief. She still remembered the feel of his skin against hers. Maybe on Saturday—or not, since he would only be the driver.

"Janna, would you take care of their horse...." Daed's voice trailed off when he noticed the Jeep. He shook his head. "Get them something to drink and a piece of pie."

Janna wished that she could sit on the porch with Kristi, sip lemonade, and listen to stories about her elopement and subsequent honeymoon in Florida. But, since Kristi was shunned, they'd have to wait until she had knelt before the church and confessed. *If* she knelt before the church and confessed.

Janna sent Kristi a furtive smile, then hurried into the haus.

Mamm gave Janna a puzzled look. "Back so soon?"

"Visitors. Daed sent me in for refreshments."

"Who?" Mamm peeked out the window. "Ach. I'll get it. You go." She motioned toward the seldom-used front door.

Janna nodded and left, despite the disappointment gnawing at her. She'd been more than a little tempted to hang around and see what Shane and Kristi had kum to discuss with Daed. *Please, Lord, let them have kum to repent....*

Janna started walking along the road. She didn't know where she was headed, but right now, that didn't matter. Getting away did. She needed a few moments of peace.

As she rounded the corner, she saw a familiar green and white pickup parked on the shoulder. A man leaned against the hood, as if waiting for her. *Troy.* Janna's breath quickened, and she hurried toward him. He was talking on his cell phone, his gaze directed somewhere out across the field. As she neared, he noticed her and grinned. But he held up a finger, asking her to let him finish his conversation.

Janna had never needed one of those devices. Her clients didn't call her. They slipped her their shopping lists on Church Sunday or gave her a new list when she made a delivery. Sometimes they sent a shopping list in the mail, or she got word secondhand that somebody needed her, and she'd stop by.

Troy made a grunting sound, then nodded. "Jah, you're almost here. Just a bit further down the road. You'll see me." He snapped the phone shut and slid it into his pocket. "Hey, Janna. What are you doing here?"

"I was going to ask you the same thing." Janna tilted her head. "I was taking a walk."

"I had a blowout, and my donut is flat." Troy motioned at a metal contraption holding the front end of the truck several inches off the ground.

"Why didn't you walk back to the farm? Daed would be glad to take you to town." She'd be just as glad to, if Daed would allow it.

"I don't need a ride to town. I need an air compressor to inflate the donut. My roommate's bringing one out." Troy smiled. "I doubt your daed has one."

She studied the metal thing holding up the truck. "Nein. I don't think he does." She lifted her gaze to his. "But we could've hitched your truck up to a couple Clydesdales and towed it home for you."

He blinked. "Jah, I remember seeing your daed do that for an Englischer before. But Joey's on his way. Danki just the same."

She nodded. "Mamm finally came home. She took over in the kitchen to give me a break." Then she frowned. She shouldn't have told him that. He'd think she rambled on about nothing, just so she could stay with him. Either that, or she could use it as an opportunity to apologize to Troy for Meghan's behavior. She took a deep breath.

His smile was slow. "So, then after Joey gets here, you'd be able to go into town with me. If you liked the koffee, I could get you another one. Or a milkshake. It is kind of warm today. We can go through the drive-through, and I'll take you back to my house. Or down to the creek."

She shouldn't. She couldn't. She wouldn't. "I'd love to."

His smile broadened. "Awesome."

Gravel scattered as a car sped over the hill. Janna stepped out of the road, closer to the ditch, as a beat-up red car skidded to a stop in front of Troy's truck. The passenger side door was dented, the window covered in sheets of plastic.

Troy smirked and approached the vehicle. "You're driving a little too fast for the conditions, Joey. Seems these back roads might be a good spot to put a speed trap."

"Yeah, if you want to catch a speeding horse and buggy." Joey got out of the car, his brown eyes widening when they came to rest on Janna. "Hey, babe. Where've you been all my life?"

Janna squirmed under his appraisal.

Troy's smirk turned into a scowl, and he almost bristled. "Back off, McCall."

"Whoa. Seriously?" Joey stared at Troy, then at Janna. "You've gotta be kidding."

Janna couldn't quite follow their conversation.

Joey hauled something out of his trunk—a machine, of some sort—and lugged it over to Troy's truck. Within moments, it was hooked up to the spare tire. It made quite a racket.

Janna stood back, unsure of its safety, but it did the job.

Joey disconnected a hose and put the cap on the stem. "Looks good now. Should be able to get you to Marshfield so you can get the old tire fixed or replaced." He carried the machine back to his car, loaded it, and got in. He looked at Janna and shook his head before glancing at Troy. "Man, we need to talk."

"Thanks, Joey. By the way, there is a speed limit on these roads."

"Yeah, yeah, yeah. I know. No faster than a crawl. Got it." His tires squealed as he drove off.

Troy shook his head. He tossed his old tire in the back, tightened a few things on the spare, then lowered the truck. He wiped his hands on his jeans as he came toward Janna. "So. Do you really want to come?"

She hesitated and glanced down the road in both directions. She knew she shouldn't, but she couldn't help it. She nodded.

"Okay, then."

She walked around to the passenger side and, with a final look at the road, climbed inside and pulled the door shut.

❧

Troy couldn't keep from grinning as he jogged around to the driver's side.

Janna pulled the seatbelt across her chest and buckled up. "I'm not used to riding in the front seat."

"Not many options in a pickup." He winked at her. "Let's go get my tire taken care of, and then we'll head for the drive-through." He glanced at the clock on his dashboard. "Or I could take you out for supper." *Say yes....*

"Nein, I'll need to get home. Chores and washing up the dishes from the canning we did. The floor should be scrubbed." She looked away. "Mamm will probably ask Meghan to do it, though. She needs to learn. But if she doesn't, then I'll have to."

"The tire might take awhile. An hour, maybe more, depending on how busy they are at the garage." He secured his own seatbelt, started the engine, and drove off before she had a chance to say she couldn't go, after all. He wanted to spend time with her.

"I got another shopping list from your mamm this morgen. Seems your sister has been craving chocolate-covered strawberries."

Troy chuckled. "She's always been fond of those. At least she's scheduling her cravings in advance, instead of sending her husband out on midnight runs for dill pickles and ice cream."

Janna made a face. "I don't even want to imagine that combination."

"Me, neither." He drove out to the highway, turned right at the light, and then continued to the village of Diggins, where he made another right onto Highway A.

In Marshfield, he pulled into the parking lot of the Walmart Supercenter and headed to the back, where the automotive department was located. When he'd parked, he got out and opened the passenger door for Janna, assisted her in climbing out, and then lifted the shredded tire from the truck bed.

Janna eyed it warily. "I doubt they can fix that."

He chuckled. "Nein, they can't. But it's still under warranty."

She raised her eyebrows. "If you say so."

"Would you want to do some shopping here? Your daed mentioned some groceries you needed to pick up for your family."

She shook her head. "I didn't bring my list, so I'll just go tomorrow morgen. Though I could pick up the strawberries and chocolate your mamm asked for."

He opened the door to the automotive shop and held it for Janna. "Sounds good. I can pay for the items and drop them off after I've taken you home." As they entered the store, Janna winced, probably from all the noise.

A service technician approached them with a smile. "May I help you?"

Troy turned his attention to the business at hand, talking quietly to the service technician, then handed him the keys to his truck. He pushed his way through another door, holding it open for Janna. "There aren't any restaurants within walking distance, but we can grab a snack at the Subway inside the store, if you'd like."

"I'm not hungry, but danki."

He watched Janna glance around as they entered the main part of the store. He wondered if she was hoping not to see anyone who might recognize her and spread the word back home that she'd been out in the company of an Englisch man. If her daed found out, he'd probably assume that she'd been with him.

On the other hand, he didn't really want the bishop to harbor any more ideas in that direction, either. He knew nothing would come of this time with Janna. Nothing possibly could.

And if his mamm found out that Janna had been with him....

He eyed an Amish couple who nodded at Janna and then looked at him, their curious expressions changing as recognition dawned. What had he been thinking? Mamm would find out, for sure.

❧

Janna walked quietly by Troy's side, feeling extremely self-conscious. She didn't dare look around, or even lift her head, for the absence of her black bonnet would make recognition that much easier. She stood out more in Marshfield, anyway, because it was populated by the more conservative Old-Order Amish from other districts. Not only that, but she was with Troy, an Englischer.

Not that she considered that a bad thing. She wanted to be with Troy. And he wasn't shunned—yet—as he was still in his rumschpringe, according to most people. The worst someone might presume would be that they were courting.

Her stomach knotted. She'd best not think of such things.

They were just friends. Still on their way to becoming friends, really.

Yet she wasn't sure she could settle for mere friendship. Not considering the way she'd felt about him for as long as she could remember.

They walked past a display of dinner dishes, and Troy nodded at them. "Suppose you have your hope chest all packed and ready, ain't so?"

Janna stifled a gasp and stumbled. He reached to grasp her elbow. Sparks shot through her and she glanced up at him.

"Steady there." One side of his mouth lifted in a wry smile.

She pulled away. "Danki. I'm fine." She ventured another glance at the display and felt her face flush. "My hope chest is none of your concern." But how she wanted it to be. Had always wanted it to be, ever since she'd knit her first item to fill the chest—a misshapen pot holder—when she'd been a little girl.

They walked in silence for several more aisles, until Troy spoke again: "When I saw you yesterday, for the first time in years, I'll confess that I was surprised to find that you weren't already married."

He seemed determined to bring up subjects that were verboden. Janna shook her head, refusing to comment. How could she? He couldn't know that her infatuation with him had chased away all other prospects.

They entered the grocery side of the store.

"Someone giving you a regular ride home from singings?" he persisted.

If she didn't know better, she'd say he was trying to find out if someone courted her. She had to be reading far more into this exchange than she should. "Does it matter?"

They walked into Subway. He ordered two soft drinks and filled the cups he was handed, then led the way to a table in the back. Troy took the seat against the wall, leaving her to sit across from him, her back to the restaurant. Maybe to protect her from being recognized. Sweet of him, really.

"Doesn't matter, nein." He shook his head. "But if someone is courting you, he needs to know you aren't in love with him."

Chapter 8

Janna stared at him with a mixture of hurt and disbelief.

He knew better. She never would've gotten into his truck if she had a beau—even one she wasn't in love with. She'd be faithful.

He'd simply wanted to verify her availability for curiosity's sake. Or maybe because his heart entertained foolish hopes.

"I'm sorry." He wanted to reach across the table and touch her hand, but he restrained himself. "I shouldn't have said that." He pulled in a breath. "To be honest, I was fishing."

She blinked. "Fishing?"

"To find out if you were seeing someone. I knew better than to ask."

"There's never been anyone," she whispered. "Except...."

He waited, but she didn't fill in the blank. Though she really didn't need to. He caught the telling glance in his direction, then her shy look down. The faint blush that colored her cheeks.

So. She felt the same way toward him that he felt toward her. Always had. If only he'd known it back then.

He would have ruined her life.

Troy looked away.

He would ruin it now, if they got involved.

Knowing that, was he wrong to spend time with her now? To encourage their mutual attraction?

He took a sip of his cola, his thoughts in a jumble. Should he? Or shouldn't he?

He wasn't typically so indecisive. Being an officer meant making a quick assessment of the situation at hand, trusting one's instincts, and following through with decisive action.

But this was uncharted territory. Even though all the signals he'd picked up so far said "Go"—or, at very least, "Proceed with caution"—he needed to take the time to pray about it for several days, or until he had heard from God. Matters of the heart weren't something to mess with unless he had clear guidance.

In the meantime, he'd be content with friendship. After all, he could never have enough friends. And whether she admitted it or not, with her niece and all her baggage, Janna needed him in her corner.

❧

Janna swallowed some of her cola, enjoying the carbonation as it burned its way down her throat. This was a rare treat.

She glanced around the seating area, sparsely peppered with other patrons, and then chanced another look at Troy. He'd wanted to know if someone courted her. A part of her wished she could've said yes. At twenty-one, she was almost an old maid. Courtship usually started at sixteen or seventeen. She'd been too ashamed to admit that no one ever called on her. But she'd never wanted anyone to. Maybe, in a subconscious effort to hold out for Troy, she had managed to discourage all of the eligible Amish men.

Then again, if someone had been courting her, according to Troy, she wasn't in love with him. That would mean…what? That Troy would back off and stop coming around? Or that he would push his way in and infringe on another man's territory?

That sent a shiver up her spine.

She took another sip of soda.

"Have you joined the church?" He openly studied her. "Have you ever considered leaving the Amish?"

Leaving? Janna blinked. Her throat swelled shut. She swallowed, hard. "I joined the church years ago. But, yeah, I considered leaving." Briefly. Right after he'd left. But she'd quickly decided it was foolishness. If he hadn't noticed her as an Amish woman, he'd never notice her as an Englisch one.

"And?" He leaned forward.

She forced a casual shrug. "And I decided to stay."

He sat back. "What's life like for you then, Janna Kauffman?"

She imagined the words he thought but left unspoken: *"No beau, and your best friend left the faith. Must be lonely."* To his credit, he kept quiet.

"Kristi may have left, but she's going to repent." She hoped that had been the purpose of her visit that afternoon.

His brow furrowed in confusion. Maybe he hadn't thought the words she'd imagined. He shook his head, studying her with a slight smile. "How did you turn into a personal shopper, anyway? Odd job for an Amish woman."

"I've always loved shopping. Mamm tasked me with shopping for our family as soon as I was old enough to go into town by myself. Pretty soon, other women started asking if I would pick up this or that, and, before I knew it, I was in business. My biggest clients are the widowers."

"I bet." His gaze skimmed over her, lingering on her lips long enough to send a thrill shooting through her. He raised his eyes to meet hers. "An attractive—no, beautiful—woman like you would get their attention. But…would you marry a widower?"

He thought she was beautiful? Her insides turned to mush. But, a widower? "Ach, I don't know. I suppose, if I marry, that'll be my only option before too long."

He nodded. But he still studied her, his forehead creased, as if he were deep in thought.

After a few moments, he rubbed his chin and grinned. "How do you think I'd look with a beard?"

Her heart pounded.

"Paging Troy Troyer." A voice crackled over the loudspeakers. "Your vehicle is ready for pickup in the automotive department."

Troy sobered and glanced at his watch. "Let's refill our drinks, and then we'll go." He stood up. "Did you want to get the strawberries and chocolate here or at the grocery store in town? I have a cooler in the back, and I can grab a bag of ice."

"We can get them here." Janna stood and popped the plastic lid off of her cup as she followed Troy to the soda dispenser.

He refilled her drink and handed it back to her before filling his own. Then, he made another movement toward her, as if he wanted to hold her hand. But he started walking, his arms at his sides.

If only he would've taken it.

❦

Troy went to his parents' later that night, after their usual bedtime. He figured he would drop off the strawberries and the chocolate undetected. He parked the car, grabbed the grocery bag, and let himself in through the unlocked door. As noiselessly as he could, he stashed the items in the refrigerator. But as he closed the fridge, a beam of light flashed across his face, blinding him.

"Hiram? What are you doing here at this hour?" Daed asked. Mamm stood close behind him.

"Dropping off something Elisabeth wanted." Troy stepped away from the refrigerator. "I didn't mean to wake you."

"We were late getting to bed." Mamm brushed past Daed and came into the room, a battery-powered lantern in one hand, and opened the refrigerator herself. She pulled out a gallon of milk. "Want some?"

"Nein, danki."

Mamm set the lantern on the counter, filled two mugs with milk, and handed one to Daed. She returned the milk to the fridge and then carried the lantern to the table, pulled out a chair, and sat down, beaming up at Troy. "Have a seat, sohn. I heard some wunderbaar news."

Something about her expression filled him with foreboding. He didn't think he wanted to know this news. Especially since he had a good idea what it would be. He'd never seen so many Amish at Walmart. So many spies. "Gut," he said cautiously, edging his way toward the door.

"Ach, nein, don't leave yet. We want to know. They say you're spending time with Janna Kauffman." Mamm studied him.

Troy shot a glance toward Daed, but his father just tugged on his graying beard, surveying him.

"Is that so." Troy didn't inflect the phrase as an inquiry. After all, Amish courting was kept secret until the banns were read. Mamm knew better than to ask.

But then, he hadn't been courting. It'd been an impromptu date, of sorts. With a friend.

"I heard you and Janna were seen together at the creek. And you went to her haus early this afternoon."

For a second, Troy hesitated. How had the news reached her so quickly? It'd been after dark. They'd sat on their boulder, drinking milkshakes from McDonald's, looking at the stars, and talking. Nothing inappropriate had happened. He hadn't even touched her hand, though he'd desperately wanted to do that—and more.

No, Mamm couldn't know about that already. She must have been referring to their first meeting at the creek the day before. But who would have seen them there?

"Listening to idle gossip, Mamm?" Troy grasped the doorknob. At least reports of their trip into Marshfield, dinner out, and second trip to the creek hadn't reached home yet. Though it was only a matter of time until they did. He'd been so focused on Janna, he hadn't paid much attention to anyone else who might have been nearby—friends, neighbors, family…. That news would spread like wildfire in dry brush.

"Abbie Kauffman said you ate dinner with their family last nacht," Mamm said, with the air of a woman who has firsthand knowledge. "She told us during the quilting frolic this afternoon."

Hmm. Had Abbie also mentioned the main reason he'd stopped by—all the trouble with Meghan? The purpose of his visit had been official business, and nowhere near as romantic as Mamm must imagine.

Troy raised an eyebrow and opened the door. He aimed a grin at Mamm. "See, you don't need the news from me. You hear it all by nightfall, anyway." He needed to get out of there before she realized he'd been with Janna and that was why he delivered the strawberries.

"Why don't you kum for dinner tomorrow nacht?" Mamm stood, picked up her empty mug, and deposited it upside down in the sink.

"Jah. Unless I have a hot date." Troy winked.

"You do." Mamm cast him a conspiratorial smile, then shuffled in her too-large slippers toward the door. "Your 'hot date' will be here tomorrow." She giggled as she disappeared with Daed into the darkness of the haus.

He stared after her for a minute. When was the last time he'd heard Mamm giggle? Not since....

Hold it. His "hot date" would be here? At his parents' house?

Troy was tempted to follow his parents back to their bedroom and demand answers. But he stifled the urge. Mamm had something planned. Something involving an Amish woman.

And he hoped he knew who that woman would be.

Chapter 9

*J*anna pushed her shopping cart out of the grocery store, thankful that the load was much lighter than usual. It wasn't her usual day to shop, but she'd needed to make a trip to the store to pick up the items she'd forgotten from her own family's list. Especially the koffee.

Her buggy was parked alongside three others. She loaded the groceries into the cooler in back, then returned the cart to the store.

Outside again, she collected the horse's reins and started to climb into the buggy when she noticed a single rose lying on her seat. She did a double take. Was this the wrong buggy? Nein; there was Tulip, stomping her foot and tossing her mane.

She hesitated before picking up the pink rosebud and bringing the blossom to her nose. As she inhaled the delicate scent, her mind filled with hopeful, wishful thoughts about a certain man.

A police car rolled to a stop beside her buggy.

Janna froze, her heart stuttering. *Not again*. What had Meghan done this time? If she kept this up, she'd be expelled from the fancy school, and then what?

She jumped down from the buggy, eyeing the vehicle warily.

The driver door opened, and Troy slid out, dressed in his uniform, a gun holster over his hips. As he approached, he slid his sunglasses down over his eyes. His smile made her heart do flips.

Yet she couldn't manage to smile back. "Whatever Meghan did, you can tell Daed. He's at home. I don't want to handle it again today."

A frown of confusion etched Troy's features. "Meghan's at school, as far as I know." He came closer. "Mamm said she…uh…."

"Your mamm hand-delivered a letter this morning." Janna wanted to remove his sunglasses, as Daed had done, so she could see his eyes. But she didn't have the nerve.

He nodded, seeming completely at ease. "Jah. She told me she invited you to dinner tonight. I could pick you up, if you'd like. We could meet in the same place where I had a flat tire yesterday."

"Jah. That'd be gut." Janna rolled the stem of the rose between her fingers, careful of the thorns. It felt as if a flock of upset hens had taken up residence in her stomach. She wished she could borrow some of Troy's composure.

Troy reached out and took the flower from her. "A secret admirer, huh?"

Heat flooded Janna's cheeks. "Appears so. There's nein card."

Smiling, he lifted the flower to her face, gently trailing the rosebud over her cheek and down to her lips. The soft petals lingered there for a few seconds, and then he pulled the flower away.

Janna's breath hitched. Her heart raced. She could almost feel the air crackling between them.

Troy took a step back. "I shouldn't have done that," he said, hoarsely. "Forgive me."

"There's nothing to forgive." Nein, this would be something to remember. To cherish.

"I need to get back to work. I'm supposed to be setting up for radar. I just wanted to see you."

She grinned. "Danki for the flower."

He handed it back to her, his fingers grazing hers. "See you tonight. Five fifteen." He turned and walked back to his cruiser. He got inside, shut the door, and lifted his hand in a wave as he drove off.

Janna let out a long sigh. Five fifteen couldn't kum soon enough. She climbed onto the buggy seat and tucked the rose stem into a pocket of her apron, hoping it'd stay. As she flicked the reins, she noticed an Amish couple in black approaching the buggy parked beside hers. She gave them a friendly smile.

They returned it with a judgmental glare. Apparently they'd witnessed—without pleasure—her unplanned tryst with an Englisch police officer.

Her smile vanished. She clicked at Tulip, and they headed for the highway.

The scowling faces of the couple had singed an impression in her mind. To displace it, she thought about how much she looked forward to being with Troy tonight—and with his family, of course. Maybe the two of them could spend a few minutes alone. A drive in his truck wouldn't last as long as a buggy ride, but at least they'd be together.

She was curious as to what he'd told his mamm and daed to warrant the invitation. What was his parents' impression of their relationship? What was Troy's? He wanted her to spend time with his family, that much was clear. And he'd left a red rose on the seat of her buggy. Did this mean he wanted to court her?

Her heart pounded at the possibility.

Troy parked the police cruiser in a turnaround between the northbound and southbound lanes and settled back in his seat to wait. An alarm went off anytime someone approached his radar driving above the speed limit, so he didn't need to watch that closely. He pulled out his cell phone and checked it for messages, then powered up his e-reader. He'd arrived at the exciting part of an action-packed thriller and was anxious to finish.

He pushed the button to lower the windows a bit, loosened the seatbelt, and settled in. He'd finished a chapter when he heard horse hooves and buggy wheels approaching. He glanced up as Janna passed on the edge of the southbound side of the road. She waved.

His grin was short-lived, as the radar alarm sounded. He tossed the e-reader on the seat beside him, refastened his seatbelt, and prepared to move. He wouldn't turn the siren on until he was well away from Janna so he wouldn't spook her horse. As soon as traffic cleared enough, Troy pulled into the highway after the red Corvette.

Lights flashing, he sped past Janna, weaving in and out of traffic.

༄

Hours later, Janna's heart still seemed to be lodged in her throat. As soon as she'd put the groceries away, she hurried out to the barn and hid in the loft. The tears she'd managed to hold at bay for the entire trip home finally escaped, making trails her face and dripping off her chin. She scooped up a newborn kitten and cradled it close.

She'd never really grasped that Troy's job sometimes required high-speed chases. That it was dangerous enough to warrant him wearing a gun strapped to his hips. *Lord, protect him. Keep him safe in those dangerous vehicles. And return him to the faith. Please.*

The last line of her prayer seemed so hopeless. As far as Troy had removed himself from all things Amish, it'd take an act of God for him to return.

Janna sighed and wiped her face.

The ladder creaked, and Daed's head appeared over the edge of the loft. He kept climbing until he was high enough to step off the rung. He turned in her direction, then hesitated.

"Janna. I didn't know you were up here. I came to check on the kittens."

"They're fine." Janna hoped he hadn't noticed the catch in her voice.

Daed sat next to her and reached for a kitten. "Everything okay?"

Janna shook her head. "I was praying."

He nodded. "You saw him in town."

"Jah. At the grocery store. He said something about radar. When I was on my way home, he passed me, chasing someone down the highway. Weaving in between all the cars. Ach, Daed, he'll never return."

"Our God is the God of miracles, Janna. Let's not give up on him yet."

"God? Or Troy?"

Daed smiled. "Both." He returned the kitten to the mama cat. "Keep praying. God has a plan."

"I know. But His plans and mine don't always mesh."

"Then you must align your will with His."

"That's not always easy to do, ain't so?" Janna glanced toward the rafters. "His parents invited me for dinner tonight."

Silence.

She looked at Daed. His grin had widened.

"I have high hopes for that bu." He patted her hand, then got to his feet. "Keep praying. Try not to push him away, even if it seems hopeless."

Janna frowned. "You're telling me to risk my heart and face potential shunning if something develops between Troy and me?"

Daed turned to face her and shook his head. "Nein. Amish need to marry Amish. You know that. But that bu needs to return to the fold. And I think you may be the one to bring him home."

"Daed, I can't. Whether he returns or not is between him and God." She couldn't do such an impossible task.

"Jah." Daed moved toward the ladder. "But God has a plan. And it involves you."

Chapter 10

*T*roy stood in front of his pickup, his anticipation building as he waited for Janna to come down the road. He glanced at his watch. 5:25. She wouldn't stand his parents up, would she?

Had something happened at home that prevented her from coming? If only she had a cell phone so he could call her.

He sighed. Maybe he should drive to her house and see what kept her. Before climbing in, he took one last look around. There she was, cutting across the fields toward him.

Troy couldn't keep from grinning. He strode in her direction, resisting the urge to open his arms and pull her close. "Hey! You made it."

"Sorry I'm late. I had to get dinner on at home. Mamm needed to take care of Grossmammi, since my aent has a bad cold."

He made a sympathetic face. "Is Meghan behaving? I have a few possibilities lined up for community service."

"Nein." Janna held up her hand. "Talk to Daed about it."

Troy nodded. "I'll come by next week sometime, then."

"Maybe stay for dinner?" A small smile played on her lips.

His gaze lingered on her mouth. He wanted to kiss her. But it was way too soon for that. Besides, affectionate behavior needed to be discreet. Here, on the side of the road, they were hardly hidden. Anybody might drive by and see them.

"Dinner, jah. Definitely." His gaze roved over her. "We should get going. Mamm likes to serve dinner promptly at five thirty." He glanced at his watch again.

She smiled and headed to the passenger side of the truck. He stood for a moment, admiring the sway of her skirts as she walked. The way the dress skimmed over her curves. He swallowed hard, then hurried to open the door for her. She slid in and buckled up.

Troy pulled in a shaky breath. He wasn't at all prepared for whatever this evening would bring.

For the first time in years, he wished for a horse and buggy, complete with the narrower seats and the slower pace, all for the chance to be close to Janna as they traveled down the dirt road for a couple of miles. The truck would get them to his parents' entirely too fast.

He had it bad.

❧

Janna's stomach churned. She'd grown up around Troy's family, gone to church with them, and attended singings at their haus when she'd been a teen in her rumschpringe. Now she did their shopping and had a friendly relationship with them. But this would be the first time she faced them as the woman Troy courted.

If that's what he was doing.

It looked as if he was, and the gossip grapevine would state it as fact. But Troy had never kum right out and asked her to be his girl.

Janna had mixed feelings about him courting her, mostly because he was deeply imbedded in the Englisch world. But it sounded like Daed was in favor of a relationship between them, based on their conversation in the barn loft. He'd basically commissioned her to bring him home.

Troy knew his way around her heart, maneuvering his way into her affections. Already. Though she'd never really stopped caring for him. Never stopped loving him.

It hadn't even been three full days since they'd flirted with each other in the produce aisle. Their relationship, however it was to be classified, moved too fast. And too slow, as aware as she was of him.

What would it be like to be kissed by Hiram "Troy" Troyer? Maybe she'd find out tonight. A thrill shot through her. Of course, he'd probably had lots of practice, whereas she had only the cold unresponsiveness of her handheld mirror and the compensations of her overactive imagination. The real thing had to be far better.

Troy stopped the truck in the driveway by his parents' back porch.

Janna swallowed her trepidation as Troy slid out of the truck and came around to her side. He opened her door and extended his hand to help her out. She grasped it, enjoying the spark of his touch, the friction of his rough skin against hers.

Ach, Troy. She stood close to him for a moment, just to see what would happen.

He stepped back with a fleeting smile. "Well, shall we?"

His mamm appeared on the porch, drying her hands on her apron. "Welkum, Janna! Elisabeth is going to kum downstairs to eat with us tonight. Isn't that wunderbaar?"

Janna blinked. "Is she feeling well enough? I know she's been on bed rest. I'm willing to go upstairs to visit with her. I don't want to jeopardize her health, or that of the boppli."

"Ach, you're sweet, but you'll do nein such thing. The midwife has given her permission to get up some, as long as she's careful not to overdo it."

Troy's hand shifted in hers, squeezing slightly before releasing it.

She wished he would have held on. She needed his strength as she prepared to see his mamm and sister under these circumstances. Besides, she really liked holding his hand.

Janna found a smile as she proceeded to the porch, ahead of Troy. His mamm opened her arms, gathered her in a hug, and gave her a kiss. "I'm so glad you could join us on such short notice."

"Danki for having me, Mrs. Troyer."

"Why so formal all of a sudden? You know to call me Rosie."

Janna smiled. "May I help you with anything, Rosie?"

"Oh, I think I have things under control. Dinner is almost ready. I'll just get you a glass of lemonade, and we'll visit. Hiram, go get your daed and Paul. They're in the barn. Tell them to kum inside and wash up."

Troy gave Janna a quick wink before he turned and headed for the barn.

Rosie sighed, watching her son as he strode away. She wrapped her arm around Janna's waist. "I'd about given up on him. And then I found out about you. I never should have lost faith. So gut to know he's courting an Amish woman."

Janna opened her mouth to correct her, because she still wasn't sure they were courting. Renewing a friendship, jah.

Rosie pulled her into another tight hug. "I'm glad it's you. So glad. Just don't let him lure you away. You bring him home."

Not Troy's mamm, too. Janna stifled a groan.

Talk about pressure.

Troy stepped into the darkness of the barn. Instead of going to find Daed and Paul, he hesitated a moment, glancing back at the haus. Mamm had embraced Janna again. He shook his head. His parents' approval was nice, and Janna did seem to be warming to the idea of being in a relationship with him, the more time they spent together. He hadn't missed the invitation in her eyes just seconds before Mamm had stepped onto the porch. And, as much as he'd wanted to kiss her, he didn't feel at peace about that step just yet.

For now, it felt right to cultivate a friendship with her. He still had a lot of praying to do about the relationship. He didn't intend to make any promises he couldn't keep.

Casually dating Janna was one thing; courting her, quite another. Being Amish, she'd expect courtship. He'd forgotten that when he told her he wanted to date her. Probably the reason she'd refused him.

He raked his fingers through his hair, and turned toward the dairy section. Male voices came from the back of the barn. He opened the door and went down the six concrete steps. Daed and Paul worked at the end of the room, on opposite sides, hand-milking.

"Need help?" Troy went further into the room.

"Nein. About finished."

"Gut. Mamm sent me out to tell you to wash up for dinner."

Paul looked up and smirked. "That girl you're courting here?"

Troy's stomach clenched. "Janna's here. But we're just friends."

"Not the way I heard it." Paul straightened. "Heard you gave her a rose this morgen."

The grapevine worked fast. Too fast. That meant his sister would be eyeing him and Janna all through dinner, trying to gauge how he felt about her, and vice versa. Mamm had already formed her opinion.

He hoped Janna wouldn't ask him to define their relationship. He hated it when Englisch women did that. Like they weren't capable of having a casual association after a certain point.

But saying he wanted to stay just friends would bring the relationship to an end. He didn't want to do that. He wanted her friendship—and more, when the time was right.

If the time was ever right.

He left the barn and went to the house—and Janna.

Through the kitchen window, he could see her standing at the counter with Mamm, pouring lemonade into glasses. Elisabeth sat at the kitchen table, fanning herself with a napkin.

When he walked through the door, his sister turned and met his gaze. And beamed as she might at her newborn baby.

In this household, at least, the relationship between him and Janna was set in concrete.

No doubt that was the case in the Kauffmans' home, too. As well as in every other Amish home in the district.

Troy swallowed. He had no defining to do. Janna wouldn't ask. She'd simply follow his lead. The way she'd been taught.

Ready or not, he courted Janna Kauffman.

A thrill of excitement rippled through him.

He. Courted. Janna Kauffman.

Chapter 11

Janna turned around to hand Elisabeth a glass of cold lemonade. She faltered when she noticed Troy standing there with an odd expression in his eyes, one she couldn't begin to understand. But his smile was gentle. Kind.

He washed up, pulled out a chair, and sat down at the table. His gaze rested on her. She set Elisabeth's lemonade in front of her, then turned to retrieve a glass for Troy. His mamm and sister had fallen silent, but both had wide, knowing grins on their faces.

Whatever they thought they knew was wrong. Discomfort washed over Janna, the way water rushed over the low-water bridge during a heavy rainstorm.

In time, maybe she would feel less awkward around Troy's family. Right now, though, they eyed her as if they expected Troy to announce his intentions—or have banns read on the next church Sunday.

Even if their relationship had progressed to that point, Troy hadn't started baptism classes.

She took a deep breath, trying to control her nerves, and carried his drink to the table.

Rosie set a plate in front of each of the six chairs. "You can sit next to Hiram," she told Janna with a smile.

She stifled a gasp. Really? Normally, men sat on one side of the table, women on the other.

Troy raised his eyebrows at the unconventional seating arrangement. But then he shrugged, stood, and pulled out the chair next to his.

"Is there anything else I can do to help?" Janna hovered next to her seat. Too close to Troy, really. He kept his hands firmly on the back of the chair, waiting.

"Ach, nein. Have a seat, dear." Rosie turned and bustled back to the stove.

Not knowing what else to do, Janna sat. Troy pushed the chair in, then gently touched her shoulder before returning to his seat.

Settled next to her, he reached under the table for her hand and gave it a squeeze. She thrilled at the contact.

Elisabeth smiled at her. "I've heard Kristi Lapp might be working as a midwife again."

Janna blinked. "It's Zimmerman now, but I didn't know she'd stopped."

Elisabeth looked away.

Ach, the shunning. None of the Amish would have contacted Kristi.

Janna glanced at Troy, then back at Elisabeth. "Daed hasn't said." That was all she could say, truthfully. She would not speculate about the reasons behind her best friend's discussion with Daed on Saturday.

Troy's hand tightened around hers. "I've been meaning to get acquainted with Shane Zimmerman. Hear he's a great vet. Guess I'll stop by his farm sometime."

Janna wondered if that meant he might take her to visit Kristi. Or was she still reading too much into his comments?

If only he'd say the words so she could stop second-guessing his intentions, as well as their relationship. And stop pinching herself to see if this were really happening to her.

Rosie was carrying the platters of food to the table when the door opened and Troy's daed and brother-in-law came in. They headed over to the sink and washed up. After a brief hesitation at the odd table arrangement, Elam sat at the end, as the patriarch of the family, and Paul sat next to his frau.

"Nice treat to have Hiram and Janna with us tonight. And to have Elisabeth feeling well enough to make it downstairs." Elam glanced around the table. "Let us give thanks." He bowed his head for the silent prayer, and everyone else followed suit.

Troy's hand released hers and slid against her knuckles on its way back to his own lap. She immediately missed the contact, though she supposed it would be hard to eat if they continued. And it would only increase the size of the grins on the others' faces. As if she didn't feel enough pressure already.

When they raised their heads after prayer, she was surprised to feel Troy's foot bump against hers and settle in next to it.

◈◈◈

Troy had been pushing the boundaries. He knew it, and Janna probably did, too. But then, he always had. A trait that'd gotten him into a lot of trouble as a bu. It had probably played a part in his departure from the faith.

Forget *probably*.

It'd had everything to do with it.

Janna shifted the tiniest bit closer. Her skirt swirled around his pants' leg. He closed his eyes a moment, relishing her nearness, a big grin on his face he couldn't remove. If only they didn't have to stay here after the meal was finished. But Mamm would expect Janna to stay and get acquainted with the family, her prospective in-laws.

He shifted as Janna passed him the bowl of buttery English peas with pearl onions. He shoved the spoon inside, cringing at the high-pitched squeak when the utensil scraped the bottom of the clear glass dish.

Mamm had gone all out with this meal. Fresh-baked bread, still warm; homemade butter; a tender, falling-apart roast; mashed potatoes; and the peas. Across the room on the counter sat a couple of coconut-cream pies—Mamm's specialty.

"Everything looks and smells delicious," he said. "It's been ages since I've eaten a home-cooked meal."

Well, not exactly. More like a few days, since he did eat with Janna's family once. Except that was marred by Meghan's behavior. And the bishop's too-seeing eyes.

"You could have them more often." Paul looked up from his plate. "Just have to make an effort to kum by."

"Or get married." Elisabeth aimed a smirk in his direction. "Though maybe that's in the not-too-distant future."

Troy's face heated. He didn't dare glance at Janna to see how she took the teasing. Out of the corner of his eye, he saw her squirm in her seat.

On second thought…. He looked up. Janna's flaming cheeks probably mirrored his own.

He turned his eyes on his sister, firming his features into the impassive look he'd mastered in police academy and perfected further through on-the-job training. "That's enough."

Elisabeth sobered and nodded, to his surprise. She leaned back in her chair and looked at Janna. "I'm sorry. I know it's too soon. But we're all just so excited it's you."

Janna swallowed and glanced at Troy. After a moment, she looked away.

Troy forced himself to relax and take a bite of meat. It *was* too soon. And if his family, as well as the community, didn't ease up on their expectations—and lay off the teasing—

they'd scare her away, snuffing out their kindling relationship before he even had a chance to win her.

And he wanted to win her.

But enough to return to the faith? He just didn't know. Things would be so much easier if she agreed to jump the fence for him.

He'd have a talk with his family about this, for sure. If Janna continued to do their shopping, she'd be walking into a ticking time bomb every time she came by. They needed to back off until his intentions—and Janna's—were clear.

Any future courting would be done outside of the community, someplace they wouldn't be known. Like Springfield. And he would stay away from the local grocery store when she might be present.

Maybe he should revert to the time-honored method of tossing pebbles at her bedroom window and inviting her on a walk down the road under the cover of darkness.

He liked that idea. Tonight, he'd ask her which window was hers.

Time to let the gossip die down.

❧

How did Troy manage turn himself into an intimidating policeman and then, seconds later, transform back into the man she'd been spending time with? Even his sister had seemed unsettled by his other persona.

Janna tried to relax. Yet she couldn't help wondering what thoughts were going through Troy's head. Did he regret having told his family about her? Or had he even done that? It could be that the grapevine had been their sole source of news about their budding relationship, and that they'd made their own assumptions, thereby placing Troy in the same awkward position as her.

Jah, that was probably the case. Nein man—especially not an Amish one—would put a woman in this situation without first announcing his intentions to her.

Otherwise, she might as well expect him to drop her off where he'd picked her up, make some excuse for not being available tomorrow, and avoid her on all future chance meetings in town. That would end things before they'd begun, to be sure.

Her eyes burned. She shouldn't react this way. She'd warned herself that Troy's world was too different from hers. But she'd allowed herself to believe the encouraging words Daed had spoken in the barn loft that afternoon. To hope Troy would fall in love with her and want to return to the Amish.

To dream of his kisses.

Janna heard a low buzzing sound. Troy leaned back in his seat and pulled his cell phone out of his front pocket. He glanced at it. "Excuse me," he said, standing up. "Got to take this." He headed for the door. "Troyer," he said as he stepped outside.

When Troy finally came back into the haus, dinner was over, and Rosie was slicing up her homemade pies. Janna studied him, noting his troubled expression. But he didn't say anything, other than another apology to the family as a whole.

The rest of the evening passed quickly. Too soon, she said good-bye to the Troyers, got into Troy's truck, and rode home.

Troy pulled into the driveway of her parents' haus and turned off the engine. "I'll walk you to the door."

"You don't need to." Still, the idea thrilled her.

"Jah, I do." He got out, came around to her side, and helped her down. But this time, he released her hand immediately.

Janna smiled away her disappointment. "Your family is really sweet. I'm glad your sister is doing better."

"Jah." He hesitated. "Listen. That phone call I got during dinner…turns out I have to work tomorrow. They need me to cover for someone. I won't be able to take you into Springfield. I called one of the Amish drivers for you. A woman. She'll be here at eight."

"Ach." It was happening just the way she'd thought.

She forced her chin up and squared her shoulders. She couldn't let him know how this rejection affected her. "Danki." Hopefully, he didn't notice the wobble in her voice.

"I have to work Sunday, too, but I'll stop by sometime to talk to your daed about Meghan." He touched her hand, briefly. "And stay for dinner, if I'm still invited."

She nodded, not trusting her ability to speak. Tears burned her eyes and clogged her throat.

He stopped by the front porch, extended a trembling hand, and let it trail over her cheek. "Janna…."

She moved out of his reach. He didn't have the right to touch her like that, even if she wanted him to. She climbed the steps.

"Danki for coming tonight, Janna. Gut nacht."

She nodded again, opened the door, and went inside. The sound of raised voices fraught with tension drifted out from the kitchen. She wouldn't count on Troy staying for dinner whenever he came to talk to Daed.

Their relationship was over.

If it had ever really begun.

She swallowed hard. Maybe she could slip upstairs and get her emotions under control before she had to face her family.

She took a couple of silent steps toward the stairs.

Daed said something, quietly, that Janna couldn't discern.

"You can't make me!" came Meghan's loud-and-clear retort. "Besides, you're just like other men, even if you are my grandfather. I know you were up in the loft with Aunt Janna today. Wonder what your 'perfect Amish community' would say if they knew?" There was an ugly, sneering note in Meghan's voice. Something in the kitchen shattered, and in the next moment, someone carried a flashlight lantern into the front room.

Why would anyone care that she'd been in the loft with Daed?

Nothing about that exchange made sense.

Janna slunk into the shadows as her niece stomped up the stairs.

Chapter 12

Saturday afternoon dragged. From his post on the southbound highway, Troy eyed every white van that passed, but he never saw the driver he'd called for Janna. He sighed, fingering his e-reader. Last night's rejection replayed in his mind in slow motion.

He'd had big plans for when he would drop Janna off. He'd intended to ask her to be his girl, getting that formality out of the way. He'd wanted to find out which window was hers. And he'd hoped for their first kiss, there in the darkness.

Somewhere between parking at the end of the driveway and walking her to the door, something had gone totally wrong.

It might have been the stress at home, on account of Meghan. He had overheard a snippet of heated conversation when Janna had opened the door and gone inside, but he hadn't been able to make out what was being said.

Jah, had to be the tension. He couldn't think of any other possible explanation.

In this case, his plans would have to be moved to another location. A safe place where she'd be more open to him, and not so bothered by whatever was going on at home. Maybe the creek.

No. As much privacy as it afforded, it was still too public. They'd already been seen there together.

He could send her a letter asking her to join him for dinner. He'd take her into Springfield, to a nice restaurant, and ask her to be his girl.

The kiss would have to wait.

God would open the door when the time was right.

He reached for his ticket pad and scribbled a reminder: *Write Janna.*

⸎

Janna's feet ached and her head pounded when the driver finally dropped her off at home on Saturday nacht. The errands had taken all day, thanks to the heavy city traffic, and her unfamiliarity with the layout of the various stores had slowed things down, too. She was glad she'd asked her clients for detailed lists.

The deliveries would have to wait until Monday. It was too late tonight, and tomorrow was a church Sunday, devoted to the service and to church meetings.

The driver helped Janna stack the inedible purchases in a pile next to her buggy in the barn before heading home to her own family.

Janna dragged her feet into the haus, dreading what she'd find there. But it was quiet. Mamm sat in a chair, doing some mending in the light of the gas lamp. Daed sat next to her, reading *The Budget*. Meghan didn't seem to be around. Janna wouldn't ask where she'd gone. She didn't want to know.

Daed looked up with a smile that didn't reach his eyes. Shadows she'd never noticed before resided in their depths, and deep wrinkles furrowed his brow. He looked tired. Discouraged.

For that matter, so did Mamm. Things must not have gone well at home during her absence. They hadn't talked at all about what had transpired last nacht while she'd been away, either. Daed had simply disappeared during the wee hours of the morning, made a brief appearance for breakfast, and then left again. Mamm had done her morning chores in silence.

"Have a seat, Janna." Daed motioned toward the other chair.

She obeyed, reaching for a ball of black yarn and a sock that needed mending. She figured she might as well help.

"How was dinner with the Troyers last nacht? We didn't get a chance to talk."

Janna hesitated, taking her time threading the needle with the thick strand of yarn. "Dinner was gut. They seemed to think we were a couple. I think it scared Tr—him." She couldn't say his name. It hurt too much.

Daed's lips turned down further. "He won't be coming around, then."

Janna shook her head, swallowing the sob that rose in her throat. "Not for me, nein. There's still the issue of Meghan's community service requirement. He'll be out sometime next week to discuss that with you."

Daed expelled a heavy breath. "Supposed to be something happening at David Troyer's farm tonight. Meghan went. You should really make an effort to go to the youth activities, Janna. You might meet a nice young man from another district."

Janna shrugged. "I had to work today. And it's too late now." Plus, she really didn't want to attend any event at the Troyers'. Rumor had it that they drew the wild ones. She was surprised Daed had let Meghan go. Though, maybe she'd given him no choice. Hadn't she yelled "You can't stop me" last nacht? That might be why Daed wanted Janna to go. To "babysit" Meghan and make sure she didn't get into trouble.

"There's a singing tomorrow nacht." Daed eyed her over the newspaper.

"It's just hard without...." *Kristi*. She wasn't allowed to speak her best friend's name. Besides, Kristi was married now. "Maybe I'll talk to Katie Detweiler, see if she's going. It'd be easier if I knew a close friend would be there."

Daed nodded. "The singing will be at Mose Detweiler's tomorrow nacht. Katie's haus. She'll be there."

"Nein choice, Daed?" She really would have liked some time to mourn over Troy. But Daed probably wanted to prevent her from moping around like she'd done when Troy had left the faith.

He shook his head. "You're going."

⁕

Troy jerked to attention when he heard the dispatcher's voice, broken by slight static, over the radio. A wild party needed breaking up. Amish address, but it was probably an Englisch neighbor who'd reported it. He secured his seatbelt and headed in that direction, another police car trailing him. Behind that one, he saw a rising dust cloud—a third officer responding to the call. Maybe they expected drugs. The thought made his heart heavy, though he knew some of the Amish youth used. The caller had reported that there were Englisch at the party, as well.

Word must have spread that the cops were coming. As he neared the field, cars sped away in every direction. Other teens whipped at horses, urging them toward the road. One of the officers made a sharp U-turn and sped after the cars. The officer behind Troy passed, going around the buggy full of teenagers. Troy slowed down and tailed a buggy whose driver whipped the horse as hard as possible. As if that would prompt it to outrun a police car.

Such behavior usually meant there was something to hide.

Troy should know.

Heaviness descended over him.

He radioed for backup when he'd followed the buggy for more than a mile, and the teenage driver had ignored his repeated commands through the bull horn to pull over.

The slow-speed buggy chase finally ended when four more police cars raced up behind him, lights flashing. One passed the buggy and skidded sideways, effectively blocking the road.

Unable to stop in time, the horse ran into the side of the cruiser, stumbled, and fell on its side. One of the wooden sidepieces on the buggy snapped in two.

The teens jumped from the buggy and started running.

Troy slammed on the breaks and vaulted from his cruiser, leaving the door open. He took off after them, tackling a boy to the ground just before he reached the woods. An older officer huffed up behind him. "I'll take him."

Troy nodded, rolled to his feet, and ran after another teen—an Englisch girl this time. When he overtook her, he grabbed her by the arm, yanked her up, and marched her back to the waiting vehicles. The lights from the cars revealed the identity of his catch.

Meghan.

She gave him her typical glare. Troy merely sighed. Another officer patted her down and then shoved her into the back of a different car. Troy was glad he didn't have to take her home. He would've dreaded facing Bishop Dave and Janna with this one. At least Meghan wasn't in possession of drugs, though he wasn't positive she hadn't been using them.

Bad enough that he was the one who'd taken Meghan down and that she'd recognized him. He didn't need further interference between him and Janna.

Chapter 13

*D*aed closed the big German Bible in his lap and lifted it onto the small round table between him and Mamm. Without a word, he bowed his head for silent prayers. Mamm closed her eyes. Janna stared out the window into the darkness. Was Troy still working? Or was he at home, doing whatever Englischers do at nacht? Maybe he was with another woman. An Englisch one.

She didn't like the feeling that flooded her heart. Jealousy, pure and simple. *Ach, Lord. Forgive me.*

She shouldn't allow herself to think of him. She tangled her hands in her apron and tried to force her mind back to the Scripture Daed had just read: *"In every thing give thanks: for this is the will of God in Christ Jesus concerning you."* How could God expect her to give thanks for the upheaval in their home and lives? Did He really expect her to be thankful that Meghan lived with them and caused such tension? Should she praise Him for Troy's messing with her heart and emotions, only to desert her? Sighing, she bowed her head. *Forgive my mood, Lord. Help me to be thankful for what You've done. To be thankful for my blessings, whatever they are.* Her attitude reared its ugly head again. She'd count her blessings when she got into bed.

Daed cleared his throat, signaling the end of prayer. "Ready, Abbie?" He stood and reached for Mamm's hand. "Nacht, Janna."

Mamm smiled. "Gut nacht, Janna. Rest well." She and Daed headed upstairs, hands clasped.

"Gut nacht." Janna followed behind them.

Midway up the stairs, she paused at the sound of gravel crunching under car wheels.

Troy? Her momentary surge of hope quickly fizzled out. He wouldn't be coming by. "Who could it be this late?" Janna turned around and headed back down the steps, Daed behind her.

Red and blue lights flashed outside the windows.

"Police?" Dread filled Daed's voice. He pulled the door open.

Meghan stood there on the porch, her upper arm in the clutches of a hard-faced police officer. At least it wasn't Troy. Janna swallowed and drew back, stunned by the open defiance on Meghan's face.

"David Kauffman? We just broke up a party. She's had plenty to drink. She wasn't in possession, but possibly used...." The officer's words didn't make sense to Janna, probably due to the pounding in her head.

Daed's shoulders slumped. "Thank you, Officer." He stepped back. "Go to your room, Meghan. We'll talk in the morgen."

Meghan's upper lip curled into a sneer, but when the officer released her, she headed upstairs without comment.

Janna turned to Daed as the officer returned to his car. "What are we going to do?" A door slammed upstairs.

"You're too young to remember, but she's just like her mother. Trouble to the core. Don't know why Sharon thinks I can handle her daughter when I couldn't handle her." He shut the door and turned away. "I need to spend much time in prayer. You pray, too."

"What was it that drew Sharon away?" Janna followed Daed into the kitchen. "You never did tell me."

He sighed. "I guess it's time you knew." He poured a mugful of milk and sat at the table. "An Amish bu courted her, and she got...in the family way, but, by that time, her young man had left the faith. So, she followed him out into the world." He shook his head. "But, after that, I don't know. He returned home a couple of years later, repented, and married someone else. He said Sharon never contacted him. And we went several years without hearing from your sister. Didn't know if she was alive or dead."

"She's still not gut at keeping in touch." Janna leaned back against the counter.

"Nein. Just when she wants something." Daed frowned. "Meghan has much to overcome." He drained his mug and pushed to his feet. "We should get to bed. Need to be rested for tomorrow." He winked at Janna. "There'll be a surprise for you then."

Janna raised her eyebrows, but Daed said nothing more; he merely gave her a mysterious grin.

Troy? Maybe he'd be at the singing. *If only.*

⁂

Troy shut his eyes against the glare of sunrise coming through his window. He hadn't bothered pulling the shades last night, preferring to stare out at the starry sky and pray for the Kauffman family. He could only imagine their reactions when Meghan arrived home in her condition. Drunk, for sure; the smell of beer on her breath had been unmistakable. And, given the drugs they'd found, she might have been stoned, as well—a condition some of the officers called "droned."

Would Meghan be stupid enough to mix drugs and alcohol? He shook his head. She seemed like a smart girl, but intelligence had nothing to do with it. If only her brains could be channeled in the right direction.

No point in trying to sleep any longer. The aromas of fresh-brewed coffee and sizzling bacon assailed his senses, as did the blaring sound of either the television or the radio, he couldn't tell which. Joey's cowboy boots clomped down the hall outside his room, accompanied by a light clicking noise.

He glanced at the clock beside his bed. He'd have time to make it to church, if he chose to attend the one where he'd been going on his rare Sundays off duty. Or was this the day the Amish community met for preaching and fellowship?

If it were, then it'd be nice to join them, maybe see Janna, if only for a brief conversation. Anything longer would fuel gossip. He could apologize again for having to bow out of the trip into Springfield yesterday.

His lips twitched. He'd never thought a woman would affect him this way—make him willing to sit through a long service on a hard, backless bench rather than the soft, cushioned chairs that furnished the sanctuary at his church.

He checked the calendar on his cell phone and tried to calculate the Amish church schedule. He shook his head. It'd been too long since he'd met with them. And Mamm hadn't talked about church in a while. She'd probably given up on him.

Even if it were a church Sunday, he had no idea who was hosting the services.

He'd go to his usual place of worship.

His focus needed to be on God, anyway, and not on a certain woman.

Troy turned the doorknob, opened his bedroom door, and shuffled across the hall to the bathroom. In the kitchen, a woman giggled. Joey'd had an overnight guest? That explained the clicking down the hall he'd heard earlier. Stilettos. Joey must have gone to a club in Springfield last night.

For the first time, this bothered Troy. Maybe due to his more conservative roots. Or maybe it was jealousy. Not caring to figure it out, he ducked back inside his room, snagged a pair of lounge pants, and pulled them on.

If only he could afford his own place. But rent was high, and houses were scarce, since Seymour was basically a bedroom community for Springfield.

He yanked a T-shirt over his head, then ventured across the hall.

A few minutes later, the hot water was washing over him, massaging muscles sore from tackling teens last night.

He had to get out of here. Daed always warned him that he would become like his friends. Troy had ignored him at the time, but now it seemed Daed was right. If he'd listened as a teen, then…

Troy's throat swelled. Tears sprang to his eyes. He straightened his posture and firmed his face. "Nein."

Would Mamm and Daed let him move back home? It'd get him away from Joey, back into the thick of things with his community, and, best of all, nearer to Janna.

On the other hand, it would put him right back in the middle of his mistakes.

He couldn't do it.

✦

During the service, Janna's tears flowed freely as she watched Kristi kneel in repentance for her sins. The Amish community would forgive Kristi, welcome her back, and never again mention that she'd left the faith for an Englisch man.

Janna fought the urge to bounce right off the narrow bench, rush up the center aisle separating the men from the women, and wrap her best friend in a hug. Instead, she grasped Katie Detweiler's hand, anchoring herself to her seat.

Kristi's ehemann, Shane, knelt before the preachers, water streaming over his face and back. Daed had poured it over his head in observance of the believer's baptism.

Janna couldn't believe he'd agreed to become Amish. Maybe someday, Troy would be the one getting baptized into the church.

Get real. Troy wouldn't return. Janna blinked away the heartbreak and tried to focus on the joy of having Kristi restored to the faith.

When the congregation was dismissed, Janna lurched to her feet, still holding Katie's hand. She wanted to push her way through the crowd to get to Kristi's side, but that would be inappropriate. She'd waited this long. She could wait a bit longer. Maybe she'd visit her friend tomorrow. She forced herself to turn to Katie. "Let's go put the meal out."

Katie nodded. "I brought the peach pie I made yesterday. It's a new recipe, and I'd love to know what you think of it. Can you stay the afternoon? You are coming to the singing, ain't so?"

"Jah." Janna sighed. "Daed said he'll arrange a ride home for me, if no one asks." And no one would. She'd attended these singings since she was sixteen, and no one had ever driven her home. Not even Tr—

Nein. She would not think of him.

"Ach, someone will ask. You're so beautiful."

Janna shrugged. "I don't know. I think I must be subconsciously sending the message that I'm not available. I don't mean to, because no one could possibly be more available than I am, but—"

Katie laughed. "Except me. Trust me, you'll get married a long time before I do. I'm too shy to even talk to the buwe."

Janna touched Katie's hand. "You can do it. When that special someone comes around...." She leaned toward Katie and nodded at an Amish man who looked their way. "What about him? He just moved to our district from Indiana. I think Daed said his name is Micah."

The man inclined his head, as if he knew she was talking about him. He said something to the other men around him, turned, and headed straight toward Janna and Katie.

Chapter 14

*T*roy took down the envelope he'd found taped to his front door. It was marked "Hiram Troyer," which meant someone in the Amish community had brought it by. He broke the seal, pulled out a single sheet of paper, and unfolded it.

Troy,

> *There's a singing tonight at the Detweilers'. Janna will be there. She might need a ride home.*

> Dave Kauffman

The word "might" was bothersome. Yet he didn't care to explore the emotions that washed through him.

He stared at the note for a few moments, then glanced at his watch. He'd be late. Hopefully, Janna didn't have a ride yet.

If only he hadn't gone into Springfield with his friends. They'd met at a steakhouse for lunch, and afterward, since no one had made other plans, they'd gone to the mall and also visited some other stores in the area. Troy had purchased something for Janna, but he wasn't sure when he'd give it to her.

If he'd gone straight home, he would have been there when the bishop had stopped by, and he could have been at the singing on time.

Interesting. Bishop Dave, matchmaking. Interesting. And for his own daughter, no less. With you. The black sheep. A chill traveled down his spine. Did the bishop know something he didn't? Had God spoken to him, revealing that Troy would someday return to the faith?

Inconceivable.

It wouldn't happen. It would take nothing less than a miracle to get Troy to kneel before the bishop and the other preachers. A union between him and Janna would require Bishop Dave to shun his daughter.

Troy was realistic enough to know that, in the long term, Janna would never choose him over her community. Even if she did agree to be his girl, it would be "for now," not "for good."

Regardless, he'd go to the singing. And he'd ask Janna if he could take her home. The long way. With a side trip to the creek.

He carried the took the note inside, laid it underneath his pillow, and headed back out the door.

The singing was already breaking up when he arrived. He parked the truck, ignoring the curious stares from the ones still hanging out, and went looking for Janna. He didn't see her in any of the small groups standing around. Swallowing his disappointment, he approached one of them. "I'm looking for Janna Kauffman. Did she come?"

The girls studied him, as if wondering what he wanted with Janna. Or maybe wondering if the gossip about them was true. "She came, *jah*, but she already left," said one of them. "With Micah Graber."

Oh. That hurt.

Troy managed a nod—curt, to be sure—and started back to his truck. As much as he wanted to, he would not trail Micah's buggy to see if he'd take her straight home. Nor would he take a shortcut to the Kauffmans' and wait for her on the doorstep.

He would go over there tomorrow, to talk to Bishop Dave about Meghan. And maybe to collect on that dinner invitation.

∽∾

Monday morning, Janna scrambled out of bed, pushing the remnants of her dreams of Troy from her mind. She really needed to get over this infatuation. She hurried into the kitchen, grabbed the egg basket, and went outside to start her chores.

"Janna?" Daed followed her into the chicken coop. "What are your plans for the day?"

Janna lifted out a warm egg from underneath a hen. "I have to deliver the groceries and supplies I bought in Springfield on Saturday. Is there something you need me to do?"

Daed shook his head. "I've arranged a meeting with the other preachers after lunch. I need to discuss a potential issue with them and get some prayer."

Janna nodded. "You want me to stay out of the way?"

"Nein, we're meeting at someone else's haus." Daed touched her arm. "You're quiet this morgen. Are you all right?"

"I'm fine." Still, tears welled in her eyes at Daed's concern.

"Hiram Troyer show up at the singing last night?"

"Nein." Why would he, considering he'd distanced himself from every Amish custom?

"Then…who brought you home?"

"Micah Graber, the new bu from Indiana. He's nice." *And about as exciting as a wet sponge.*

Daed nodded, then opened his mouth, as if about to say something else. But he simply shook his head as he stood there, studying her, a sorrowful look on his face. Before she could ask what bothered him, he turned and left.

Eggs collected, Janna headed back to the haus, just as the school bus growled to a stop on the road. Meghan climbed on, sporting her bright orange backpack.

Mamm came out on the porch as Janna mounted the stairs. "I'm headed to the Fishers' for a work frolic. Want to join me?"

"Danki, but nein. I have too many things to do." Laundry, dishes, and deliveries would help to keep her mind off of Troy. Or should.

So much for distracting herself with work. All morgen, Troy hovered there at the edge of her thoughts, leaving her agitated.

That afternoon, she started the supper preparations. She planned to try her hand at a stir-fry, using carrots, fresh asparagus shoots, and some of those cute snow pea pods, along with home-canned chicken. As she sliced the carrots, watching them drop into the kettle of water, a pang hit her heart. She'd enjoy this chore a lot more if she knew Troy would be joining them for dinner. She closed her eyes briefly, prayed for strength, and then finished the job.

As soon as the supper preparations were complete, she grabbed her Bible and headed up to the barn loft to read and pray in private. Meghan would be home soon, and Janna was not in a mood to put up with her drama.

She should try, though. Maybe if she took some interest in her niece, instead of trying to avoid all contact, she could influence her life in a positive way.

An hour later, the noisy school bus sputtered down the road and stopped at the end of the drive. Janna scooted further back into her corner of the loft. Dinner would be soon enough to face Meghan. She'd try to be over her own heartbreak by then so she could focus on her niece.

The few seconds' silence after the bus's departure was shattered by the rumble of a motorcycle coming down the drive and stopping outside the barn.

Most likely one of Meghan's new friends. She wouldn't bother checking to see which one.

❧

Troy hung his helmet from one handle of his bike and strode up the porch steps to the door. No one had appeared to see who'd driven in, so he knocked and then stepped back. He'd planned his visit close to the dinner hour, hoping Janna's invitation still stood. Two days without her had nearly sent him into withdrawal.

Especially after last nacht, when....

He pulled in a breath and knocked again.

No one answered his summons, so he opened the door and peeked inside, calling out his presence.

Meghan stood by the stove, spooning the contents of a jar into a steaming kettle. He studied her warily. Probably poisoning the soup. But that was thinking the worst. Most likely, she was helping with supper. Nice of her. He smiled.

She scowled in return, her fist going to her hip. "What are you doing here?"

"I'm looking for your grandfather."

She gave an exaggerated glance around, her scowl still firmly in place. "Not here. Maybe in the barn."

Troy nodded. "I'll check in there."

"Probably up in the loft with Janna." Her voice dripped with disdain.

Troy backed up a step, hating where his mind had gone. Meghan was up to no good, insinuating nonsense. He'd better clear out before she directed it at him. "Okay. Thanks for the tip."

He walked out to the barn and went inside. One of the buggies was missing. "Bishop Dave?"

No answer, except for a shuffling sound in the loft.

Troy hesitated, his mind flashing back to Meghan's insinuation. *Surely not.* Even so, his jaw clenched as he climbed the ladder. Somebody was up there. If not Bishop Dave, then Janna. And he wanted to see both. For different reasons.

It took him a moment to find Janna. She sat on a hay bale, her knees curled up to her chest, in the shadows near the wall. Alone. A flashlight lantern was beside her, unlit. Was she trying to hide? From him? She must have recognized his voice.

Troy forced a smile and headed in her direction.

When she looked up and saw him, she cringed.

He tried to ignore the pain that knifed through him. "Hey. I'm here to talk to your daed. Meghan said he might be up here." He tried to play it cool, even though he knew the bishop would have answered if he'd heard him calling for him.

"Daed's not home." Janna swallowed. She stretched out her legs and reached over to light the lantern. "He left around two to meet with the other preachers. Said there was a potential situation he needed to address."

"Hmm. I came to discuss Meghan. Do you know when he'll be back?"

An odd thump sounded behind him, but he ignored it. He was in a barn. With animals. Could be any number of things.

Janna shook her head. "Can't say. When the preachers get together, they tend to talk for a long time."

Troy motioned toward the bale of hay. "Mind if I sit down?"

She lifted one shoulder and moved the lantern to the floor.

He sat next to her. "Have I done something to upset you? I thought things were going pretty gut on Friday nacht. But somewhere between the truck and the haus...."

She glanced at him. And then away.

He longed to reach out and touch her hand. Maybe even grasp her chin and turn her face so he could look into her eyes. "Was it my family? Did they scare you? I know they can come on pretty strong."

She shook her head, looking down.

He sighed. This was going nowhere. Still, he had to find out where he stood. "I had a note stuck to my door when I got home Sunday afternoon. It mentioned a singing at the Detweilers'. I drove out there, planning to offer you a ride home. Then I found out you'd left. With someone else." *Micah Graber.* Troy frowned and reminded himself again that he had no claim where she was concerned.

"Jah. I think he likes Katie, but he didn't ask her, probably since it was at her haus. I was his second choice, I'm sure. And I didn't know how else I'd get home. Daed had indicated that I'd have a ride, but I didn't know what he'd arranged." She gasped and looked at him, her eyes widening in horror. "He tried to force you to take me home, didn't he?"

Troy didn't quite know what to think or how to feel. Joy that Janna wasn't being courted by Micah warred with fear of what her panicked look might mean. He swallowed hard. "He hardly needed to force me. I wrote you a letter. You should get it tomorrow." He didn't want to face rejection, but, after a moment's hesitation, he decided to ask anyway. "Since I'm here, I might as well say it myself. May I take you out for dinner sometime? I suggested Friday in the letter, but anytime will be fine."

She shook her head before looking at him. "Why?" Her voice was barely louder than a whisper.

He clasped his hands over his knees and sent up a silent prayer for help overcoming her cold shoulder. "Because I want to know if you'll be my girl. I want to court you, Janna."

Chapter 15

Janna's breath caught. "Really?" She twisted to face him. "You're not just saying that because you feel you have to?"

Troy shook his head. "I don't have to; I want to. But I don't want us to be the subject of gossip any longer. I don't want you suffering for choosing a man who left the church. I want to keep it quiet, to get to know you the way the Lord intended."

Which meant...what, exactly? He wouldn't return to the faith?

Mamm's longtime counsel echoed in her memory: *"Amish marry Amish."* Yet Daed's advice had been to the contrary: give Troy a chance, even if it seemed hopeless.

He leaned closer and lowered his voice. "I want to toss pebbles at your bedroom window at night and go for walks in the darkness. Take you on buggy rides in the evenings. Take you home from singings, if I'm able to go."

Her smile surfaced.

"And I want to take you out to dinner in Springfield. To a ball game, maybe, or a cultural event of some sort."

So, both worlds. His and hers. That was only fair. But she'd joined the church, which meant that participating in his world would require her to kneel and confess at some point. She pictured Kristi this past Sunday, tears streaming down her face. But then, maybe Troy would kneel beside Janna for believer's baptism, as Shane had done.

On the other hand, it could lead to heartbreak.

"I want us to make a decision without any pressure being put on us," he whispered. "The way it's supposed to be."

Buggy wheels crunched over gravel outside the barn.

Troy reached over, grasped her hand, and waited.

Below them, Daed led his horse back to its stall, talking quietly the whole time. After a few moments, the rustling sounds faded, and silence fell.

Indecision ate at her.

Troy bumped her shoulder with his. "So, what do you say? May I court you?"

❧

When she didn't answer for a few more seconds, Troy released her hand and stood. "You can think about it awhile, if you need to. I know it's a big decision."

But he would rather she had cried "Jah!" and flung herself into his arms.

He walked over to where the ladder was usually propped, but it was gone. Had someone moved it? He glanced around. It was then that he noticed a rope hanging from the rafters. As a teenager, he'd often swung by a rope from the loft to the ground. No reason he couldn't do the same as an adult. He'd go down there and find where the ladder had wandered off to, then set it up again so that Janna could climb down.

She came up behind him and clutched his arm. "Should we call for Daed?"

Troy shook his head. "We'll be okay." He walked over to the rope and grabbed it, giving it a good tug, to make sure it was secure. "I'll go find the ladder."

Her eyes widened. "That isn't safe. Where will you land?"

He pointed to a mound of hay. "I'll be fine." He patted her hand, then took a deep breath, swung out into the barn in a wide arc, and let go of the rope. He hit the pile of hay and rolled.

Getting to his feet, he glanced up at the loft, where Janna stood with one hand over her mouth.

He grinned. "See? I'm fine! I'll find the ladder for you. Be right back." He went outside the barn. Nothing. He walked all the way around it. There was no sign of the ladder anywhere. No way it could have wandered off, or very far, without help.

Meghan. Had she removed the ladder, hoping to trap him and Janna in a compromising position? To get Janna in trouble with her daed? No doubt about it. Probably hoped they'd be stuck up there and the bishop would discover them.

He wasn't sure what that would that accomplish, though. He was still in his rumschpringe, since he'd never joined the church, and nothing would be said. But Janna...she could end up in disgrace.

Not happening on his watch.

Troy took a deep breath and went back inside the barn. "I couldn't find the ladder. Why don't you just swing down, like I did?"

Janna backed away from the edge. "Ach, nein. I couldn't."

"I'll catch you. Either that or you'll have to wait until the ladder magically reappears."

"You'll catch me?" She looked doubtful.

"I promise, Janna. Just be sure to let go when I tell you to."

"I won't be injured or killed?"

He smiled. "You'll be perfectly safe."

"I guess I have always wanted to try...." After a long moment, she went over to the rope, grabbed it, and then stood there, completely still. Maybe praying. A minute later, she took a deep breath and swung out into the barn.

"Atta girl. Perfect." He waited. "Okay, jump."

It took her a moment to let go, and he moved into position. The force of her landing took him off balance. He took a couple of steps, trying to find his footing, and fell backwards into the hay.

For a moment, Troy lay on his back, holding her tight, while he mentally evaluated himself. He felt fine. Nothing broken or hurt. But he hated being pinned, and Janna wasn't moving.

"Hey."

No answer. He couldn't see her face. His was positioned too near certain places where he had no right to be. Not that he would object. But he hoped she hadn't been knocked unconscious. He gently shoved her off of him and turned her over. Her eyes were squeezed shut.

"Hey. Janna." He tapped her cheek.

Her eyelids opened a crack, studied him a moment, and then slowly widened, welling with tears.

"Are you hurt?" He brushed at the dampness under her eyes.

"I'm alive?"

"Jah." Troy chuckled. "You've never done that before?"

"Nein. Katie Detweiler's brother was killed when he landed on a pitchfork, remember? The preachers warned us not to."

"Guess that never stopped me." Troy's thumb slid over her cheek and stopped at the corner of her mouth.

A heartbeat later, he became very aware of where he was. Where she lay.

And that she didn't push him away.

Janna gripped the side of Troy's shirt, fear and adrenaline still pumping through her veins. "I'm alive," she said again, and tentatively moved her arms. Nothing hurt. She wrapped them around his waist. "Jah." She grinned. "Jah, I'll be your girl."

"Gut." Troy shifted against her, and his thumb traced her lips. With his gaze settled on her mouth, he started to lower his head.

A thrill coursed through her, and she trembled. She felt her pulse increase. Her heart raced. She'd dreamed of this moment for years.

The next second, he rolled away and sat up. "I'm sorry."

"Don't be sorry. You saved my life." Janna fought a wave of disappointment.

"Nein," he whispered. "Your daed came in here. I caught a glimpse of him."

She looked around. "Are you sure?"

"Jah, I'm sure."

A door slammed. "Wonder how that ladder got out in the tool shed," Daed said, his voice loud enough to wake the mice. Seconds later, the ladder banged against the loft. "Better make sure it's secure." Another bang.

Troy reached out and plucked a piece of hay from her hair. "Told you."

Janna swallowed. "Danki." And then, despite Daed's proximity, she leaned over and planted her lips on Troy's. She wanted his kiss.

His eyes bulged. Not exactly the romantic response she'd imagined.

Janna pulled back, humiliated. She scrambled to her feet and darted out of the barn, shame flooding her. Why had she done that? Had she honestly thought he'd follow through with Daed standing there, possibly watching?

And, worse, she hadn't known what she was doing. It must have been obvious that she was a beginner.

How could she face Troy again?

Chapter 16

*T*roy jumped to his feet, then froze. Bishop Dave stood on the far side of the barn, next to the ladder, looking after Janna. His gaze shifted to Troy, and he opened his mouth.

Go after her! screamed his every male instinct.

Ignoring Bishop Dave, Troy ran out of the building.

He caught up with Janna halfway across the yard. Firmly but gently, he grabbed her arm and spun her around to face him. And opened his mouth to tell her...what? That he'd kiss her later?

Something in her eyes stayed him.

He sucked in a breath. "Janna." Exhaled. "May I kiss you?"

It'd be a brief one. A peck, really, considering how exposed they were right now.

She stared at him, not answering. Her teary eyes shone with hurt and humiliation.

"Ach, Janna," he whispered. He cupped her cheek. "Close your eyes."

She remained motionless and kept her gaze on him.

"Please. It was kind of...unexpected. I can do better."

She licked her lips, drawing his attention to them, and then her eyelids fluttered shut.

"Now, part your lips a little. And...move them some. Stay flexible."

It'd be the smallest kiss possible....

His lips brushed hers, just enough to feel her softness. To catch a hint of watermelon. And to ignite something big. His belly clenched as a shiver worked through him. He pulled back for a brief second. Her eyes opened, and he lost himself in their green depths. He lowered his head and slid one hand from her cheek to the back of her head, while his other hand pressed against her lower back, drawing her nearer. His mouth moved back to claim hers.

He tasted her hesitation. Her insecurity. Her fear. And then, her surrender, as he coaxed a complete response from her.

She made a tiny sound, and he lost all restraint. He held her against him, deepening the kiss, and felt her arms fling around his neck. She whimpered again, and he groaned deep in his throat.

"Janna," he whispered, his hand sliding from her back to her waist, his mouth making an exploration of its own to her ear...and lower.

He nuzzled the tender skin on the side of her neck, then started to reclaim her lips, when ice-cold water splashed the side of his face and dripped down his shoulders, soaking him to the skin.

He gasped and pulled back.

Eyes wide, Janna wiped her hand over her wet cheeks, even as they reddened.

His gaze shifted slowly to the one who'd broken up his oh-so-inappropriate advances on Janna. Behavior that should have been reserved for their wedding night.

Meghan stood there with a now-empty pail and the scowl that seemed like a permanent fixture.

Truthfully, she'd done them a favor, as public as their embrace had been, and as quickly as it had flared out of control. He nodded at her. "Thank you." Then, he glanced at Janna, her face flushing every shade of red. "I'm sorry. I didn't mean to do that."

She spun on her heel and resumed her dash for the house. This time, Troy let her go.

"I'm sorry," he said again to Meghan. Then, he turned and headed toward the barn—and Bishop Dave.

⁂

Janna shut the door behind her and pressed her palms to her burning cheeks. Who knew kissing could be like that? Her wildest imaginings hadn't kum close. Hadn't been anywhere near reality.

The door opened again. *Troy?* Janna spun around.

Her hopes plummeted when she met her niece's glare.

Meghan slammed the door. "Seriously, Aunt Janna? Get a room."

Janna gasped, her face heating, more at the implications of the comment than its mean-spiritedness. She pulled in a breath, then moved to the stove and stared, unseeing, at whatever was in the kettle.

She opened her mouth to say something about the cold dowsing from the bucket of well water, but then she shut her mouth. After all, she'd been in the wrong, allowing Troy the liberty of kissing her the way he had. Clinging to him the way she had.

She should take a page from Troy's book and apologize to Meghan.

Unless his apology had meant he was sorry he'd kissed her. That her inexperience had turned him off. And that his thanks had meant he was glad Meghan had interrupted Janna's too-wanton behavior and put a stop to it.

Ach, Troy.

He'd be sorry he'd asked her to be his girl.

Janna shifted the kettle and rice came into focus. She turned on the gas burner. Hopefully, Troy wasn't planning on joining them for dinner.

She wouldn't be able to face him ever again without thinking about....

She closed her eyes.

That man could kiss.

⁂

Troy tried to shake off his shock at the entire encounter. That first time, in the barn, she hadn't moved her lips; she'd merely pressed them against his. Definitely inexperienced. And then...then.... He pulled in a breath. *Wow.* He could get addicted to her. Fast.

Troy went back inside the barn and found the bishop leaning against the ladder, his head bowed. His coloring looked rather ashen.

"Bishop Dave?" Troy touched his arm. "Are you all right?"

The bishop shook his head and blinked, then focused on Troy. "Just a lot on my mind." He sighed. "You came to talk about Meghan. I need to talk to you."

"Okay." Troy stepped back. "Regarding...?" Janna? And the embrace they'd shared? The one Meghan had stopped? He glanced down at his wet shirt. If he were the bishop, this conversation would be simple. One-sided. *Stay away from my dochter.* Dread filled him.

"Let's take a walk. Out in the fields."

With a nod, Troy followed the bishop outside, his own manner growing more solemn. He tried to prepare himself, mentally and emotionally, for whatever Janna's daed had to say.

The bishop rubbed his beard. "This is...um, what would you say? Off the record?"

"Okay." Troy nodded. *Odd start.* "What's on your mind?"

"I talked to the preachers this afternoon, and we spent a gut bit of time in prayer. I feel I must talk to you, too. The preachers didn't tell me to do this. I need to." He took a deep breath.

The preachers were involved? Troy's dread mounted. He wished the bishop would just get to the point.

"My granddaughter suggested that I am…how do I say this? She accused me of acting in an inappropriate manner toward Janna. Suggested we do something immoral when we are together in the hayloft."

Troy had a flashback of his brief conversation with Meghan in the kitchen when he'd been searching for Bishop Dave. He hated himself for reading more into her words this time. "You're saying that Meghan believes you are involved in…immoral acts? With Janna?" His fists clenched.

A tear trickled down the older man's cheek. "It's a lie from the devil. The thought sickens me. Troy, you've known me for many years. You know I would never do such a thing." He looked at him with tortured eyes. "Janna loves spending time in the hayloft. I talk and pray with her there, on occasion. That is all. God knows this is the truth. I'm appalled that Meghan could even think of such an atrocity."

Troy's brow furrowed. It was an awful thing to accuse someone of.

And then, he recalled Janna's inexperience. Her hesitancy. He was the only man who'd ever kissed her—he would bet on it. "I would never believe that about you for a heartbeat, Bishop Dave. But, I'm thinking…."

He took a deep breath. What was he thinking? He wasn't prepared to counsel a leader in the Amish community about matters like this. He bowed his head. *Lord, give me the words to say.*

They walked in silence for a few more minutes. Finally, Troy stopped and put his hand on the older man's shoulder. "Something must have happened in her life to put that idea into her mind. And with Meghan's issues…maybe it even happened to her. I don't think she would even conceive of a father treating his daughter in such a way unless she'd experienced something similar herself."

"I'm afraid you might be right. One of the other preachers suggested the same possibility."

"Do you want me to talk with a counselor at the school she's attending? Try and get her some help?"

The bishop frowned. "You know that's not our way, Troy."

"A Christian counselor, then? There must be several in Springfield."

"Nein."

Troy nodded. He'd let it go. For now. The bishop's thinking was colored by the Ordnung and other, unwritten rules. Troy understood that. But there were times when the Amish needed to look outside their own community for help. Now, for example. But he didn't know what he could say to convince them of that.

Bishop Dave inhaled. Wiped his face. "Okay. You came to see me about something else…Meghan's community service. She's already worked a few evenings at the school, cleaning and making other improvements."

Troy kicked at a clump of dirt. "I know. But with this accusation in mind, and with the drug bust on Saturday…."

"The officer who brought her by said she hadn't been in possession of any drugs."

"She wasn't. I was there. But when we stopped the buggy she was riding in, she ran. Two of the other kids with her were in possession, and I think Meghan was using, too. We didn't issue a drug test. I would have, but it wasn't my call.

Regardless of whether she was using drugs, she knew about them; otherwise, she wouldn't have run."

"So. The community service?"

"I need to talk to a few more people. Volunteering at the recycling center and the local library won't cut it. Hard labor with the Amish might."

Bishop Dave heaved another heavy sigh. "Probably not. Do what you think best, Troy. I'm in over my head with this one." Another sigh. Then a half grin at Troy. "You and Janna, rolling in the hay…care to explain that?"

Troy cleared his throat. "Someone removed the ladder, so we had to use the rope swing. Janna didn't exactly have a smooth landing."

"You caught her."

"About the extent of it." In more ways than one. But he wouldn't admit that to her father.

"You're staying for dinner, ain't so?"

"If I'm invited. Sure." But then, Troy remembered Meghan standing over the stove, suspicious jar in hand. He wasn't so sure he wanted to eat whatever she'd fixed.

But for Janna….

He'd stay.

Chapter 17

Janna arranged the table settings, including a place for Troy, just in case her worst nightmare came true and he joined them. And if he did, and if he offered her a look of pity, she'd be tempted to pour the pitcher of iced tea in his lap. Tempted. Not that she actually would.

Meghan grabbed a handful of forks and spoons and carried them to the table. "So, you actually like *him*? Are you two, like, dating? Are you getting married? Please don't tell me *he'll* be my uncle."

Janna swallowed. "We don't talk about such things. A relationship...it's private, and—"

"It is hardly private if you're gonna make out in the driveway. Everyone saw you. Sheesh."

"Everyone?" Her breath caught. Surely, Meghan was exaggerating.

"Yeah, everyone. Grandpa followed him out of the barn when he came charging after you. Grandma was just coming home, and she hurried upstairs. Probably went to bed to sleep off the shock. And I don't know how many people drove by while I was pumping water into that bucket."

Nein. If that were true. If anyone knew it was her... Who else would it be? She opened her mouth, worked it, but nothing came out. Daed had seen them? Mamm, too?

Janna pressed her fingers against her lips, then jerked them away. The pressure reminded her too much of Troy.

"How was school?" Maybe changing the subject would work.

"My algebra teacher hates me. She gives us a quiz every day. And there's a test on Friday. I think the English teacher has it in for me, too. I've got a book report due the end of the week, plus a five-hundred-word essay to write. *Five hundred words.* That's almost a whole book." Meghan gave a heavy sigh. "Biology is right after lunch, and it's so gross, I can hardly eat a bite. I'm always afraid I'll throw up in class."

Janna wrinkled her nose at the thought, then quickly composed herself. This was the longest conversation she'd had with Meghan since her arrival. She didn't want to discourage her niece.

"And then, there's world history. Really, is it necessary to memorize the names of all these people who are dead, along with the dates when they did something? The only fun class is P.E." Meghan sighed again. "I wish I could drop out of school, like you did at fourteen."

"I didn't drop out. Amish schools only go up to the eighth grade. And I had to go to…different classes…after that, to learn basic homemaking skills."

"Yeah. Much better than what I have to do." Meghan set a napkin beside each plate.

She kind of agreed with Meghan about the irrelevancy of certain classes. But Sharon insisted on her daughter having a well-rounded education. And Janna didn't think Daed would allow Meghan to drop out. After all, that would give her nothing but time on her hands, a sure recipe for disaster.

Unless Mamm took her under her wing and started imparting all the things a maidal needed to learn. So far, Mamm had charged Janna with teaching Meghan a few skills, such as jam making. But Janna had made only a halfhearted attempt with her instructions, mostly because Meghan was Englisch and wouldn't stay long. No use mastering skills she wouldn't need. That was probably Mamm's reasoning, too.

But maybe they needed to make another attempt to teach Meghan about running a home. It couldn't do any harm. And it might even help. Especially since Meghan had agreed that those topics were "much better" than her current subjects. She might actually be interested enough to keep busy outside of school hours.

The door opened. Janna turned, holding her still-wet skirt away from her legs. She really should've taken time to change instead of dripping all over the kitchen floor as she stood there, fixing supper and trying to carry on a civilized conversation with Meghan.

When Daed and Troy trudged through the door, Daed seemed to scrutinize Meghan with sorrow-filled eyes.

Troy looked at Janna, his gaze skimming over her, probably noticing the immodest way her dress clung to her. He looked up and met her eyes. Something about his gaze made her blood heat.

Not pity. Something more…more…she wanted to say passionate.

"Dinner will be ready soon," Janna announced. "I need to go change. Meghan, can you get Daed and Troy something to drink?" She released her skirt and plucked at the upper part of her dress, pulling it away from her skin.

Daed shook his head. "I want to wash up first. And find some dry clothes for Troy. I think we still have a few outfits of your brothers' and nephews'…."

Troy grinned. "That's okay. I'm not sugar. I won't melt."

❧

"You can't be very comfortable." Bishop Dave looked him over.

Troy arched an eyebrow. "I'll be even less comfortable in borrowed clothes." Not to mention, he would feel like he was living a lie, dressing Amish when he was anything but. Besides, he didn't think he'd be able to handle wearing…. He wiped his forehead with his sleeve.

And avoided the bishop's too-penetrating gaze.

The demons of his past lurked in every corner of this house. Or maybe it was God Himself, peering at his soul. He needed to escape. To get out of there.

His breath came rapidly as he backed toward the door. "You know, I…I think I need to go." He wasn't ready to face his demons. Nor the stares from the assembled members of the Kauffman family. What had made him think he could court an Amish woman and remain unscathed? It couldn't be done.

Troy raked his fingers through his hair, wishing for his sunglasses as he avoided Janna's hazel eyes, narrowed in confusion. They were greener today, matching her dress. A dress that, thanks to Meghan, clung to her in all the right places. He sucked in a shaky breath and looked away. Make that all the wrong places.

He had no excuse he could give them. None, except the truth, and he couldn't face that. Couldn't face them.

He straightened his spine. Took another step backward. "I need to go," he said again. Then, he turned and tried not to bolt out the door. He didn't succeed.

The door opened and shut again behind him as he fumbled with the helmet his trembling hands couldn't pull off the handlebar.

"Hiram." The bishop's voice behind him was calm. Quiet.

Troy shook his head. "Troy."

"Hiram." The bishop repeated it, as if Troy would shuck his Englisch veneer if he answered to his Amish name. "You're shaking. I don't think you're in any condition to drive. You'd be an accident waiting to happen."

"It's Troy." He couldn't keep the hard edge from his voice. "And I'll be fine." The strap finally slid off the handlebar, and he pulled the helmet over his head. Straddled his bike seat.

And roared off, leaving Bishop Dave standing in the dust.

❧

Janna stood at the kitchen window, staring at the dirt that rose behind Troy. Daed watched him go, his shoulders slumped, as if the weight of the world had settled on him.

Maybe it had. She felt the heaviness, too.

Something about the mention of finding dry clothes for him had changed the entire atmosphere. Changed him. She didn't understand how the thought of borrowing clothes could be so…so…she wasn't sure what the word was.

And not to mention he'd left. Without saying good-bye.

She should feel relieved. They wouldn't be facing each other across the table, trying not to look at each other. Trying not to relive the moments they'd spent wrapped in each other's arms.

Her gaze moved to Daed, still standing in the driveway, looking after Troy.

Had he and Mamm really seen her kissing Troy? Or had Meghan lied about that? She would know, if and when Daed decided to say something about it. But, even if he hadn't seen them, he at least knew that she and Troy had both gotten wet. He'd probably ask her if something had happened that she'd care to explain.

She watched Daed's chest rise and fall before he turned and headed toward the haus. Janna turned and fled. She needed dry clothes—and space.

Chapter 18

*T*roy shook his head. How embarrassing to have had a full-fledged panic attack right there in front of Janna and Bishop Dave. He'd never had one of those before. And he sure didn't want to have another one—ever.

Troy parked his motorcycle in the driveway beside his house and hung the helmet from the handlebar.

He wasn't ready to face the past. He'd kept that portion of himself locked up tight, allowing admittance to no one. Not even God.

His parents didn't even know his secrets.

They didn't know what had pulled him away so soon, after—no. *No!* Troy turned away from his bike, marched past his truck and Joey's beat-up blue car—he still hadn't gotten that window fixed—and went into the house. The aroma of Kentucky Fried Chicken welcomed him. His stomach rumbled a return greeting. An almost full bucket sat on the wobbly card table where they rarely ate. An open brown bag held the biscuits, along with a disposable cup full of some sort of cold drink, judging by the condensation pooling around the bottom.

Dare he hope it was for him?

In the living room, the TV blared. "Joey?"

"In here."

Troy followed the voice. There were Joey and the girl of the week, snuggling on the couch in front of the TV.

"Hey." Joey looked up. "Picked supper up in Marshfield. Help yourself. Got you a drink, too."

Troy grinned. "Thanks."

"Thought you'd appreciate it."

Troy went after a paper plate and piled it with food, snagged the soft drink, and then returned to the living room and collapsed onto the other end of the couch. Apparently, she wouldn't be around long enough to warrant an introduction, as Joey didn't bother.

Even though Troy tried to ignore the two of them, he couldn't help but notice their frequent kisses, and the fact that the girl was almost sitting on Joey's lap. He wished he could make Janna magically appear beside him.

Or maybe not. He respected Janna. And would never treat her the way Joey treated his women. Especially in public.

He felt again the rush of emotion as he remembered the out-of-control kiss—*kisses*—they'd shared outside the barn. Then he cringed at how public they'd been.

Make that "never again."

❦

After Janna had changed clothes and taken time to pray, she came downstairs to find Meghan setting dinner on the table. Daed and Mamm were already seated. Mamm looked up and smiled, but there was an undercurrent of something undefined in her expression. Was it wariness? Disappointment? Fear?

Janna's heart lodged in her throat. Meghan hadn't lied. Mamm had seen them kiss.

Her gaze darted to Daed, who busied himself arranging a cloth napkin on his lap, one she'd sewn from some scrap material. That done, he bowed his head. "Let us pray."

Janna sat and obediently bowed her head, thanking God for her food, for His blessings, and even for Troy's asking to court her, though she wasn't entirely certain where that would lead, or even if it would last. Would he be willing to give up his police career for a farm? Not likely, considering how he'd freaked out over being offered Amish clothes.

She already knew the answer. Her appetite fled the scene, and tears welled in her eyes.

He'd made a commitment to court her, but it wouldn't be a lasting promise that led to marriage. Because she wouldn't leave.

Was this an Englisch way of getting a girl to date him even after she'd declined?

Either way, he needed her prayers. Especially regarding whatever had caused him to bolt at the mere mention of Amish clothes. She didn't understand.

He didn't want the reminder of his Amish roots. The past he'd cast off. She wiped her moist eyes with her finger.

Meghan took a helping of rice, then ladled a spoonful of the chicken and vegetable stir-fry on top. "I haven't had Chinese food in forever. I'm glad you put it on the menu today, Aunt Janna. I added a pinch of red pepper, to give it some flavor. Hopefully, it isn't too spicy."

Daed took a cautious bite. "It's ser gut, Meghan. You did wunderbaar."

Meghan grinned. "Aunt Janna got the vegetables ready and started the rice, but I did the stir-fry all by myself."

Daed nodded. "We'll have to let you cook more often, for sure."

Janna forked up a bite of her meal, even though she wasn't hungry. "It *is* gut."

"Thanks." Meghan took a sip of tea, then leaned back in her chair. "I never saw a cop freak out before. He's ex-Amish, right? What happened to him?"

Troy stared at the TV but couldn't focus on the pictures flashing across the screen. Joey and his girlfriend had abandoned their seat on the couch in favor of more privacy, which was fine with Troy. He didn't need to watch them.

He sighed. He really needed to get a place of his own.

He remembered his cousin Becky saying one time, "If you drink much from a bottle marked 'poison,' it is almost certain to disagree with you, sooner or later." She'd quoted it from one of the books she constantly carted around, during a discussion about some of the bad decisions they'd made. He still made bad decisions.

Right now, it seemed as though he'd had too much to drink from that bottle marked "poison."

Going home seemed the best choice. And the worst.

Maybe he'd go scout it out and see if Mamm and Daed were open to his returning home. He would have some adjusting to do. Getting accustomed to living without electric again, in the same house as his sister and her husband and Mamm and Daed. Sleeping in the room where….

He crumpled the paper plate around the bare chicken bones.

Who was he kidding? He couldn't go home again.

The demons had followed him from the Kauffmans' house into Seymour. He didn't know where to go to escape.

Shuddering, Troy stood up and went to the kitchen, where he shoved his crumpled plate into the overstuffed trash can and stashed his soft drink, still full, in the refrigerator.

Troy closed his eyes and rubbed his forehead. "God, I'm fine with the way things are now." *Not really.* "I don't want to revisit the past." *Can't. I'll go insane.*

It'd been awhile since he visited his cousin Becky. He hadn't seen her since she married Jacob Miller last fall. Her daed, his onkel Daniel, was a reliable source of sage advice.

Not that he'd be able to talk to him about his issues.

But it'd be a temporary escape. Maybe.

Troy checked his pocket for his keys, got back on his motorcycle, and headed for Amish country again. A different district from Janna's, with a different bishop, but a similar lifestyle.

How could it be that the thing he ran from still drew him?

Fifteen minutes later, he pulled into the driveway, noting the "Closed" sign on the door of the blacksmith shop, though the scent of smoke still lingered. Kids spilled out of the house and surrounded his bike. He climbed off and picked up the littlest one—Becky's daughter, Emma—and set her on the seat. She squealed, giggled, and kicked her legs in delight.

Onkel Daniel emerged from the house next. "Corrupting my grandchild, jah?" His smile softened the words.

Troy looked around. "More than one, it appears." He lifted another toddler and placed her on the seat behind Emma.

"Sadie's kinner are here, jah. She and Becky both added to their families this week. Both had buwe. Becky had hers early this morgen. First in the family." His smile widened. "But that's not what brought you by. Kum on up to the porch. We'll talk."

Becky would be resting in bed, and thus unavailable to talk. Troy's hopes sank. But at least Onkel Daniel was there.

Becky's husband, Jacob, came out of the house he'd built for Becky and joined them. When Troy lifted Emma down, she promptly ran to her father, who swung her up in his arms.

Troy glanced at Jacob. "Congratulations on your new little one."

He grinned. "Jah. Bex named him Jacob." He laughed. "That'll be confusing, for sure."

"So, what brings you by, Troy?" Onkel Daniel sat in a wooden chair.

Troy shrugged and leaned against the porch rail. "Haven't been out for a while. Just thought I'd catch up with you." He was glad Onkel Daniel didn't call him Hiram. He was the only Amish relative who had accepted his Englisch identity without question. "How's business?"

"Ach, gut, gut...."

A couple of hours later, Onkel Daniel excused himself to go bed down the livestock. He patted Troy's shoulder. "We're praying for you, sohn. Remember, you cannot change the past, but you can change the future."

Troy nodded. "Danki." He should've figured he wouldn't get off so easy. Was it that obvious he ran from his memories?

Jacob gave Troy a good-natured slap on the back as he straddled the bike. "I don't know what's troubling you, but, as a wise police officer once told me, 'Might want to start with God. And then forgive yourself.'"

Troy stifled a grin at the irony. "Not sure how wise that officer is, but danki. I'll keep that in mind."

"One more thing," said Onkel Daniel as Troy fastened his helmet. "You need to get up high enough and step back far enough to see the whole picture."

Troy could say with absolute certainty that he didn't want to see the whole picture. The portion he saw was seared into his mind. Branded on his memory.

Any more of it would kill him.

Chapter 19

*J*anna wished again that Daed would have shared what he understood of Troy's strange actions last nacht. She reached her hand under a chicken, pulled out a warm egg, and set it in her basket. All he'd done was make a vague comment about its being Troy's story and then said he wouldn't stoop to gossip. That had been the extent of their discussion about it at the dinner table. Meghan had appeared as unsatisfied as Janna still felt.

Okay, so Troy wouldn't have been there to defend himself. But, surely, shedding a little candlelight on the subject wouldn't constitute gossip.

Or maybe that had been Daed's way of admitting that he, too, knew nothing of how Troy's brain worked. That he wasn't privy to the man's secrets, either.

Other than a comment he'd muttered as he'd left the room—something about God pursuing Troy—he'd refused to say another word on the subject.

To Janna, the concept of God chasing Troy—or anyone, for that matter—made no sense. Did the Almighty hunt for anyone? Did He run after them in the barnyard, grab their arms, spin them around, and force them to pay attention?

Not that the attention was undesirable.

Her lips tingled. She raised her hand to touch them but dropped it when she remembered that her fingers were dirty from chicken feed and fresh eggs. *Yuck.*

She resumed her mental meandering. The point was, God didn't chase you down. He waited for you to kum to Him. Didn't He?

She grabbed another egg and put it in the basket beside the first. And then picked up a third. Positioned it next to the others.

Wait. What about the story of the apostle Paul's conversion? It seemed like God had actually pursued him. Striking him blind on the road to Damascus. And the story of the shepherd going out to look for his lost sheep. But, if God were chasing after Troy, how did Daed know about it? He may be a bishop, but that didn't make him privy to God's thoughts, too, did it?

Would God chase after her if she wandered away, like a shepherd seeking out a lost sheep? Or would He take her for granted, like the father of the prodigal son, who sat at home and then celebrated when his son came crawling back? Daed would remind her that the other son wasn't taken for granted. He was valued. All that the father owned was his, too. And she was every bit as important to God as Troy. He'd also add that if something isn't lost, you know exactly where it is.

That kind of made her feel gut. God knew exactly where she was. Had been. Would be.

She collected the rest of the eggs and then exited the chicken coop, just in time to see the big yellow school bus drive off. Mamm was in the garden already, picking leaf lettuce and putting it in a mixing bowl to wash later.

Janna carried the eggs into the haus, then went out to the shed to get the hoe. She joined Mamm in the garden, digging the blade into the soil to start the work.

Mamm looked up. "I need to talk to you." A frown creased her forehead as she turned her attention back to the lettuce. "This is rather difficult, but, regarding what I witnessed yesterday...." She stopped and met Janna's gaze again. "You need to be careful. He left the faith. I don't want you to be pulled away, or to get hurt, if he's only playing with you, like a cat with a mouse it's about to kill."

Sudden tears burned Janna's eyes. She nodded. "I know. I'll be careful." She sighed. "I know it's silly, but I've dreamed of being courted by him since we were in school together. Maybe I'm the one toying with him."

"Ach, Janna." Mamm gave her a sad smile. "Perhaps you need to spend some time in prayer about this, instead of jumping at what appears to be a dream kum true. We don't need either of you getting hurt."

❧

Troy blew out a breath of boredom as he stared out the window at the steady stream of cars driving past his Thursday morning post on the highway. He flipped on his turn signal and merged into the traffic. He'd get a cup of coffee, stop by the station for a doughnut, and then cruise awhile.

No one had ever warned him that police work was long hours of tedium, punctuated by moments of pure panic. Of course, if anyone had warned him, he probably wouldn't have listened. His hero—his savior—had been an officer. He'd helped Troy escape the Amish, paved his way through training, and mentored him. And then he'd died, short months after Troy had joined the force. He was taken down by a bullet at what should have been a routine traffic stop. A wooden cross jutting out of the shoulder served to honor his memory. Troy drove by it often and kept it covered in flowers.

Blinking away the moisture in his eyes, Troy merged into the turning lane for McDonald's.

His intercom crackled to life. "Just got a tip. Something going on in the high school parking lot. Need a couple of officers to check it out stat."

Troy bypassed the driveway of McDonald's and reached for the radio. "Troyer. On my way."

"O'Dell. En route."

When Troy pulled his cruiser into the school parking lot, he saw Officer Pete O'Dell approaching two girls who stood with their hands behind their backs, as if hiding something. Not that they would get away with it.

As Troy got closer, he saw that each girl had a handful of license plates. And that one of the girls was Meghan. Did she always go looking for trouble? Or did it just seem to find her without fail? And why on earth would she steal license plates? Maybe to switch them around, as a prank?

He parked the cruiser behind Pete's. Sure enough, the entire row of vehicles were missing their plates, front and back. He pressed the button to lower the window. Meghan glanced his way and winced.

Pete glanced back at him. "Look what I found. Cordless screwdriver." He dangled the tool for Troy to see. "Go notify the school officials. I'll have the girls start putting the plates back on."

Troy shook his head at Meghan, then drove over to the building, parked in a visitor's space, and went inside.

A woman in a business suit and black high heels met him at the office door. "Can I help you, officer?" Her tone was less than friendly.

"I hope so. You've got two students, both girls, removing license plates in the parking lot."

"Plates...plural?" She narrowed her eyes.

"Almost an entire row's worth." Troy drew in a breath. "We'll need to check vehicle registrations to make sure they're putting the plates back on the correct cars."

The woman set her lips in a thin line and silenced him with a glare. As if this was his fault.

Troy arched his eyebrows in a frown and stared right back.

"I'll have my secretary dig up the student parking permits so you can get them matched up." She spun on her heels and headed back toward a private office.

Troy didn't bother waiting for the secretary. After all, police had access to license plate registration records.

He drove his cruiser back to the crime scene, parked it beside Pete's, and joined his partner, who leaned against his vehicle, peering at his phone, while Meghan and the other girl worked at reattaching the plates to the vehicles—at random, it seemed.

Troy peeked at the screen of Pete's phone. He was accessing the vehicle registration listings. Sure enough, the plate Meghan was attaching right now was on the wrong vehicle.

The police and the school had their job cut out for them.

Janna kept an eye on the road as she hung the laundry out to dry. Troy hadn't stopped by since Monday, when he'd asked her to be his girl and then bolted. She didn't know what to think. Of course, if theirs were a typical Amish relationship, it would be normal not to see each other for a week. But Troy had kum around almost every day until he'd made their courtship official.

Her task completed, she went inside, washed up, and gathered the grocery shopping lists that she'd been handed on Sunday, along with those that had been delivered throughout the week. After hitching her horse to the buggy, she headed toward town.

Before she realized what she was doing, she had turned onto the road where Kristi lived, and stopped directly in front of her haus. Her friend was working in her herb garden, which occupied a plot of land on her parents' farm that bordered the Zimmermans' property.

Kristi glanced up and smiled. She pushed herself up off the contraption she knelt on while gardening, stood, and started toward Janna's buggy.

Janna grinned to see how well Kristi walked. She'd made significant improvements since the buggy accident that had nearly crippled her.

"I'm glad to find you at home," she said, stepping down from the buggy. "It's been so long since we last talked."

"Forever," Kristi agreed. She brushed the dirt off her hands and wrapped Janna in a hug.

"I have some shopping to do in town but decided to visit you first."

"I'm so happy you did. Can you stay awhile?"

"For a little while, jah."

"Gut." Kristi started toward the haus. "Shane's sister, Sylvia, is still staying with us, but she went into town for some baby diapers and pop. And to McDonald's for a chocolate shake." She rolled her eyes. "I've been trying to convert her to herbal tea, but she and Shane are both addicted to caffeine, I'm afraid." She held the door open for Janna. "I'm going to wash up for a minute. Please, have a seat." She gestured at a sofa in the sitting room. "Do you want some tea? Or lemonade?"

Janna grinned, remembering Kristi's affinity for herbal teas—and her denunciation of chocolate milkshakes, even though she knew her friend secretly indulged in them from time to time. In fact, a chocolate shake sounded wunderbaar. Janna would stop and get one for herself when she was in town.

"Lemonade would be great."

When Kristi left the room, Janna ignored her directive to sit and instead stepped into the spacious kitchen. She got out the ice cube tray, dropped a couple of cubes into two glasses, and then carried them to the table. She filled them with lemonade from the pitcher as Kristi came back into the kitchen.

"Danki, Janna. You didn't need to do that." Kristi sank into a chair and rubbed her leg. "But I'm glad you did. My leg is getting to be a great weather forecaster. I think a storm must be coming in."

Janna sat down across from Kristi. "I've missed you so much. How have you been? And how is married life?"

Kristi grinned. "Ach, marriage is wunderbaar. Shane is so gut to me. He just about bends over backward to do things for me, especially since we found out that...." She moved her hand to her abdomen and looked down, blushing.

Janna blinked. *A boppli?* "Ach, Kristi! Really?"

She beamed up at her. "Jah. Sometime in late January, I figure." She reached for her lemonade. "I overheard some talk on Sunday. They say Hiram Troyer has noticed you, finally. I know you always hoped he would. But, didn't he jump the fence?"

Janna squirmed. She remembered the conversation she'd had with Kristi several months ago, when she'd found out her friend had fallen in love with an Englisch man. She had warned Kristi to be careful, to avoid getting too involved... and Kristi had defended her decisions.

Now Janna knew how her friend had felt. She wished she hadn't judged her so harshly. "He did jump the fence. And he asked if he could court me. But...." *He hasn't kum around.* She wouldn't say that. "I'm not sure what to do. Mamm thinks he's just playing with me, like a cat with a mouse. I know our relationship can go nowhere. He won't return; I won't leave.

So maybe I'm the one toying with him." She pulled in a deep breath and shook her head. "I hate admitting that. It makes me doubt my motives."

"So, your mamm's against it. Has your daed said anything? Or does he know?"

"Daed thinks I should give him a chance. He actually said I might be the one to bring Troy home."

"Troy?"

Janna tucked several loose strands of hair back behind her ear. "Hiram goes by Troy now. Can't get a much more Englisch name than that."

Kristi gave her a sympathetic look. "I'll be the last one to caution you. After all, it might turn out the way it did with Shane and me. Or it might not."

Janna drained her lemonade. She didn't want to talk about Troy or their doomed relationship any longer. "I need to go. I'll be sure to stop by again, and stay longer next time." She gave Kristi another hug, set the empty glass upside down in the sink, and headed for the door.

She didn't want her romance to be exactly like Kristi's. She wouldn't be strong enough to handle it if Daed kicked her out and shunned her. Or shunned her and then kicked her out.

Besides, given Daed's recent efforts at matchmaking, he wouldn't be likely to punish her that way. He was meddling with matters of the heart. He shouldn't punish her, at least in that way, if she fell in love.

Chapter 20

$\mathcal{T}$wo hours later, the last of the license plates was replaced on the correct vehicle. Pete escorted the girls into the school building, where the principal informed them that they were suspended for the rest of the school year. Then, he drove them to the police station, where they were written up while their parents were notified. In Meghan's case, this involved looking for either the bishop or Janna. The girls were placed in a holding cell until their guardians arrived.

Troy hoped he found Janna first.

Or maybe not, since he really didn't want to be the one to deliver the bad news. Again.

Still, knowing Thursday was her shopping day, he drove past the grocery store. No sign of a buggy overloaded with coolers.

He stopped at home to grab the teddy bear he'd bought for her when he'd gone to Springfield with his friends. She'd need the encouragement, especially after finding out about Meghan's latest caper. He tossed the box in the back of his cruiser, then drove back to town, passing McDonald's as he entered the square. He crept past the fabric shop and around the square to Dollar General, then returned to the grocery store.

He smiled. Janna's buggy was there.

He pulled up beside it, got out of the car, and deposited the contents of the box on the buggy seat. He'd wait for her outside the store. That would be better than interrupting her shopping…right?

He wasn't sure.

Maybe it would be better to talk to her before she finished, so she wouldn't be worried about any perishables she'd purchased sitting too long in the heat.

He maneuvered his police car into a parking space, slid out, and walked into the store. He spotted Janna almost immediately, in the produce section, loading apples into an empty cart. Good. She'd just started shopping.

He headed toward her, and then his steps stuttered, along with his heart, when an Amish man carrying a straw hat walked up to her. Could that be Micah Graber?

"Hi, Janna."

She looked up as Micah stopped in front of her. "Hi." She found a smile, then turned her attention back to the apples.

"I…uh…saw you kum in here. I wondered if I could take you on a buggy ride sometime."

Janna blinked at the Gala apple in her hand. She'd been sure Micah liked Katie, not her. She'd seen him watching her, at church and at recent frolics and singings. She must have misread his attentions. "A buggy ride?"

She was already committed to someone. Troy was supposedly courting her. Could she decline politely enough that Micah would ask her again? A backup plan, of sorts, in case Troy stayed away?

Her heart broke to consider the possibility. It had been three days.

"Janna Kauffman." A familiar yet stern-sounding voice came from behind her.

She closed her eyes a moment. *Ach, Lord. Nein.* She pulled in a fortifying breath, opened her eyes, and turned around.

The scary Troy stood there, his lips in a hard line, his jaw firm, his eyes impenetrable. Had he overheard Micah's offer?

"I need to take you in to the station."

"Was ist letz?" She searched his gaze for some indication of what was going on.

He looked at Micah. "You'll have to excuse us."

Micah shot a startled look in Janna's direction as he backed up a step. "Jah. Um, yes, sir."

She was pretty sure this exchange would be translated as "Nein buggy ride." Would Micah spread gossip about her around the community, stating he'd witnessed her arrest? If only Troy hadn't worded it that way.

Micah hesitated. "Is there something I can do, Janna? Should I get your daed?" He frowned at Troy. "Actually, Officer, I know you've got the wrong girl. Whatever the charges are, Janna is innocent."

Troy's smile was slow. Dangerous. "Oh, I've got the right girl, all right. And she won't need her daed. She's a…." His gaze slid back to Janna. "Person of interest."

Ach! Her heart pounded.

Micah's nod was tentative. "Then, I guess I'll see you later, Janna." He turned and walked away.

Janna looked back at Troy. Should she ask about his absence? Or would that embarrass him, considering his awkward departure on Monday? Maybe she'd been unrealistic, expecting him to kum see her every day.

His gaze softened. A little. "I do need you to come into the station." His tone had gentled.

"Meghan?" She almost choked on her niece's name.

"I'm afraid so."

She let out a sigh. "I have lots of shopping to do. Can't I just pick her up on the way home?"

Troy rubbed his jaw. "That should be fine. The officer on duty at the station will give you the details. I'll stop by tonight to talk to your daed."

He raised his hand, let his fingers trail over her cheek to the corner of her mouth. His gaze dropped to her lips, but then he stopped, raised his eyes and looked around. His hand lowered back to his side and he turned and strode away.

Janna watched him go, her heart breaking. He'd kum to see Daed, and not her? Or maybe the fact that he wanted to see her as well was understood. If only he'd state his intentions. After a moment, she turned her attention back to her list.

She hoped she wasn't being a bad aent, leaving Meghan at the police station like this. But, considering her history of shoplifting, Janna didn't exactly want her along while she shopped for groceries.

"He didn't take you in?" Micah appeared again, this time carrying a ready-made sandwich, a bag of chips, and a soft drink. Lunchtime. She'd have to pick up something for herself. And Meghan.

"Nein, but I need to stop there when I finish shopping. My niece—" She stuttered to a stop, embarrassed to be airing her family's dirty laundry to a relative stranger. How would it reflect on Daed, the local bishop?

"What did he mean when he said you were a person of interest?" Micah's eyes narrowed a moment, then widened as comprehension dawned. "Ach, Janna. He's Englisch."

She rubbed her arms, suddenly chilly. "I thought you liked Katie Detweiler."

He surveyed her. "I do. But she won't talk to me. And I guess you're taken, ain't so?"

Her heart ached for him. "Jah," she whispered. "But you shouldn't give up on Katie. She's really shy."

"I'll remember that." He started to turn. "If you change your mind, let me know." He headed to the checkout, paid for his lunch, and left the store.

Janna stood there a moment longer, her eyes burning. Micah was a man Mamm would approve of. Amish to the core.

She no longer felt like shopping. It would give her too much quiet time to think about men, plural. Troy and Micah. Whoever would have thought she'd have *that* kind of trouble? She could shop later this afternoon. Right now, she'd go pick up Meghan from the police station, take her to McDonald's, and talk about her latest problem over lunch. Somehow, she needed to reach her niece. She'd settle her own heart issues later.

She pocketed her lists, emptied the bag of apples into the bin, and returned her cart on her way out the door. Back at her buggy, she untied the reins and went to climb into the seat. She found it was already taken, by a two-foot-tall, plush pink teddy bear covered in tiny red hearts.

Her pulse pounded as she reached for her new furry friend. There was nein note, but it had to be from Troy.

She held it close to her chest as she looked around, willing him to appear.

Troy never did get his coffee or doughnut. And now, he was off duty, with plenty of time for both. He toyed with the idea of changing into street clothes and then heading to the grocery store to hang out with Janna. But that would border on being too...something. Especially after he'd come on so strong when he saw her talking with another man. A man who'd asked her out.

She hadn't refused.

But then, Troy hadn't exactly given her the chance. He'd barged over there, all official, and stated his business, probably scaring both of them. It beat acting jealous and informing the other man that she was already taken. By him.

He frowned. *For now.* Because, in the long run, she'd choose a man like Micah Graber. One who was Amish.

It was in her best interests to remain open to that opportunity.

He went home and changed clothes, then headed out again after he'd searched the fridge and found nothing suitable for lunch. He drove to McDonald's, parked his truck, went inside, and got in line.

He never should've left that teddy bear in Janna's buggy. It would be better for her if he stepped out of her way. Before they fell in love. It'd hurt something fierce, but....

Before they fell in love? Too late. He already loved her. Maybe he always had.

"I'm afraid they don't sell doughnuts here, Officer." A female's voice broke into his thoughts.

Troy turned his head. There was Meghan, in the next line over, a smirk on her face. Behind her stood Janna, holding the teddy bear.

He grinned. Gone was all compunction about giving her the bear.

She blushed, a pretty shade of pink that almost matched the stuffed animal. "Danki. I didn't want anyone to take it."

He nodded and checked to make sure no one was behind him. "Join me. My treat."

Meghan glanced at Janna. "Cool." She stepped over beside him.

Janna waited another beat.

He couldn't keep from reaching for her hand. "Come on."

She allowed him to tug her over next to him.

He entwined his fingers with hers. "No point in all three of us standing in line. Why don't you two tell me what you want, and I'll order for you? You can find us a seat."

Janna took a breath. "Just a side salad, please." Her face brightened. "And a chocolate milkshake."

He chuckled. "Got it. Meghan?"

"Big Mac Extra Value Meal. Hold the mustard."

"Since they don't have doughnuts, what would you say to a pie?" He winked at her. "Your choice—apple or cherry."

She grinned. "Cherry. Thanks!"

Wow. She *could* smile. And be polite. He hoped this meant he'd scored some points with her. She did seem pretty cheery around him, especially considering she'd just been caught breaking the law and had spent another morning in lockup. Did she think that being chummy would reduce the severity of future punishments? Or did she really enjoy watching him with her aunt, if only as a source of juicy gossip?

He gave Janna's hand a squeeze, then released it. "There's a booth free back there." He nodded at it. "Save me a seat."

She smiled.

To resist the urge to stare after her, he turned his attention to the line ahead of him.

When the order was ready, Troy carried the tray back to their booth. Janna slid over to give him space next to her. The teddy bear sat on the table, propped up against the wall.

"How come you went with a teddy bear?" Meghan nodded at the toy. "'Cause you figured she'd sleep with it?"

Janna gasped. "Meghan!"

He caught Meghan's gaze and gave a stern shake of his head. He wouldn't go down that path. He would not. He would...not. He...would...not.

His thoughts arrested, he looked at Janna. "I thought you had a lot of shopping to do. You can't be done already."

She shook her head. "I decided to get Meghan and grab lunch first. Then shop. I didn't want to think."

He wouldn't ask about what. Or who.

"I thought Meghan and I would talk about what she'd done."

He raised an eyebrow and looked at Meghan.

She hung her head in a show of repentance. Whether it was sincere or not, he wasn't sure.

"Should I move to another table, then?" He made a move to gather his food.

"You can stay." Meghan lifted her gaze to his. "If you promise to keep your mouth shut. I already heard it from that other officer who caught me, and from you, when you noticed we put the plates back wrong, and from the principal. Then, the other cop went over it again at the station when Aunt Janna got there. And now it's her turn. I guess later I'll hear about it from Grandpa." She scowled. "My mom is so going to kill me when she finds out."

Troy slid the bag containing her meal across the table. "I won't say a word." He handed the salad to Janna, along with a packet of utensils, and then the chocolate milkshake and a straw. He bowed his head for a quick, silent prayer, then opened his own sandwich carton.

Janna raised her head and studied her niece for a few moments. Then, she took a deep breath. "Why, Meghan? Why?" She shook her head. "Never mind. Let's just have a regular conversation. I haven't been spending enough time with you, and I'm sorry. That's going to change."

Troy smiled. Then frowned. Would his life have been different if someone—other than his hero—had taken him under his wings and spent time with him?

Chapter 21

After lunch, Janna drove the buggy back to the grocery store, Meghan in tow. She nestled the teddy bear in the child seat of her shopping cart, which provoked plenty of teasing from her niece.

Janna pulled her master shopping list out of her pocket and headed back toward the produce section. She cringed when she saw the bins of Gala apples. Where she'd been when Micah—and Troy—had approached her.

"What can I get, Aunt Janna?" Meghan bounced on her toes beside her. Clearly, being suspended from school wasn't an effective punishment. "I know I can't go off by myself, and have to stay right by your side, but can I gather things you need if they're in the same area?"

Janna thought for a moment. "I guess. As long as I can see you." She scanned her list. "Let's see...I need ten five-pound bags of carrots, fifteen ten-pound bags of potatoes, two bags of yellow onions, and ten oranges."

Meghan stopped bouncing. "Seriously? Um, that's a lot of food for four people."

Janna blinked. "I shop for others in the community. Widowers, shut-ins...." She'd thought Meghan knew that. But, when it came to that girl, nothing surprised her.

"I guess that explains all the coolers piled in your buggy. How'd you get them all, anyway? Do you go around and pick them up before you shop?"

157

"Nein. My clients deliver them with their lists at church on Sunday or when they kum visit. If they mail their list, then I stop by and pick up their cooler, if I need to."

Peering at Janna's list, Meghan shook her head. "You're gonna need another cart. Am I permitted to go and get you one?"

She didn't sound sarcastic or saucy. Just accepting of the current terms.

Janna hesitated. "I guess so. I can see the carts from here."

The process went a lot faster with two shoppers. When they had paid for the purchases, Meghan helped Janna sort the orders into the proper coolers.

"Now we have to deliver everything, right?" Meghan climbed into the buggy. "Mind if I hold your bear?" She picked it up from the seat. "Ooh, it's soft." She looked at the tag. "Build-A-Bear! I so can't imagine him going in that store. He must really like you." She chewed her lip. "I'm sorry for throwing water on you guys last week, but Grandpa told me to."

And Daed hadn't said anything about the kisses to her. Not one word. Had he spoken to Troy about it? Janna glanced at Meghan. "It's okay." *Not really.* But there wasn't anything she could do about it now.

A short time later, she pulled into Amos Kropf's driveway. He lived in a different district, but he'd been one of her first customers—and continued to be the most frequent. Amos came out of the barn and hoisted one of the two coolers that belonged to him. He gave Meghan a passing glance, then headed for the haus. Janna followed him with the other cooler, but not before reminding Meghan to stay put.

He held the door open for her. "Who's the girl?"

"My Englisch niece." Janna glanced at him. "She's here for the summer." Or longer.

"Mm." Amos set the cooler down on the kitchen table, dug inside his pocket, and pulled out a handful of cash. "How much do I owe you?"

She consulted the receipt and told him the amount.

He handed her the money. "Danki. Don't know how I'd manage without you." He looked around. "Well, you and the maud. She helps out a few hours every week, fixing meals in advance for me and the buwe. I have seven, you know. She's the one who comes up with the menu and writes my shopping lists."

"I'd noticed you've been ordering some different items." Janna smiled and backed toward the door. "I should get going. I have other perishables to deliver."

He nodded. "Sure would be a lot easier to have one woman doing all the work. You ever think of getting married?"

Janna choked. To quote her niece, *Seriously?* He was as old as Daed and had lost one frau after another—four in all, Janna thought. He had a reputation for seeking out young women to wed. Women who gave birth to a bu or two, then mysteriously died in some random accident. Suspicious. "Danki, but I'm seeing someone."

⁓

Troy arrived home to find a buggy parked in front of his house and Janna's father pacing near the front door. He parked his motorcycle, hung up his helmet, and went to greet the older man. "Bishop Dave! What brings you by? I'd planned to stop at your place later this evening for a talk."

"I saved you a trip, then, ain't so?" The bishop followed him inside, past the rickety card table and the two metal folding chairs in the kitchen, and the trashcan overflowing with garbage. At least no dishes waited to be washed in the sink.

And at least his roommate wasn't making out with a girl in plain view.

Troy ushered his guest into the living room. "Please, sit down."

The bishop looked around, taking in the long, sagging couch, which was the only seat available, and the flat-screen TV mounted to the wall across the room. He shook his head. "I'll stand, danki. What about Meghan?"

"Can I get you something to drink?" Troy asked, evading his question. "We have pop and bottled water, or I could make some coffee."

"I'm fine." Bishop Dave waved his hand. "Get to your point so I can get to mine."

Troy raised his eyebrows, surprised at this stern variation of the habitually soft-spoken bishop. "All right, then. The short version is, Meghan was suspended for the rest of the year, and fined, for changing out license plates on vehicles parked on school property. We placed her in a holding cell until Janna was able to pick her up. She's with her now."

"That brings me right to my point, Troy." Bishop Dave speared him with his gaze. "Regarding Janna. I saw what happened inside and outside the barn on Monday. I probably should've said something right away, but I was distracted by other things. I did ask Meghan to throw a bucket of cold water on you, for several reasons: she was loitering outside the barn, and I knew she would be glad to do it. But the primary reason is that, had I gone anywhere near you two, I would've done a whole lot more."

That explained why the bishop hadn't commented on Troy's wet clothes during their walk in the field. "I'm sorry, sir. I—"

Bishop Dave held up his hand. "Since you're courting Janna, holding hands with her is fine. A brief kiss on the cheek to say gut nacht is fine. However, lip-kissing, and touching her anyplace other than her hand, is *not* fine. Are we clear?"

Whoa. At least he wasn't being ordered to stay away from her. But hadn't the bishop smiled and even chuckled when he'd asked about their romp in the hay? Troy grinned. "You're kidding." Did the bishop really expect him not to kiss her?

"The correct response is 'Yes, sir.'"

Troy sucked in a breath, his smile fading. Maybe he wasn't kidding. "Yes, sir."

"Gut. We understand each other. And if I should find out that you have disobeyed me, Janna will no longer be in business buying groceries for the community. She'll stay close to home, under my watchful care. And you'll no longer be welkum. Any questions?"

"Nein. You've made your position clear. But…." He'd be disobeying.

"But what?" Bishop Dave stared at him.

Troy shook his head. "Never mind."

"You're wondering when you can kiss her." The bishop chuckled. "If God wills it, on your wedding day. Then and only then is lip-kissing fine."

Our wedding day? As passionate as their kisses had gotten, the bishop was being a wise father. Troy couldn't fault him for that. Not at all.

Nor could he control the warmth that spread through his body at the thought of a wedding day—and night. When he would take the place of the teddy bear. That the bishop seemed to approve of the possibility gave him a burst of hope.

But then, Bishop Dave didn't know about….

Troy sucked in a breath.

The bishop looked around the living room one last time, then walked into the kitchen, put his hand on the wobbly table, and watched it shift. Shook his head. "You still think this is better than working for a living?"

"I work." He put his life on the line every day. And he felt justified in resenting the implication that his job didn't count as work.

"You could have a farm. A barn full of animals. Crops growing in the fields. A haus, a frau—maybe my Janna—and kinner. And yet you gave up all that for...." He waved his hand around. "This." He pulled out a metal chair and sat. "I'll take that drink now, Troy."

Troy raised an eyebrow. Bishop Dave had delivered his warning as a strict, stern father of his beloved, and now he planned to relax into the role of friend/confidant/counselor and demand hospitality?

Troy's chest rose and fell. A muscle ticked in his jaw. But he nodded. "What can I get you?"

"Water will be fine."

Troy opened the refrigerator, pulled out a bottle, and handed it to the bishop.

"Have a seat, Troy."

He wished he hadn't come home. Hadn't seen Janna's daed. Hadn't heard his latest lecture. He didn't want to spend any more time with him today. Still, he pulled out the other chair, turned it around, and straddled it. "Yes?"

The bishop frowned pensively. "What happened to pull you away from the faith? When your brother, Henry, died in the accident—"

Troy shot to his feet, his heart pounding. "My past is not open for discussion."

The bishop rose slowly. "If you're going to be my sohn-in-law, we need to have this talk."

"I don't remember proposing."

"You haven't been gone that long, Troy. You know that courtship is one step away from a permanent arrangement."

Troy strode over to the door and yanked it open. "Thanks for stopping by."

❦

Janna's head throbbed as she pulled the buggy into the shed. Probably the combination of heat and humidity, stress over Meghan's latest problem, and fatigue from her niece's nonstop chatter during the long buggy ride. Meghan had wanted to know everything about each family to whom they'd delivered food, and her interest had peaked when they'd reached the Troyers' and she'd learned that Elam and Rosie were Troy's parents. She'd even gone inside with Janna, helping carry the coolers, met the family, and sat down to visit awhile.

Janna didn't understand Meghan's sudden fascination with Troy. Something had changed since this morgen, when he'd found her getting into mischief again. Or maybe the change had happened before that. Perhaps when Troy had bolted from the haus before dinner.

She put away their own family cooler, now emptied and wiped clean, then scooped up her teddy bear and started toward the haus. Daed stepped out onto the front porch as she approached. "I didn't realize you were home until I heard Meghan kum upstairs." He eyed the bear. "Who's your friend?"

Janna smiled. "Troy put it in my buggy. Isn't it sweet?" She hugged it close. "And so cuddly."

Daed frowned. "Troy?" He came closer, eyes fixed on the bear. "It's pink. With…hearts. Lots of hearts."

"Jah. Very cute, ain't so?"

Daed sighed and wiped a hand over his face. "You need to help your mamm with the meal. We're having guests for supper."

"Jah, Troy said he'd kum by to talk to you about Meghan. She got in trouble again today, and—"

"We talked in town. Troy won't be here tonight."

"Ach." Janna slumped. "Well then, I'll put this in my room and be right down to help." She hurried upstairs, gave the bear one last hug, and set it on her pillow. After washing up in the bathroom, she went back downstairs. Mamm stirred something in a pot. "What's for supper?"

"I'm making spaghetti. Young people always seem to like that." Mamm looked up and smiled. "You can toss a salad to serve with it."

"Young people?" Janna reached for a bowl, then grabbed the bag of leaf lettuce from the refrigerator. "Are you planning to introduce Meghan to someone?"

"Not exactly." Mamm shrugged. "Your daed asked the Graber family to join us. They recently moved here from Indiana. Do you know Micah? His sister Emily is close to Meghan's age."

"Micah?" Janna frowned. "Jah, we've met." She glanced out the window at Daed. He sat on the front porch, his head bowed, as if in prayer. What had he and Troy talked about, exactly? It must've gone badly, for Daed to go invite another single young man and his family to join them. Or was this just an honest attempt to get to know the newest family in their district?

Coming so soon on the heels of their buggy ride, Micah's approach in the grocery store and Daed's "talk" with Troy, it smacked of matchmaking. And not the kind of matchmaking she wanted.

Maybe her love life would turn out like Kristi's, after all. Because she'd get kicked out of the haus by her daed before she married Micah Graber.

Chapter 22

Troy jolted awake to some racket. He grabbed his gun with one hand from its perch on his bedside table, then rubbed his bleary eyes with the other. Maybe it had been only a bad dream. Still, he listened for the noise to come again.

There it was. A stealthy step. A burglar? Someone knocked on his bedroom door. Trespassers didn't knock. Troy lowered the gun. But who could it be? Joey always let him sleep, knowing Troy often worked odd hours. The police department and first responders called his cell phone when they needed to reach him.

He rubbed his blurry eyes again and checked the time on his digital watch. 8:00. Joey should've left for work by now.

Troy sat on the edge of the bed, groaning when the knock sounded again. Really, who would be here this early? Okay, it wasn't exactly early, but he'd been called in for an extra shift at the station last night and hadn't gotten off work until six. Two hours ago.

"Troy?"

His fuzzy brain didn't recognize the voice.

"You in there?"

Must be someone from the station. Had he missed a call? He reached for his cell phone to check.

The bedroom door opened. Troy snatched the blanket from his bed and pulled it around his waist, high enough to cover his boxers.

"Troy?"

He sighed when the bishop's face came into view. What could be important enough to mandate a visit at this hour?

Bishop Dave came into the room and studied him. "Late nacht, sohn?"

"More like a very short night. I was called in to work. What brings you by? And, more important, how'd you get in?"

"The kitchen door was open, and the screen door was unlocked. I let myself in. Easy enough to figure out which bedroom was yours." The bishop wandered further into the room, pausing to straighten something on the dresser.

"That's breaking and entering."

"I broke nothing. I just entered." He walked over to the window and opened the blinds a crack.

Troy winced at the bright light flooding the room. "Fine. Trespassing."

"I need to talk to you."

Troy fell back on the pillow and closed his eyes. "Can't you come back later?" He cracked open an eyelid and squinted at the other man. "Unless it's important."

The bishop chuckled. "Ach, it's important. I owe you an apology, sohn, for pushing when you weren't ready. For making assumptions I shouldn't have made. And for overstepping my bounds as a concerned father by inviting another man to dinner and allowing him to take my dochter on a walk last nacht. Please forgive me."

Troy sat up again, suddenly wide awake. "You—. Another man—. What?" He pressed a hand to his forehead, feeling the beginnings of a tension headache. "Micah Graber."

Bishop Dave turned away from the window and frowned. "You know him?"

"He took Janna home from singing on Sunday nacht. They'd already left when I got there." His gut churned. His fist began to close, but he forced it to relax.

The bishop's frown deepened. "I thought you didn't show up."

"I showed up. You should've known I would." He met his gaze. "I saw Micah at the grocery store yesterday. Overheard him ask Janna on a buggy ride." It hurt to mention that. But the bishop might have put Micah Graber up to that, too.

"What'd she say?" A wave of emotions crossed the bishop's face. Looked like a mixture of guilt and regret, with a tinge of curiosity.

"She didn't say anything, because I interrupted them. I wanted to tell him to get lost. Janna's my girl. I'm the one who's going to marry her." He sighed. "But you and I both know he'd be the better choice for her. Not me. I'm the black sheep."

"You don't have to be."

Troy gave a bitter laugh. "You don't know what I've done. I can't go back." He plopped back on the bed and closed his eyes. He was beginning to feel like a yo-yo. Sit up, lie back. Sit up, lie back. He wished he could go back to sleep and pretend this really was a bad dream. He at least wished he weren't dressed in only his underwear, so he could get up and pace about the room. But that might offend the bishop.

"Why don't you tell me, Troy?" The bishop's voice was calm. Quiet. Almost like a figment of his imagination.

"I've never been good at following rules. I want the right to kiss her. Because I'll probably do it, regardless."

Silence.

He may as well have been alone. Maybe he'd dreamed up Bishop Dave. Which would be a good thing, because that'd mean he was actually sleeping. Having a nightmare, maybe. But that'd be better than spouting off incendiary things to the bishop. Admitting he lusted after his daughter. A sin.

He took a deep breath. "I killed my brother and my best friend—your son."

No answer.

None was needed. He must be dreaming.

Because Bishop Dave would have had something to say in response to that admission.

Troy sighed in relief and pulled the covers over the rest of his body. He'd rather dream up a conversation with Janna's daed than relive the nightmare of the real event. "I've gone too far to go back," he muttered.

"Not so far to say 'far enough.' You can't outrun God. He wants you, Hiram Troyer." It sounded like the bishop's voice, but it might have been God.

Troy rolled over. Reached for the other pillow and pressed it over his head to shut out the voice. Listening to it and believing it would open his raw wounds again.

The pillow lifted off of him. "You didn't kill either Henry or Zach." The bishop's voice broke. "If you did, you'd be a convicted murderer, serving time in prison instead of serving on the police force. Why don't you tell me what really happened?"

Troy squinted at him. "Are you really here, or am I just dreaming up this conversation?"

Bishop Dave chuckled slightly. "Which would you rather?"

"A dream. I'm not talking about the past." Troy sat up again.

"You need to get over the past in order to embrace the future."

"Didn't you just say you were sorry for pushing?"

The bishop tossed him the pillow, opened the door, and looked back at him. "I'm going to get you some koffee. And then we're going to talk."

❧❧❧

The second bunch of tomato starts were finally big enough to be transferred to the garden. Janna had planted the first ones earlier in the season, and they were now producing tomatoes. She showed Meghan how to carefully remove the seedlings from the milk jug bottom she'd used to start the seeds and how to plant them, spacing them properly and patting dirt around the roots. "These seeds are for heirloom tomatoes, not the kind you find in the grocery store. I ordered these from a store at Bakersville Pioneer Village my friend Kristi told me about."

Meghan shrugged. "Where'd Grandpa go so early this morning? He didn't even finish breakfast. He just did his chores and left."

"He didn't say. I expect he had some business to tend to. And someone will feed him, wherever he goes. Part of Amish hospitality."

"So, did you have a good walk with that guy who came to dinner last night?"

Janna nodded. "Micah's nice enough." Except that he wasn't Troy, and she didn't feel a thing for him. Not even the tiniest spark of attraction.

Meghan sat back on her heels. "Does this mean you and Troy broke up? Or just that you aren't seeing each other exclusively?"

Janna patted the dirt around a tomato plant. What was with Meghan's sudden interest in Troy? Didn't matter. Her curiosity seemed to improve her attitude. "I don't know. Daed told me yesterday that he'd talked to Troy in the afternoon, so he wouldn't be coming by. And that Micah and his family were invited to dinner. I'm not sure if it was just a friendly, neighborly thing, or if Daed was trying to match me up with Micah."

"Grandpa wants you to marry Troy. He says that boy's in love with you."

Her face heated. She had nothing to say to that.

"Besides, Grandpa says he likes him."

"When did he say this? And why were you listening? Eavesdropping is a sin, you know."

Meghan laughed. "It's not a sin if someone's talking in English right in front of me. Well, kind of. I was in the next room."

"Did he know you were there?"

Meghan shrugged. "So, is that why Grandpa was upset last night? Because Micah was here and Troy wasn't?"

"I don't know."

Her niece sighed. "So, after we get the tomatoes planted, what's next? Onions?"

Janna laughed. "They're already in. Right over there." She pointed. "We're going inside to scrub the kitchen floor."

"Seriously? It looks clean enough to eat off of. Not that I'm going to."

"Meghan, did Daed—Grandpa—really tell you to throw a bucket of water on us?"

"Yeah. But not quite the way it happened. He said you were in the barn, but, by the time I got the bucket filled, you'd gone outside. Which is probably a good thing, because I don't know how I would have gotten a bucket up in the loft."

"We weren't in the loft."

Meghan stared at her. "Then, how'd you get down? Oops! I mean...."

"I figured you'd taken the ladder." Janna smiled at the memory of swinging into Troy's arms. "We used the rope swing. Troy caught me. We landed in the haystack."

"Ooh. Guess that's what Grandpa meant when he said something about you two rolling in the hay. Really, Aunt Janna?"

"It wasn't exactly the way it sounds." Janna's face burned. What must Daed think of her? And why hadn't he said anything? Maybe he'd talked to Troy, instead.

No wonder Troy hadn't kum around.

❦

A knock sounded, jarring Troy from his doze. He sat up as the bishop pushed the door open. "I have koffee and breakfast in the kitchen, if you're hungry. Picked up the 'Big Breakfast' at McDonald's. It's not so big."

Probably not, compared to Amish breakfasts. But then, most Englisch didn't work half as hard as Amish farmers. Troy stumbled to his feet. The sooner he got this over with, the faster he could go back to bed. He really should've gotten up in the bishop's absence and locked the door instead of rolling over and going back to sleep. But he doubted that would've stopped the bishop. He would've pounded on the door or gone around and knocked on Troy's bedroom window. Most Amish wouldn't understand the luxury of sleeping till eight. Even if they were up all night with a cow in labor, they still got up before dawn to start their daily chores.

Troy stepped toward the doorway. The bishop stood there, looking down at the floor. "Carpet's loose. I'd offer to help you replace it, but I suppose you'd tell me it's the landlord's job, ain't so?" He gave a short laugh.

"Jah. Danki." Troy scratched his chin, feeling the stubble. He really should shave. Maybe after he got his sleep.

The bishop frowned. "You need to get dressed. At least put something on your bottom half. I don't think it's possible for me to carry on a serious conversation with a man in his underclothes."

Troy's face heated. He must be more exhausted than he'd thought, to have overlooked his lack of clothing. He'd need to drink the whole pot of coffee if he was going to participate intelligibly in this conversation. He grabbed a pair of jeans from his dresser drawer and pulled them on.

Bishop Dave led the way into the kitchen. He shoved the brimming trash can out of the way, transferred Joey's dirty breakfast dishes to the sink, and sat on one of the metal folding chairs. "We still need to talk. You want the right to kiss my dochter. I want answers before I'll content to your marrying her."

Troy took a deep breath. "I still don't remember asking her to marry me." Even though he remembered telling the bishop he'd wanted to tell Micah to get lost because Janna was taken. Because he was going to marry her. No matter. "Assuming I do propose, it's not like we'd be getting married tomorrow."

"You could. Missouri has no waiting period."

Troy's breath hitched. Had the bishop just said what he thought he'd heard? Impossible. "But Janna would be shunned. Do you really want that, and this"—he nodded at their surroundings—"for your daughter?"

Bishop Dave gave him a long look, one that communicated things Troy's tired brain couldn't begin to comprehend. "I saw the stuffed bear you gave her. Pink. And covered in hearts. You are in love with my dochter, ain't so?"

Troy swallowed. "I'm infatuated with her. I haven't known her long enough to be in love." A lie. He loved her with everything that was in him. But he still didn't know how to get beyond….

"Difference between infatuation and love. Infatuation, you wouldn't want what's best for her. You'd be interested in self-gratification only. Love, you look out for the other person. Buy her little gifts. Do things for her." Bishop Dave frowned. "You've known her all your life. She's always dreamed of marrying you. I can't tell you how many scraps of paper I've kum across over the years bearing the names 'Janna Kauffman and Hiram Troyer' inside a scribbled heart."

Troy's heart swelled. "I've always wanted to marry her, too. Ever since I was old enough to notice girls." Might as well be honest. "But I'm the last person you want for your daughter. Micah would be a much better choice. He's a decent man."

"Jah, he is." He shrugged. "Ultimately, the decision is Janna's, but...you want the right to kiss her. If she marries Micah, you'll never have that right. You know my rules. I know you haven't asked her to marry you. But you did ask to court her, ain't so?"

Troy nodded. "I know your rules. You know I'll eventually break them. Have already done so, in fact." His mouth quirked. "Truthfully, sir, I know this is just for now. She needs to choose a worthier man. A man of honor. Which I'm not."

"See? You *are* in love with her. But let me be the judge of whether you're worthy or not. I want to know what happened. You said you killed Henry and Zach. It's time for that conversation now."

Troy shook his head. He still couldn't talk about it. He pushed his breakfast away, too weary to even lift the fork to feed himself. Too tired to chew. He yawned, so wide his jaw popped.

The bishop sighed. "Okay. Sleep some more. I'm going to clean up a little of this pigsty before I go. My gut deed for the day." He smiled. "Who is your landlord? Maybe I'll pay him a visit. See if he'll hire me to fix that carpet and make some other needed repairs."

"Joey's aunt owns it. She lives on the next street over, on the corner."

The bishop nodded. "Ach, Bobbi Jo Smith. She'll hire me. She probably hasn't been by to see what's needed. You go to bed. We'll talk more after you're rested. I'll be here."

There'd be no getting out of this conversation. At least it had been postponed. Troy stood and patted the bishop on the shoulder. "Danki."

Janna's daed needed to know what happened to cause his son's death anyway. He knew the particulars, but not the details. Troy shook his head and headed back to his room. Moments later, he was back between the sheets. He heard faint sounds from the other room, then nothing, as darkness overtook him.

⚬⚬⚬

The door swung open so hard, it banged against the wall and bounced back. Was he dreaming? No, this was real. An intruder? He saw only the dark outline of the trespasser. Troy jumped out of bed, scattering his blankets. He grabbed his gun, leveled it, and fired.

The prowler standing in the doorway grasped at his shoulder, stumbled back against the wall, and slid to the floor. Blood soaked his shirt.

Troy's eyes widened as the veil of sleep lifted. *Oh, dear God. Bishop Dave. What's he still doing here?* His heart ceased to beat.

The bishop stared at the gun, then raised his pain-filled eyes to meet Troy's. "Why, Troy? I only wanted to serve you."

Chapter 23

Janna sent Meghan to sweep the bathroom while she scrubbed beneath the kitchen table on her hands and knees. She was making a mental checklist of the remaining rooms to clean when tires crunched over gravel outside. Seconds later, someone pounded on the door. What a time for visitors.

But maybe it was Troy. Janna looked down. Not exactly the way she wanted him to see her. She scooted forward.

A moment later, the door opened, and a pair of tennis shoes and a blue jean skirt appeared. Definitely not Troy. Janna looked up. *The driver?* She fought disappointment.

She crawled out from under the table. "Kimmy." She stood. "What brings you by?"

"Troy Troyer just called. He said your dad's been taken to the hospital in Springfield and you'll need a ride. Is your mom home?"

Janna stared at her in shock. "Was he in an accident? Is he okay?"

"I'm not sure. Troy said something about a shooting." Kimmy shook her head. "I couldn't hear him very well; I think he was probably driving through an area with poor reception when he called. Maybe he meant they shot the horse."

Janna gasped. "I'll get Mamm. She's upstairs sewing."

She turned and dashed into the other room, almost running into Meghan, who stood there with her hand over her mouth. "Grandpa...?"

Janna shook her head. "I don't know. Do you want to kum along to the hospital?"

"Of course, I do. I'll get Grandma. You need to put some shoes on." Meghan started to climb the stairs. "Grandma!" she hollered. "Come quick! Grandpa's been in an accident!"

Janna shook her head. She could have shouted just as easily. Except that she'd been trained not to. She grabbed her shoes and slipped them on. *Please, Lord. Let Daed be all right.*

When they arrived at the hospital, Mamm hurried over to the front desk. "Dave Kauffman," she said to the woman seated there. "Do you know how he is?"

The woman checked something on the computer, then turned to the man sitting beside her. "Can you take them to the waiting room?"

He led them down a maze of hallways and through a set of doors into a spacious area that looked like a lobby. Most of the seats were empty, except for a group of people huddled on a sofa near the TV.

Troy paced the floor in front of the entryway, a distraught look on his face. When Janna entered the room, he met her gaze with bloodshot eyes.

"Troy?" Janna rushed to him, trailed by Mamm, Meghan, and Kimmy. "What happened? Will Daed be okay? They wouldn't tell us anything at the front desk."

Troy looked away and made a move for his shirt pocket, where he usually kept his sunglasses. He patted his pocket and kind of shrugged.

She was glad he couldn't hide behind them.

"I hope he'll be okay. He was shot in the shoulder." He pulled in a breath and glanced back, still avoiding her gaze. "I shot him."

"What?" Janna took a couple of steps backward. Distancing herself. "You shot my daed? Why?" Daed liked him. She more than liked him—had agreed to be his girl. Seems that would have counted for something. Wasn't the first rule of courtship "Don't shoot the girl's father"?

"It was an accident. He woke me from a sound sleep, and I reacted on instinct, without thinking. I never would have otherwise." He swallowed. Tears tracked down his cheeks. He didn't wipe them away. "I didn't mean to."

"He woke you…?" She shook her head. It made no sense.

"He came to my place." Troy frowned. "He wanted to talk."

"He wanted to talk, so you shot him?" Meghan crowded in beside Janna.

Troy sighed. "It's not like that. It's…." He glanced over Janna's shoulder. She turned to follow his gaze. *Mamm.* "I'm sorry," he said to her. "I'll take care of the farm while he's laid up."

"It's a nice thought," Mamm said. "But I'm sure the community will step in."

"I'm sure they will." Troy exhaled. "But I shot him. I need to do this."

Mamm made a slight sniffing noise—the one she made when she disagreed with something but wouldn't argue. Probably because she knew they would need help.

If Troy took over the farm work, it meant he'd be coming around more. Every day, at least a couple of times. Janna brightened a little. The community would probably need to help some, though, especially if Troy continued working his regular job.

Mamm said something in a low voice to Kimmy, and they went to the nurses' station across the hall. Probably to ask about Daed's condition, since Troy hadn't said anything about that.

"I have to know what Grandpa wanted to talk about with you." Meghan moved closer. "Was he wondering why you ran off the other day? 'Cause, if he was, we're all curious. And if he wasn't, we still want to know. Or maybe he wanted to lecture you about kissing Aunt Janna."

Janna rolled her eyes. "Meghan, please. This is serious."

Troy rubbed his hand over his face. "Both reasons, okay?" He gave Meghan a half grin, and then his gaze flickered to Janna for a second before darting back to Meghan. "But this is neither the time nor the place for either discussion."

"Why not?" Meghan frowned. "It'd be a way to kill time while we're waiting for an update on Grandpa. How is he, anyway? Have you heard anything?"

"Nothing, other than they took him back for surgery. The bullet lodged in his shoulder. I know he'll need to stay in the hospital a couple of days, but anything more depends on whether the bullet hit bone or muscle; whether it exploded or stayed intact; and…." Troy sighed and looked at Janna again. "I really am sorry."

She pulled in a breath. "I forgive you." Assuming Daed would be okay. If he died, it'd be a struggle to move past it. But she would. She'd forgive, as God had forgiven her. "I do forgive you," she said again, to cement it in her mind.

Troy lifted one corner of his mouth. "Danki, Janna." He reached for her hand and gently squeezed, then leaned forward and quickly kissed her cheek. Right in front of Meghan.

"You might forgive him, but I'm not sure if I do or not." Meghan planted her fists on her hips. "I might, if you tell us why you ran out the other night."

His smile was unconvincing. "You are as tenacious as your grandfather. But I don't want to talk about it. Sorry."

Janna sighed as he turned and walked away. He was right. This was neither the time nor the place. And Meghan probably didn't need to know.

But how could she and Troy have any hope for a future if he wouldn't share his past?

❧

"Want me to get you a Coke?" Troy stopped about three feet away and glanced over his shoulder. He hadn't dared stand there with them any longer. He'd wanted to take Janna in his arms and comfort her. But how could he, when he was the cause of her pain? Not to mention, hugging her would be a breach of her father's rules. And even though he'd already expressed his doubts about following them for an extended period of time, it seemed wrong to defy the man he'd just shot, who lay in a hospital bed, his family awaiting word on his condition. *Lord, please keep Bishop Dave alive. You know I didn't mean to shoot him. Forgive me.*

"A Coke sounds good. I'll go with you." Meghan hurried to his side.

"Janna? You want something?"

She shook her head. "Nein, danki."

He nodded, then turned and headed toward the vending machines he'd seen in the hallway, Meghan close by his side. He would have preferred to be accompanied by Janna rather than her niece. Then again, it was nice that she seemed to be warming up to him. He didn't know what had brought about the change, but it was positive, so he wouldn't complain.

"So, you did something terrible," Meghan stated rather than asked. "That's why you won't talk about it. Bet it's nothing like what I did."

Troy gave her a sharp look. His breath lodged in his throat. He didn't dare say a word.

"I was a cheerleader in California, before my mom got involved with...*him*. Sometimes we'd have parties, and my friends would bring roofies, and we'd put them in people's drinks. It was really funny to watch how they acted when they were all strung out."

Who was the mysterious "him" she'd referred to? Was it the man Troy suspected had done something to Meghan to make her believe the bishop might be doing the same thing to Janna?

She seemed to have forgotten he was a cop; he didn't think she would have volunteered that information otherwise. So, she'd had some involvement with drugs, whether just distributing them to unsuspecting people for her own amusement or using them herself, he didn't know. He was glad he hadn't grown up Englisch. The Amish had their share of misfits, but he hadn't been one of them; had never been the brunt of anyone's joke. He'd been a leader—the one the other buwe followed.

When they reached the vending machines, Troy fed one a few coins. He turned to Meghan. "What do you want?"

She tilted her head, considering her options, then reached out and pushed a button. With a loud clattering, a green can of 7-Up appeared at the opening in the bottom.

Troy inserted a few more coins and pushed a button for his own drink. Mountain Dew. He thought he needed the extra caffeine.

"Should I get one for Janna?" he asked Meghan.

She shrugged. "I don't think she drinks pop. Her best friend is some kind of health nut. Herbal tea and lemonade—not the kind from a mix—are all she'll drink." She grinned at him for a few seconds, until her smile faded into a frown. "Hey...what I told you? I was just kidding. I never did that."

Right. She must've remembered who she was talking to. But he nodded, pretending to believe her. "I think I'll get Janna a drink just in case." He fed the machine some more money.

"So, what's the real reason you shot Grandpa? Because he made me dump water on you?"

Troy's face heated. If only he hadn't kissed Janna that day. He should have kept it to a tiny peck. Or, better yet, selected a private place. But he hadn't. He wouldn't make that mistake again.

He glanced at Meghan out of the corner of his eye. "Like I told you, it was an accident. Someone who's been trained to respond to violent emergencies isn't responsible for his actions until seven seconds after a startling event. Your grandpa woke me from a sound sleep. I'm not saying I'm not to blame, don't get me wrong. I did it. I'll own that. But I'm saying I reacted on instinct. I didn't act with an intent to harm him."

Meghan sighed. Maybe she'd expected some juicy confession from him, since she'd given him one.

Not happening.

He owed the bishop an explanation, especially since he was Zach's father. He'd probably be shunned, even though he'd never officially joined the church. Confessing to Janna would ruin their relationship. She'd been close with her brother Zach, in age and as friends. He could only imagine how Meghan might react if she found out she had an uncle she'd never met—and never would, thanks to him.

Troy clenched his jaw so hard it hurt.

He shouldn't have spilled that bit of news to the bishop. If he survived, he wouldn't let it rest.

Even so, he prayed he would survive. He couldn't handle the additional load of guilt.

A nurse stepped into the waiting area. "Kauffman family?"

Janna shot to her feet.

The woman motioned for the group to follow her. She led them into another, smaller waiting room. "Have a seat. The doctor will be in shortly."

Meghan plopped down in a chair. Mamm stood, wringing her hands, by the door the nurse had just closed behind her. Janna wasn't quite sure what to do. She wished she could cling to Troy's hand and absorb his strength. He wasn't family, but he'd followed them into the room and now stood stoically beside her.

She jumped when his fingers slid against hers. She grasped at them as if they were a lifesaver. And maybe they were. If he'd killed Daed....

Nein, she wouldn't think that way. Troy was too gut a person. He'd never kill anyone.

Then again, he was a police officer. He might.

He moved closer, his chest brushing against her right shoulder. If only she could lean against him.

The door opened, and a man wearing bluish-green scrubs stepped into the room. He looked around at them, keeping his face impassive. "Mr. Kauffman suffered...." Those three words were about all Janna understood of his explanation. They should have sent along a translator. His update apparently over, he scanned the room again. "The nurse will come and get you once he's settled in a room."

"Settled in a room" meant he was alive, right? Relief washed over her.

"Danki, Lord," Troy whispered beside her. His thumb slid over the top of her hand, sending tingles through her, until he stilled it mid-motion.

If only he'd repent of his worldly ways and return to the faith.

She couldn't allow herself to dream of a future with him until he did.

Janna looked up and met Mamm's disapproving glare. If only she could see what Janna saw, instead of a cat baiting a mouse. At least Daed shared her perspective. Maybe. She supposed his opinion might have changed, since he'd gone over to Troy's to discuss the matter of his kissing Janna—and left with a bullet lodged in his arm.

Chapter 24

*T*roy followed the Kauffmans into Bishop Dave's hospital room. His gaze landed on the paste-white man lying in bed, hooked up to an IV. The large bandages on his shoulder peeked out from the neck and sleeve of his hospital gown. Troy choked on his emotions and fought the urge to weep.

Janna's mamm wrung her apron as tears streamed down her cheeks. The bishop fixed his eyes on his wife, and he extended his good arm, reaching for her hand. She clasped it and sat down beside him on the bed, making no move to dry her face.

Janna stepped over to the wall and leaned against the windowsill, while Meghan plopped into the only chair.

Bishop Dave's eyes flickered over the rest of them—Meghan, Janna, Troy. He froze when the bishop's gaze met his, hoping the man wouldn't order him out. Or, worse, demand answers now.

His eyes burned. For a moment, he was tempted to rush forward, fall on his knees beside the bed, and beg forgiveness. For shooting him. For killing Henry and Zach. For every wrong thing he'd ever done, including kissing Janna the way he had. Well, he really wasn't sorry about that. He'd do it again if he had half a chance.

He took a step forward, then forced himself to stop. He wouldn't humiliate himself in that way. Not here. Not now.

Maybe not ever. It was bad enough that he'd cried in front of Janna—in front of everyone. That he'd made this huge mistake—make that *mistakes*—to start with. If only he could go back and do it over.

He sucked in a breath. *It is as it is.* He couldn't change anything. A verse from Isaiah flashed in his mind. *"This is the way, walk ye in it."*

Bishop Dave held his gaze. "I forgive you, sohn. It was an accident. Now you must forgive yourself."

Troy's heart warmed with relief. If only his forgiveness included everything. Troy wasn't sure God had forgiven him everything—especially the parts he'd never confessed. The parts locked up tight inside of him.

Bishop Dave looked at his wife. "Troy will handle the farm work while I'm laid up."

She pursed her lips and nodded. Troy supposed she'd rather Micah Graber come and fill in for him. In fact, he wouldn't be surprised if Micah showed up to help out. And if he did, there'd be nothing Troy could do about it. Even if Micah got invitations for dinner and wanted to court Janna. Micah was the better man, by far.

Troy's chest rose and fell and he backed toward the door. He'd go. He needed to stop by the station to talk to the police chief about the accidental shooting. He would be suspended from his job, pending an investigation. Assuming the penalty wasn't more severe. After that, he'd take care of some of the Kauffmans' farm work, then return home and go to bed. Starting tomorrow morning, he'd be expected to follow the schedule of an Amish farmer.

Bishop Dave narrowed his eyes. "You aren't leaving, sohn?"

He nodded. "I need to go. Kimmy's in the waiting room. She'll take everyone home."

"I'll go with you." Standing up, Janna turned to her father. "Ich liebe dich, Daed."

Bishop Dave glanced at his daughter. "Ich liebe dich, Janna." He looked at Troy. "Take gut care of my girl."

Troy nodded with a gulp. He almost basked in the undeserved trust Janna's daed displayed. It might take all his strength, but he'd honor that trust—at least for tonight.

&cso

Janna planted a kiss on Daed's cheek, then hurried after Troy out the door and into the hallway. "You do have your truck, ain't so?" she asked.

He caught her hand in his. "Jah. I'd have refused to take you on my bike."

"I would've gone." She still dreamed of wrapping her arms around his waist and holding on tight, like she'd seen Englisch girls do.

His smile was fleeting. "I don't have a helmet for you."

"Is that important?" She'd seen plenty of people riding without them.

"It's against the law to not wear one. Not to mention dangerous." They pushed through the front doors of the hospital and headed toward the parking lot.

When they reached the truck, Troy opened the passenger door for her and then closed it when she'd climbed in before getting in himself. "I need to go by the station. I can take you home first, or you can wait for me at my place. It's nearby. I'll take you home when I go to do the chores."

It'd be a bad decision, but she wanted to see—and to know—where he lived. Though she might be tempted to steer her horse down his road whenever she took the buggy to town, in hopes of catching a glimpse of him. Or even his truck. *Pathetic.*

"Nein point wasting gas. I'll wait at your haus." She certainly didn't want to wait at the station. Too many bad memories there.

He nodded. "I'll give you the key so you can let yourself in. I told the chief I'd be in as soon as I got back to town." He swallowed. "They confiscated my gun. I know I'm going to be suspended, at the very least."

"What will you do if you lose your job?"

Troy shrugged. "Give Joey notice and move home, if Daed will let me. And if he won't, then...I don't know. I'll worry about it later. My only skills are law enforcement and farming." He gave a short laugh. "Though I guess I could always do construction."

She hated the bitter tone she heard in his voice. She shouldn't have asked such a depressing question. But, in a way, she'd wanted to know if he'd consider returning home if his career came to an end. And it sounded as if he would, assuming his parents permitted him to. She couldn't think of any reason why they wouldn't. After all, they loved Troy, even though they hated that he'd left the faith for the world. They looked forward to his visits, and his mamm had told her they prayed daily for his permanent homecoming.

He merged into the bumper-to-bumper traffic on the bypass, traveling at an unreal speed. Janna grasped the handle on her door with her right hand, so tightly that her knuckles turned white. "This traffic is awful. Scary." *Terrifying* was more like it.

He nodded. "Bad enough in Seymour. But this is lunch hour. It should get quieter as we get out of the city." He sighed. "Speaking of which, are you hungry?"

"Nein. But danki."

"I'm not, either. Your daed brought breakfast, but I was too tired to eat. I just shoved it away." His mouth quirked, and he cast her a sidelong glance. "Janna. I'm so sorry."

"I know." She wished she could scoot closer to him. If they were in the buggy, she would have, at least a little. But they were separated by a plastic boxlike thing—a console, she thought it was called—and a gear shift.

They drove into Seymour, and Troy maneuvered the pickup down a couple streets, then stopped in front of a small white haus. Daed's horse, Briar Rose, and his buggy were tied in the front yard. Someone had given Briar Rose a bucket of water.

He took the keys out of the ignition, worked a key loose, and handed it to her. "I don't expect this to take very long." He shrugged again. "Fifteen to twenty minutes, tops."

She looked at him. "I'll be praying."

He glanced away. "Danki. Appreciate it."

She took the key he handed to her, slid out of the truck, walked up the uneven concrete walkway to the front door, and inserted the key. It took a couple of twists of the doorknob before it opened. She glanced around behind her and watched Troy drive down the road.

Janna blew out a breath and entered the haus, finding herself in the living room. Along one wall was a long brown sofa; on the opposite wall, a huge television screen. A single floor lamp stood in one corner. And that was it. A bachelor pad, for sure.

The polite thing to do would be to sit on that sofa and wait for Troy. But curiosity won out. She tiptoed down the hall and peeked in the first room she came across. There was an unmade bed, the covers all a jumble. She recognized Troy's uniform draped over the back of a chair. No need to look in the other bedroom. She glanced left and right, making sure she was alone, and then stepped into the room and picked up his pillow. Troy's scent, kind of piney, met her nostrils. She hugged the pillow to her heart for a moment, then plumped it slightly and placed it neatly back on the bed. She didn't dare tidy up, as tempting as it was to make his bed. That would leave evidence of how inappropriate she'd been by going into his room in the first place. She didn't want her transgression made known.

She looked around for anything that might clue her in on the details of the shooting accident. But there were nein discarded medical supplies, nein blood, nothing. *Danki, Lord, that Daed's going to be okay.*

Janna went back down the hall to the kitchen and looked around the small room. There was a card table pushed up against one wall, with two metal folding chairs jutting out from under it. The space was clean, relatively speaking, except for the floor. She thought she could mop it without the results being obvious. She opened the closet and found a broom but no dustpan or mop. Better than nothing. She swept the dirt, dust, and debris out the back door and down the steps.

Not knowing what else to do, she sat on the couch. Maybe she should have gone home. She could have taken Daed's horse and buggy. They had to get back there somehow.

A vehicle roared into the driveway and then fell silent. A moment later, the back door slammed, and Troy appeared in the kitchen doorway. "You didn't have to clean, you know. That isn't why I brought you here."

"I didn't do anything except sweep the floor." And plump his pillow. But she didn't dare admit that to him. Of course, he'd find out soon enough. Her face heated.

Troy frowned. "Your daed must have done it, then. He said something about wanting to straighten up this 'pigsty.'"

"So? What did they say at the station?"

Troy shrugged and sat down at the other end of the sofa. "What I'd expected. Suspension pending an investigation. But the chief said I'll probably be exonerated."

"Ach." She didn't want him to lose his job, but she couldn't help feeling a slump of disappointment. She wanted him to return home. To the community…to her.

She scooted across the sofa toward him and touched his arm. "This is gut, ain't so?" A lie. She dared to move close enough to snuggle, if he wanted. Or kiss. A thrill shot through her.

He jerked his arm away and jumped to his feet. "I'll get you some lunch, if you're hungry, and then take you home." He set his mouth in a firm line. His jaw tensed.

The scary Troy.

Had she done something to upset him? Maybe he no longer wanted her to be his girl. She'd probably given in too easily to his advances. She should have made his chase more of a challenge. Or possibly he'd been repulsed by the kisses she'd found so satisfying. Her stomach churned. She didn't think she could keep anything down. "Nein. I'm not hungry. And I'll take myself home. Daed's horse is out front, ain't so?"

He looked away from her. "Danki for sweeping the floor. I'll be over later, then, to do the chores."

She had to give it one last shot, so she'd know. She peeked up at him. "You'll stay for dinner, jah?"

"Nein. Can't. Danki."

Tears blurred her eyes. She didn't know what she'd done wrong. All she knew was that, next time, she wouldn't cave so quickly. Nor would she kiss another man till they were married. That way, he wouldn't discover her lack of skill in that area until it was too late to back out.

She forced her chin up. Squared her shoulders. And headed for the front door. "I'll be seeing you, then." Hopefully later rather than sooner. She needed to keep her distance until she'd regained control of her heart.

❦

Troy watched her from the front window. He enjoyed the way her dress clung to her curves, how the hem swayed against her legs, and the tantalizing glimpse he got of even more of her leg when she hiked her skirt to climb into the buggy.

Ach, Janna. Keeping his distance would be one of the most difficult things he had ever done. But he needed to try, out of respect for Bishop Dave.

Still, when she'd sidled up to him on the couch and brushed his arm with her fingers, it'd been all he could do to move away. He'd desperately wanted to pull her into his embrace. To kiss her. To….

His breath lodged in his throat.

He'd have to devise some different ways to show Janna how he felt about her. But he didn't know where to start, beyond leaving the occasional gift in her buggy.

He watched as she flicked the reins and the bishop's horse started toward the street. For a moment, he was tempted to race after them, beg her to stay awhile, and tell her he'd go with her to the farm later.

But he'd need a way to get home later. And the bishop's horse and buggy had to be returned to the Kauffmans'. Not to mention, being alone with her was entirely too tempting.

Plus, he was really too tired to be pleasant company. The rush of adrenaline he'd experienced this morning after the accident had long since faded, and the exhaustion from his overnight shift was overtaking him again, with a vengeance. He locked the front door, then went through the kitchen to the back door and locked it, as well. He didn't want any more surprise visitors. Then he headed for his room. He'd nap for a couple of hours before going out to the Kauffman farm and seeing what needed to be done.

Maybe he'd be able to figure out his messed-up life by then.

Chapter 25

Janna was helping make supper when she heard the roar of a motorcycle. *Troy.* She had no intention of going out to talk to him. He could either figure out what to do on his own or ask Mamm. Well, to be truthful, she wanted to march out there and demand answers. Why had he asked her to be his girl and then dropped her without warning? Was it something she had done—or hadn't done? Or could his accidental shooting of Daed be to blame for his odd behavior? She'd tried to be supportive of him on that issue, going with him to his haus, where she hadn't found as much as a speck of blood. Not that she'd looked that closely.

Mamm rinsed her soapy hands under the faucet and looked up from the sink. "Who could that be?"

Meghan peered through the curtain and scowled. "It's *him.*" Apparently, her sudden interest in Troy had vanished in the hours since she'd returned from the hospital, and she'd reverted to her not-so-pleasant self.

Janna shrugged it off. She'd been a teenager herself not so long ago. She knew how hormones made one's mood shift—sometimes hourly.

"So, did you hear? Grandma stopped at the Grabers' and told Micah that—"

"Meghan." Mamm's voice was sharp. She wiped her hand on a towel and shook her head.

"What?" Meghan rolled her eyes. "It's not like Aunt Janna won't figure it out when he starts coming around every day."

Janna stifled a sigh. It seemed both Mamm and Daed were determined to marry her off. She supposed she should let it happen. Especially since romance with her choice of a man had fizzled as quickly as it'd begun. On and off. Maybe she'd have better luck with Mamm's choice. It wasn't her fault Micah didn't excite her. Didn't make her stomach do flips. Didn't make her heart sing.

Though, to be honest, her heart wasn't doing much singing now. Unless it was singing the blues.

She turned her attention to the chicken legs and thighs she had frying in the iron skillet. Mashed potatoes with cream cheese stirred in were keeping warm on the back of the stove, and she had corn heating in a saucepan.

"Smells wunderbaar, Janna." Mamm touched her shoulder.

"I suppose Micah's joining us for supper?" Janna glanced at her.

Mamm smiled sheepishly. "He should be here any minute." She walked over to the window and looked out at the yard. "I understand Hiram's conviction that he needs to help us, even though, in my mind, shooting someone is reason enough to stay away from his family. But I don't know how to tell him to go home. Especially since your daed sanctioned it. I would be disobeying his wishes."

Janna frowned and poked at one of the chicken pieces. Breaking her heart would be a gut reason to stay away, too. But he hadn't.

Maybe someday, when she felt brave enough, she would ask Mamm what she had done to win Daed's hand. Because, whatever the trick involved, Janna had failed miserably.

"I'll go tell him what to do," Meghan announced. She dropped a stack of plates on the table with a clatter. "It'd be more fun than this job, anyway. Besides, we don't even know how many places to set."

"Janna cooked plenty." Mamm set a couple of jam jars on the table. "And you don't need to go out there. We've already discussed all that needs to be done. Besides, Micah's a farm boy. He knows what to do."

With a shrug, Meghan opened the door, anyway. "*Troy's* a farm boy, too." She slipped outside and shut it behind her.

"Ach, that girl," Mamm muttered. "She never listens."

Janna glanced outside and saw Meghan dash inside the barn. "She probably wants to play a practical joke on him. Lock him in a stall, perhaps."

That would be unkind. Especially if no one came to rescue him.

Because she certainly wasn't about to.

She wouldn't be going anywhere near the man. Not today. Not tomorrow.

Not ever.

⁗⁔⁗

Troy heard a door slam. He poked his head out of a stall and saw Meghan come bounding in. "Hi, Troy. The cows are lining up outside the gate."

Troy chuckled. "They always come home, to be sure."

"Grandpa says that cows line up all on their own. That's just too weird. How do they know when it's time?"

"Cows have good internal clocks. Mostly, they know when it's close to milking time when their udders become full."

"So, they just come home themselves? You don't have to go get them?"

"Not usually."

"So…." Meghan leaned forward against a wooden beam. "Are you staying for supper? Grandma told me to set the table, and I need to know for how many."

"I think not, but danki." Troy wanted to, of course, but he didn't know how he could, as big of a temptation as Janna was. Now that she was essentially off-limits, it made him want her even more.

Meghan bent closer and whispered, "I think you should stay. Grandma invited Micah Graber. He'll be here soon to help with the chores."

Troy looked up sharply. Not that he was surprised. Micah was the better man. And the more he reminded himself of that fact, the less pain it would cause him. He hoped.

"Then, your grandma won't want me taking up space at the table." Troy aimed his best attempt at a smile at Meghan. It was probably more like a grimace, though.

"Yeah, but after you kissed Aunt Janna like that, I think you guys deserve a chance at love. I mean, it's, like, forbidden, according to Grandma. And that is just so-o-o romantic."

He laughed. He couldn't help it.

"And what about that teddy bear you gave her? It's covered in hearts. That's romantic, too."

Good thing she didn't know about the rose. About the way he'd brushed the petals against Janna's lips, wishing the whole time he could do more. He swallowed. Hard.

"So, see? You need to stay for dinner. I'll set a place for you."

Troy didn't quite follow her line of reasoning. "I…." He almost said "I'm not invited," but that wasn't true. Janna had asked him. And now, Meghan had seconded the invite. Bishop Dave would expect him to join them, he was sure.

But he had to face the facts. "I think romance is...nice. But if I stay, it'd be out of jealousy. And that isn't so nice."

"Jealousy's a perfectly fine reason to stay. Besides, if you don't, what'll you have for dinner?" Meghan bounced on her toes. "Aunt Janna is serving fried chicken with mashed potatoes and gravy, and I think there's some pie. There's always pie. Not sure what kind, though. Aunt Janna might have mentioned peach."

His stomach made a loud rumbling noise. No wonder it was said that the way to a man's heart was through his stomach. How could he pass up a home-cooked meal for a TV dinner warmed in a microwave and eaten alone?

"Okay. You win. I'll stay. But not because of Micah." He flashed a grin. "Because I'm hungry."

"Whatever." Meghan turned away. "I'll set a place for you."

"Hey, Meg? Um, wait a second."

She looked back.

"Which window is Janna's?"

She blinked at him. "Why? Are you some kind of pervert? She always pulls the shade down."

His face heated. "If an Amish couple's dating, the guy often tosses pebbles at the girl's bedroom window at night, to get her attention, and then the two either talk in the kitchen or go for a walk." This was too awkward. He wouldn't have asked if he'd expected to be grilled on courtship rituals.

"But you aren't Amish anymore."

"But she is."

"So, if I'm courted by an Amish boy, he'll come throw rocks at my window?"

"Toss pebbles, yes. Throw rocks, no." He grinned.

"Oh. Cool. Aunt Janna's window is the first one on the north side of the house. Second floor. Obviously."

"Thanks."

"Should I tell her you asked?"

His cheeks were so warm, he feared they might ignite. "No. That won't be necessary."

She giggled. "You're blushing!" Then, she shrugged. "Well, she might need to know so she doesn't go downstairs in her nightgown. But...okay. I'll ring the dinner bell when supper's ready."

She ran out of the barn, leaving him to wonder what Janna would look like in a nightgown. To keep his imagination from getting carried away, he got back to work. He finished up in the first stall, then moved on to the next one.

Not five minutes later, he heard footsteps approaching. He turned around, expecting Meghan again. It was Micah Graber.

He suppressed a sigh. "Hi, Micah."

Micah nodded. "I didn't know you'd be here. Abbie Kauffman stopped and asked me earlier today to kum help."

Troy nodded. "I heard. It's been a while since I last did farm chores. Guess they figured I'd need assistance." *Untrue.* "I'm almost finished with the horses, and I've already taken care of the hogs. Meghan said the cows were lined up, if you want to bring them in and get started on milking. I'll be there in a few minutes."

Micah nodded and headed off. Moments later, Troy heard the door of the cow barn slide open.

Troy finished feeding the horses, then followed Micah back to the cow barn. He went down the cement steps into the dusty room pervaded by animal odors. The cows were all in their areas, waiting, as Micah filled the concrete water troughs lining both walls.

Micah looked up as he approached. "Heard about your mishap this morgen." He smirked.

Troy sighed. "Guess I'll forever be known as the man who shot the bishop, ain't so?"

"Jah. At least until somebody does something to top it. And that'll take some doing."

Troy reached for a small wooden stool and a pail. "That's what I'm afraid of. Are you staying for supper? Heard Janna's fixing fried chicken."

Micah shrugged. "Might. Abbie asked me to. But...I don't know. With you here, and with both of us interested in the same woman...."

"May the best man win." Troy swallowed the lump in his throat. *Micah is the best man.*

"You're courting her already, ain't so?"

He had to be honest. Even if it killed him. "I asked. She accepted. But we haven't officially courted. And my accidental shooting of her daed probably changed everything." He blinked at the unexpected moisture welling in his eyes. *If it didn't, my other mistakes surely will.*

⁊⁊⁊

The door slammed. Janna jumped, splattering hot grease on her hand. She swallowed a yelp but couldn't keep the tears from springing to her eyes. She glanced over her shoulder at Meghan.

"He didn't need my help. Not only that, but he knew everything to do. He even knew why the cows come home on their own."

Mamm raised her eyebrows at Janna, shrugged, and then lowered the knife into the loaf of bread she had started slicing before Meghan had barged in.

"And now, Micah's here."

Janna flipped another piece of chicken, then moved to the sink to run cold water over her hand.

Meghan huffed. "I guess I'll just finish setting the table."

Mamm's eyebrows slid higher. "That would be helpful. You could slice the pies, too."

"Troy's staying for supper, too, you know. So, we'll have him *and* Micah making eyes at Janna across the table. No fair."

Janna's heart jumped up into her throat. Troy was staying for dinner? He'd declined when she'd invited him. Rather curtly, too. *"Nein. Can't."* Monosyllabic, single-word sentences. How should she interpret his apparent change of mind?

Maybe Troy wanted to take it slower. That could be why he'd pulled away. Or maybe he had decided to stay when he'd found out Micah was invited, too. Maybe he was jealous.

She shook her head. His reasons didn't matter. All that mattered was her impartial hospitality. She needed to focus on that rather than on her relationship with the most confusing man she'd ever met.

Meghan started filling the glasses with iced tea. "Why can't you invite someone over who'll look at me like that? Like…um, that one boy with really dark eyes? William Kropf? I think he's really cute, even if he is Amish. Besides, did you notice he cut his hair and wears normal people's clothes?"

Janna stared at her in disbelief. She liked an Amish bu? She tried to summon what she knew of William. He seemed a bit wild. But then, she could've said the same thing about Hiram—Troy—at the same age. She swallowed. "Ring the dinner bell, please. We'll be ready to eat in about five minutes."

Meghan set down the pitcher of iced tea and hurried over to the big metal bell hanging on a peg by the door. She lifted it down and stepped outside.

Janna checked the last piece of chicken and removed it from the frying pan, adding it to the platter of others. Then, she smoothed her hands over her apron and took a deep breath. Troy would stay for supper. Micah would stay for supper. Two men, only one of whom she wanted. If only she knew for certain what he wanted.

The dinner bell made a loud clang. Several minutes later, but long before she was ready, the door opened, and Micah came inside, followed by Troy, whose blue gaze met hers and held it. He winked, and her heart pounded into overdrive. Maybe he was still interested. Maybe he wanted to slow things down, as she'd suspected earlier, or had simply felt uncomfortable having her in his home. That had to be it.

He bent over near the door, took off his shoes, and lined them up neatly next to Micah's. "Smells delicious, Janna." He grinned at her as he made his way to the sink to wash up.

"I'm glad you changed your mind about supper." Did she hear a tremor in her voice? She hoped he hadn't noticed.

His grin widened. "Meghan talked me into it."

He'd agreed in order to get Meghan off his case, not for the chance to be with her. So much for hoping. And Meghan talked him into it how? Why? So she could see him bolt from the room like he had on his last visit? Curious.

She stood there, pondering all this, like a lump of cold mashed potatoes, holding the platter of fried chicken in midair. It was only when Troy approached her that she snapped out of her musings. He slid his hands alongside hers, lifted the plate from her grasp, and leaned forward to whisper, "I'm tossing pebbles at your window tonight." His breath tickled her ear and sent shivers down her spine. Or those might have been from his message.

She'd dreamed of hearing those words for years.

Those and *Ich liebe dich*, followed closely by *Marry me*....

Too soon to be thinking like that. Especially since she still had no clue where she stood with him.

He set the chicken on the table, while she remained standing by the stove, still rooted to the ground. Mamm shoved a serving bowl and a spoon into her hands. "Stop staring." Jarred out of her trance a second time, Janna turned, set the bowl on the counter, and filled it with mashed potatoes. Meghan came up beside her and started transferring the corn to another bowl.

Would Troy like her cooking?

She carried the potatoes over to the table and slid into her chair, carefully averting her gaze so as not to make eye contact with either man sitting across the table. She closed her eyes for the silent prayer. *Lord, please bless this food. Be with Daed at the hospital. Help him to get better, and—*

Someone's stocking-covered toes slid across her bare ones. Janna's head jerked up. Warmth coursed through her when she met Troy's gaze. If only they could be seated side by side, as they'd been at his parents' haus. Holding hands, bumping knees, and thrilling to know he'd be taking her home later. Dreaming of their first moonlit kiss—which had never happened.

Instead, they'd parted abruptly, leaving her confused and hurt by his apparent rejection.

But tonight…. Tonight, he'd kum by. Would he be content to sit in the kitchen and talk over koffee and pie? Or was his aim a walk in the darkness?

Either one was fine with her, as long as she'd be with him.

Unless he was just toying with her, as Mamm suspected, and planned to officially break things off between them.

She slid her feet away and tucked them under her chair, out of reach.

Chapter 26

Troy tiptoed into the darkened room and slipped quietly past the first bed to the other side of the curtain, closer to the window. He peered down at the bishop, his left hand still hooked to an IV. He appeared to be asleep. The moonlight bathed his face in eerie shadows.

Troy lifted the lone chair in the room and carried it closer to the bed. When he set it down, it bumped gently against the bedside tray.

The bishop stirred and moaned. His right hand slid across the blanket a few inches.

Troy swallowed and leaned forward, watching the even rise and fall of his chest. He wasn't supposed to be here, as visiting hours were over. But he hadn't come across any hospital staff ordering him not to go in. And he needed to be sure the bishop was going to be all right before he went back to the Kauffmans' farm for his under-the-cover-of-darkness call on Janna.

If only hospitals weren't so fastidious with record-keeping. He remembered Mamm saying that Grossmammi's files had been kept in a transparent folder at the end of the bed for her family members to thumb through, and for nurses to record information easily. But there was no folder or chart anywhere in sight. In fact, this bed didn't even have a space for one. Probably due to the patient privacy act.

He sighed. He wanted to check on the bishop's prognosis, see what the doctor had said about the damage to his shoulder. He vaguely remembered bits and pieces of the conversation after the shooting, but he'd been numb, scared, and confused.

The bishop moaned again. This time, his eyes opened and rested on Troy. He stared at him, blinking for a few moments, until comprehension dawned. "Sorry. I must've fallen asleep." His voice sounded raspy.

Troy stood and reached for the cup of water on the bedside table. He held it so that Bishop Dave could take a couple of sips.

"They must've given me a sedative when they came by earlier with some pills. My head feels kind of groggy." He pushed the cup away. "Danki. What brings you by?"

"Just checking on you." Troy hung his head. "I did some of the chores on your farm. But your frau invited Micah Graber over to help, too. Perhaps you'd rather have him there than me. I…I want to do this for you, especially since I'm the reason for your injury. But I don't want to cause discord." He glanced up.

"You stay. Micah goes." The bishop pressed a lever, and the head of the bed rose a little. "You stayed for dinner, ain't so?"

"Jah."

"Had to be better than what I ate. Green Jell-O was the best part. There was some kind of meat that didn't look or taste like anything I recognized. And some instant mashed potatoes and overcooked green beans."

Troy managed a grin. "I don't want to make you jealous, but jah, ours was much better. Janna prepared fried chicken. And peach pie for dessert."

"Micah stayed for dinner? How was the company?"

"Micah and Abbie talked. Meghan seemed to be upset and kept glaring at everyone. I guess that's no surprise. And Janna wouldn't look up from her plate." She hadn't, ever since he'd made the bold move of touching her toes with his and she'd jerked her foot away.

Which had really been a wise move on her part.

The bishop grunted. "Must've been uncomfortable for Janna. Wonder what bothered my granddaughter? But then, she's always bothered."

Troy shrugged. She'd seemed to be in good spirits when she'd come out to the barn to invite him for dinner.

A woman wearing scrubs with a stethoscope hanging around her neck padded into the room, pushing a portable monitor. Probably to check the bishop's vitals. She frowned at Troy. "Visiting hours are over, sir."

Right. He knew that. He stood up and smiled at Bishop Dave. "I'll be out again tomorrow to check on you."

"You should call first. I'm going to try to talk the doctor into letting me go home. I'll recover faster there than here, where I'm interrupted at all hours." His glower at the woman seemed a bit exaggerated, considering how cheerful he sounded.

"I'll take you home if they release you. See you tomorrow." Troy nodded at the nurse, slipped out of the room, and strode down the hallway to the elevator. He glanced at his watch. 9:00. He still had time to go to the Kauffmans'. Everyone should be asleep by the time he arrived—except, he hoped, for Janna.

It was an hour later when Troy tossed a handful of pebbles at the window Meghan had told him was Janna's. The window was open, so he aimed at the glass in the upper half. The small stones struck the surface with soft pings, then fell. An eternity seemed to pass before Janna finally stuck her head out.

Troy directed the beam of his flashlight toward him, so that it would illuminate his face. Janna disappeared back inside the dark room. How he'd dreamed of this moment… before he'd made mistakes.

He wiped his sweaty hand on the leg of his jeans. Nerves caused his pulse to jump, as if he were on his very first date. He wasn't, to be sure. Far from it. Though this was his first time tossing pebbles at an Amish girl's bedroom window. *Calm down.* He stepped around the side of the building and waited for Janna to appear on the porch.

"Do you want to talk out here?" she whispered, tilting her head to indicate another open window on the second floor.

Maybe they could go for a drive in his truck, to the creek. *Or not.* "Let's take a walk." He kept his voice hushed.

She nodded, then stepped back inside and immediately reappeared carrying a pair of shoes. She slipped them on her feet, then started down the steps. Troy's heart pounded as she came closer and closer, till she was near enough that he could smell the fruity scent of her hair.

His breath caught. He wanted to reach for her hand, but he feared that if he gave in and touched her, he wouldn't be able to keep himself from tugging her into his arms. From kissing her the way he'd dreamed of since holding her in his arms for the first time, in the barn. From finding out if her lips were as sweet as he remembered.

He couldn't. He shouldn't.

Good thing he'd never promised not to. He'd spoken candidly and warned the bishop that he'd fail.

Because he would. He raised his gaze to the heavens.

Lord, help me.

Janna hesitated a moment beside him, then started toward the road. He hurried to catch up, then slowed to match her pace. He kept a respectable distance between them, just in case anyone happened to be spying on them. He didn't want the bishop to find out and then ban him altogether.

"I bought you a chocolate shake at McDonald's. Hope that's okay." He kept his voice low. "It's in my truck. I parked at the end of your driveway."

"Perfect." He heard a smile in her voice.

When they reached the truck, he opened the door and grabbed Janna's shake and a straw, which he handed to her. Then he grasped the coffee bought himself and shut the door. "I visited your daed tonight, after dinner." He set his coffee cup on the truck bed.

She took a sip of her shake and leaned back against the door. "Is he doing okay?"

"Jah. Seems to be giving the nurse a hard time, though. He really wants to come home tomorrow." He stood facing her, with one shoulder pressed against the door. "I'm sorry. Really."

She grinned. "I forgive you. Really."

He sighed. "Not just for that. For making you uncomfortable at supper. Embarrassing you in front of Micah." He swallowed. "Do you…you know, like him? Do you need me to step out of the way?"

She stiffened. He somehow sensed her withdrawing from him, emotionally and mentally.

Not what he'd intended. Instinctively he raised his hand, reaching out. His fingers touched the softness of her cheek.

She made a sharp intake of breath.

He moved in a little closer, allowing his hand to fully cup the curve of her face. "Nein, I didn't mean it like that. Janna. I…I want to keep seeing you. I still want you to be my girl." And someday, Lord willing, more. If she could forgive him. "But if you think you'd rather be with him, I'll understand. He never left the Amish. He joined the church early. Never got into any trouble at all." He chuckled, though there was nothing remotely humorous about what he felt he had to say. "He's pretty much perfect. Unlike me."

"I never expected perfection." She moved into his touch.

His hand slid around the back of her neck, and he felt a shiver work through her. Seconds later, her body touched his. He felt the icy coldness of her milkshake through his shirt as the cup pressed against his side.

Just her cheek.

He lowered his head, anticipating brief contact between his lips and her smooth skin. But she turned slightly, and his lips met her mouth instead of his intended target.

He trembled. *Ach, Janna.* Her lips were ice-cream cold and tasted of chocolate.

❧

Janna thrilled as Troy drew her nearer, his lips settling firmly on hers, exploring, familiarizing themselves again. She wrapped her arms around his waist, transferring her milkshake from one hand to the other, then fumbled for a flat surface somewhere on the truck where she could set it down, in order to more fully enjoy this assault on her senses. She located the hood, somewhat sloped yet flat enough, and abandoned the drink there, freeing her hand to return to the hard smoothness of his muscular back. To the curls of hair above his collar. None of the Amish men cut theirs that short.

His kisses changed. Became harder. More insistent.

She moaned, her arms rising around his neck, as he moved against her, pressing her into the side of the truck.

His lips left hers, roaming over to her ear, then across her cheek, on her eyelids, down along the curve of her jaw, down her neck....

She yelped. Ice-cold liquid soaked the back of her dress.

He jumped away. "Janna? I'm so sorry! I didn't mean…. Did I hurt you?"

"My milkshake spilled on me."

"Your…milkshake." He exhaled. "I'm sorry. I'll get you another one sometime soon." He moved further away. "I shouldn't have done that, anyway…ach, Janna. Your daed told me he doesn't want me touching you anywhere except your hand. He definitely doesn't want me kissing you."

"Doesn't want you kissing me?" She caught her breath. "Daed said that?"

"I failed. He must have known I would." Troy's hands grasped hers. "He said I wasn't to touch you again until our wedding nacht."

Despite the cold stickiness still seeping into her dress, Janna warmed. "You and Daed spoke about us marrying?" And about his returning to the Amish? Because Daed would never agree otherwise.

She couldn't keep from grinning. This was wunderbaar gut news. Troy must be planning on completing the membership classes and joining the church later this summer. He'd probably return home to live with his parents until they married, maybe in early December, and—

"Jah. He kind of suggested you and I just go get married."

"I accept!" She flung herself into his arms. Two seconds later, his words sunk in, and she backed away. "Wait a minute. You mean…elope?" Like Kristi and Shane had done? Resulting in her being shunned? "Nein. We can't do that."

"I figured you'd say—"

"Daed suggested that? My daed? Seriously?"

"Jah, your daed said—"

"Why would he suggest such a thing? Where would we live? I suppose we could live in the dawdi-haus. It's empty, after all. But, more important, you aren't Amish anymore. What about our—"

"Janna. You're overreacting. I wasn't proposing. I just said he suggested it."

"You weren't proposing?" Her hopes deflated.

He chuckled. "So, you'd accept?"

❦

"I'm overreacting?" She fell silent.

He managed to swallow the laughter that sprang from his lungs. Turning away, he picked up his coffee and took a long swig. Then he reached inside his pocket for his cell phone and checked the time. Almost eleven. They'd spent more time in each other's arms than he would have guessed.

He set down his coffee, then opened the truck door again and pulled out the plastic shopping bag containing a gift he'd bought for Janna at a shop in Seymour. It was a cream-colored ceramic serving bowl with roses along the edge. "This is for you." He pressed it into her hands. "It's for your hope chest. I hope you like it."

"Troy...." Her voice broke.

He draped an arm around her shoulders, drawing her nearer. "Are you crying?"

"You want to marry me? Really?"

He'd thought that's what the household gift meant. That he looked forward to starting a home with her. But he hadn't dared consider it—much—until her daed had made his cryptic comment. Troy still wasn't sure what he'd meant. Or why he'd said it. But he could hardly go to the bishop and demand an answer when he wasn't prepared to reciprocate with answers of his own for Bishop Dave's questions.

But maybe, if Janna's daed was presented with the done deal.... He sucked in a breath. "I think I'm asking you to consider it."

210 Laura V. Hilton

Besides, if they were married, he'd have an easier time taking care of the farm work. He'd be living on the premises. He'd also be able to keep a closer eye on Meghan. And the best part, of course, was that Janna would be his. No chance of losing her to Micah Graber. Pure selfishness, he knew, but he couldn't help it.

"I'll be out again early tomorrow to do the chores. Maybe, if you think you can, we can go into Marshfield after that." He almost couldn't dare to hope he'd have the right to hold Janna again in less than twenty-four hours. To be able to take her to the hospital to visit her daed—as his frau.

Shooting Bishop Dave and then eloping with his daughter— would that be adding insult to injury? Troy suppressed a smile. He'd have a lot to live down in the community.

"Gut nacht." He leaned forward and kissed Janna's cheek, resisting the urge to do more. "You can give me an answer in the morgen."

Please, say jah.

Chapter 27

Janna stared at the ceiling of her darkened room, wishing she were still with Troy. He wanted to marry her. Not break things off. And if Daed had suggested marriage, it meant she wouldn't be shunned. Unless the condition of Troy's joining the church had been implied. If that was true, then marrying beforehand would bring the usual repercussions. The latter was more likely.

She shivered, remembering the passionate moments she'd shared with Troy, neither of them nearly long enough. Something cold and wet had interrupted them on both occasions.

Would Troy join the church if she married him? Or would he keep both feet firmly planted in the fancy world? Would he expect her to move into his little haus in town?

So many questions.

And her answer? She wished she knew. The logical choice would be "Nein." But if she followed her heart, then it would be a resounding "Jah."

She reached for the pink teddy bear he'd given her, hugging it close. *Lord, what do I do?*

She remembered the conversation she'd had with Kristi just few short months ago, when she'd tried talking her friend out of her infatuation with Shane—and failed. If only she'd been more understanding. More supportive. She'd hated having to shun Kristi. And now the tables were turned.

She didn't know if she was strong enough to withstand a shunning. Not even with Troy by her side. It wasn't as if he would be shunned. He'd never joined the church. He could converse freely with anyone. While she'd be invisible.

Not to mention, she didn't want to move to his haus. Didn't he have a roommate? Jah. Joey. She'd met him that time Troy's tire had blown out. Living with him would be awkward, for sure.

She wasn't any closer to reaching a decision when she heard the rumble of his truck in the driveway—two seconds before the rooster crowed.

Time to get up.

Time to collect the eggs, face Troy, and give her answer.

Marry him now and risk being shunned, or risk losing him.

❧⤳❧

Troy took another gulp from the large coffee he'd bought at McDonald's. He didn't feel at all rested, but at least he'd slept, dreaming of Janna saying "Jah," dreaming of eloping with her—until reality had butted in.

He didn't need to guess what her decision would be. He knew. Despite the passion they shared, she would say "Nein."

And he'd need to honor that. Respect that. Step back, move completely out of the way, and let Micah woo her and win her.

Even as his heart broke anew, he firmed his jaw. Time to man up and take on the challenges of the day. *Show no emotion.*

He carried the coffee into the barn and started the morning milking. After that, he'd put the cows out to pasture.

After his chores were completed, he'd pay a visit to the bishop and tell him he was too busy to keep it up—a lie, but one that would be accepted. After all, Bishop Dave didn't know that he'd been suspended from work.

He needed to find a new place to stay. Not that Joey was kicking him out. When Troy had gotten home last night, Joey had informed him that Reese would be moving in. He'd assumed Reese was the name of Joey's latest female—the one hanging on his arm and giggling as he'd delivered the news. Troy had no desire to stay in their love nest. He'd told them he was moving out, loaded his motorcycle into the bed of his truck, boxed up his stuff, piled it around the bike, and left. He'd parked by the creek and spent the night in the driver's seat.

If nowhere else, he'd sleep in his parents' barn tonight.

Or maybe camp out under the stars by the creek.

How had life suddenly become so complicated?

Right now, he'd give almost anything to rewind back to boyhood for a do-over—a chance to prevent the incidents that changed everything.

But that wasn't possible.

He heard a light step behind him. *Janna.* He'd be plunged into the depths of misery in mere seconds.

He sucked in a breath, squared his shoulders, and turned. *Meghan?*

"You're jumpy." She studied him. "Expecting someone else?"

He tried to find a smile. "Maybe so."

"Aunt Janna, perhaps?" She tilted her head and grinned. "She went into the dawdi-haus for some reason. I told Grandma they should put electric in and rent it out, but she said she'd probably live there someday. Not sure why she'd want to downsize like that, though." She shook her head.

She'd move there when Janna married Micah. Probably this very year. With both of them members of the church, it'd happen fast.

She was lost. Over. Done with. He would be a man and accept it. Wouldn't let it bother him.

At least, not until he was alone.

"So, aren't you going to go?"

Troy frowned. "Go where?"

She huffed. "I just said. Don't you listen? To the dawdihaus."

"Why would I need to go there? Do I look like a grandpa to you?" His attempt at teasing fell flat.

She rolled her eyes. "But Aunt Janna just went in. Don't you want to surprise her?"

Troy shook his head. "I think it's best if I stay away from your aunt. She'll be marrying Micah."

"Did she tell you that? Or are you just giving up because he came over last night and you think he's better than you?" Meghan's hands went to her hips. "If so, you're not the man you pretend to be."

Ouch. Troy gave a bitter chuckle. "Sometimes, life doesn't go the way you want. You just have to accept it."

"Or roll over and play dead." A strange expression crossed Meghan's face.

He tried to decipher it but couldn't.

"But I guess you know all about that, don't you?" She gave him a knowing look.

His heart stuttered. Had she somehow stumbled across his secrets?

He put down the pitchfork and picked up his coffee, then took a long swallow, staring at her. Waiting to see what she knew. What she'd say.

She studied him with a pensive look, then shrugged. "Did you have breakfast? There's some oatmeal left."

"I ate at McDonald's, but thanks."

"I have to help Grandma hang out the laundry."

He watched her go.

Exhaled.

She was right. He had to face Janna sooner or later. If she was in the dawdi-haus, she'd be alone. Her answer would still be "Nein," but at least he wouldn't have witnesses in case he fell apart.

Janna wiped the kitchen counters with a damp rag, not that they were really dirty; nobody used this haus much. It'd been unoccupied since the passing of her paternal großeltern, and they used it only for work frolics, when a lot of women gathered to help put up the garden produce. They'd be canning peaches later this morgen. At least, that's what Mamm had said at breakfast. Janna had volunteered to clean the space, with the ulterior aim of scoping it out as a potential future home for her and Troy.

Hearing heavy footfalls on the steps outside, she turned just in time to see the door open.

The scary Troy stepped in, sunglasses shading his eyes. He turned his head in her direction and froze. A moment later, he reached behind him and pulled the door shut with a click. "Meghan said I could find you here."

"Is something wrong? It's not Daed, is it?"

"Nein. Everything's fine, as far as I know." He swallowed, his Adam's apple bobbing. "Have you reached a decision?"

Janna put down the rag. "Jah, I have." It wasn't supposed to be this way. She'd dreamed that he would tell her he loved her. That she'd proclaim her love for him, in return. Not that they'd discuss their elopement in a businesslike manner. *But maybe*…. She moved toward him, summoning her courage. When she was close enough, she reached for his sunglasses and lifted them off.

For a brief moment, she thought she read stark fear in his eyes. Then, he blinked, and it was like a mask had fallen. What was he afraid of? Her? She took a breath. "I'll marry you."

The scary Troy disappeared. Vanished, in an instant. He smiled and held out his arms.

Her heart rate accelerated as she melted into his embrace, enfolding him with her arms. He hugged her tight, his own pulse pounding in her ear.

"Gut," he whispered. Then he drew back, cradling her head in his hands. He lowered his head, and his lips settled on hers, as if they belonged there. She couldn't wait to hear his whispered confessions of love. She kissed him back with all the affection she felt for him—with all her pent-up passion.

He groaned, and his kisses hardened, his hands roaming over her back.

Somewhere deep within the recesses of her mind, a clicking sound registered, but she dismissed it subconsciously.

Then came a voice she couldn't ignore—"Janna? When you finish here, will you bring up the jars from the cellar so Meghan can start washing them?"—followed by a sharp gasp. "Janna!"

She jerked out of Troy's embrace, her face heating. "Sorry, Mamm. Jah, I'll do that."

Troy turned around, a red blush creeping up his neck. He snatched his sunglasses out of Janna's grip. "Gut morgen, Abbie. I was going to check on Bishop Dave…bring him home, if he's ready. If it's okay, I'll take Janna with me."

Mamm blinked in confusion, as if deciding whether to scold him for kissing Janna or thank him for checking in on her daed. She stared at them another moment, then managed a smile. "That'd be nice of you. I didn't realize he'd get to kum home today. I was going to try to find a ride into town after we'd finished the canning."

Troy lifted a shoulder. "He was talking about it last nacht when I was up there. I told him I'd give him a ride." He glanced at his watch. "Let me know when you're ready to go, Janna."

He turned and walked out, leaving her to face the fallout by herself. Janna watched him go, then glanced at Mamm, waiting.

Mamm blinked again. Pulled in a breath. Opened her mouth, then shut it again. Shook her head. "Are you promised?"

"We're promised." She studied her feet. What was the correct protocol here? Confess to Mamm that she would be eloping with Troy this very morgen? Or let it go for now and pray she'd find the words to break the news to her later?

"So, he'll be joining the church. Gut." A smile flickered on Mamm's face. "I'm thinking this wedding had better take place quickly. As soon as he's a member."

Janna studied her. "You aren't upset that I didn't choose Micah?"

"I never expected you would." Mamm pulled her into a hug. "You've always loved Hiram. And we love him, too. I kind of hoped that having Micah around would spur Hiram into action. I was worried he'd disappear after accidentally injuring your daed." She released her and stepped back. "We need to get some material for a blue dress. I'll talk to Elam Troyer's Rosie today when she's here. Ach, so much to do."

"We're eloping." Janna held her breath.

Hopefully, Mamm wouldn't lock her in her bedroom until Troy joined the church.

Chapter 28

Troy had just finished mucking out the stalls and was pushing the wheelbarrow out of the barn when Abbie Kauffman marched up to him and grasped his arm, causing him to lose his grip on the wheelbarrow. It thudded down on the ground and wobbled, the shovel tumbling out beside it. She pulled him into an empty stall.

"Janna is cleaning up. You will do the same. But I won't have my dochter living in town. The dawdi-haus is empty. You can stay there until the boppli start to kum. It'll give you some time without Meghan in the same haus."

So, Janna had told her. "Danki, Abbie. I…I hope this is okay." He shouldn't have said that. Especially since he intended to do it, anyway. But if Abbie said nein, well, he'd need to respect that.

She frowned. "You realize everyone is going to assume this is a forced marriage. That Janna is in the family way. She'll have to kneel and confess, even though she's assured me that she isn't…that you haven't…." Her face stained fuchsia.

His blush from before came back with a vengeance. "Jah. I mean, nein."

"Gut. There's a work frolic starting here in under an hour. I have six bushels of peaches to put up, and we're making jam. I suggest you transfer all those boxes in the back of your truck to the dawdi-haus. Put them in the bedroom, where they'll be out of the way. And then shut the door. I'll have your mamm help me get the haus ready for you after everyone leaves. But let's keep this elopement quiet for now, until we can give you a proper wedding. After you join the church."

"After you join the church." Troy's stomach clenched, but he nodded. What else could he do? He supposed that if he ended up losing his job, he'd have no choice. But, in the meantime, maybe it'd be best not to rock the boat. He'd do what needed to be done. And being married to Janna would be worth it, as long as she forgave him once she learned his secrets.

He sucked in a breath and shook his head. He couldn't believe her mamm was this accepting. Not after she'd invited Micah over with such clear intentions. She probably wouldn't be this agreeable if she knew the truth.

Abbie patted his arm, then started for the barn door. "Get busy, then."

"Jah." He grinned as he hoisted the wheelbarrow handles again. If only the bishop would take the news so well. Troy's family would be thrilled, once they'd gotten over the initial shock. They loved Janna already.

After he'd emptied the wheelbarrow and put it away, he unloaded the boxes of his belongings from the truck and carried them into the dawdi-haus, stashing them in the bedroom. He dug through them to find some clean clothes, then took a hot shower. He was glad that the housing issue had been so simple to work out. More than glad Janna had said "Jah." He couldn't wait to marry her. And, since they'd be wed by a judge in an Englisch ceremony, he'd have the right to kiss her immediately after they'd been pronounced man and wife.

He dressed, then headed outside, where Janna was waiting.

He would be marrying the woman he loved. It was a dream come true. Just not exactly the way he'd imagined it back when he'd had the right to think about it.

"I now pronounce you man and wife."

Janna tightened her grip on Troy's hand when the man in the black robe spoke the magic words that made it true. A thrill shot through her.

This ceremony was so different from the Amish weddings she'd attended, but the outcome was the same. She was now Hiram "Troy" Troyer's Janna. His frau by law. Though this marriage would be considered unofficial in the eyes of the community. Hopefully, Mamm's plan to keep it hushed played out. That way, she would avoid being shunned. And then, when Troy joined the church, they could marry again. The Amish way.

She glanced around at the strangers who'd been called into the judge's chambers to witness their marriage. Every single one of them was an Englischer. They all peered at her as if she were some freaky sideshow. What—did they think that the Amish didn't marry? Or that they observed the Old Testament practice in which the woman simply moved into the man's tent? Ach, jah. That'd work. Another warming sensation coursed through her.

"You may kiss the bride."

Troy leaned forward and brushed her lips with his, then pulled back. Her mouth tingled. She wanted to pull him back to her for another kiss, one like they'd shared earlier this morgen. But maybe that would be inappropriate, even in the Englisch public. She glanced up at him, and he winked. His eyes held the promise of things soon to kum.

"Sign here." The judge slid the marriage certificate toward them, and Troy wrote his name—Hiram Troyer—in bold black slashes. Janna added hers, using her maiden name. Then the witnesses and the judge signed.

"Congratulations!" Kind words and well-wishes rained on them as Troy grasped her hand and led her from the building out to the truck. The whole experience had been overwhelming. She wished she could find a quiet moment to process it. But even at an Amish wedding, the festivities continued all day long, beginning with a sermon and ending with a singing in the barn.

Troy opened the passenger door for her and helped her in, chuckling. "Guess now we should go to the hospital to pick up your daed. We're probably the only couple ever to do that first thing after their wedding."

There was no "probably" about it. She'd never heard of such a thing before. And it would be another awkward experience, telling Daed they'd eloped. After the fact. Would he comply with Mamm's plan to keep it quiet? Or would he shun her on the spot and insist on finding another ride home? She'd jumped into this too hastily. Remorse ate at her. But she couldn't undo her actions. And, to be honest, she wasn't sure she wanted to. She loved Hiram Troyer. She wanted to be his frau. Even if he continued going by "Troy." She'd grown accustomed to calling him that, even in her mind.

Her stomach started to cramp as they got closer to the hospital. She wanted to ask how they would break the news to Daed. But she didn't dare say a word, too afraid of distracting Troy when he needed to pay attention to the road. Traffic was so heavy, she hung on to the door handle with white-knuckled fingers. They arrived in Springfield, followed a maze of streets to the hospital, and then parked in what looked to be the last available parking spot.

She heaved a sigh of relief as Troy came around to her side to open the door for her. She wanted to collapse into his arms, but even here, there were too many people. Too public for an embrace, even if she needed one for courage. Maybe they'd have a moment alone on the elevator. She grasped his hand, trying to absorb his strength, as they walked side by side into the building.

But people were everywhere inside the hospital, too, even in the elevators. Too soon they were on Daed's floor, and they hadn't had a minute alone to talk.

If only they'd thought this through instead of acting in the heat of the moment. But it wasn't as if Troy hadn't given her time. He'd asked yesterday, giving her all nacht to think. To plan. To refuse. And she hadn't.

Troy released her hand just outside the door. Somehow she managed to stay on her feet. How could she face Daed with this? It'd been easier to tell Mamm. Daed wielded so much power.

The first bed was empty this morgen, freshly made, awaiting a new patient. A blessing they wouldn't have an audience for this discussion. On the other side of the open curtain, Daed reclined on the bed, thumbing through a newspaper that someone must have brought him.

Janna found a smile as Daed looked up. He glanced quickly from her to Troy and then back again, his gaze narrowing, his lips parting slightly. Did they look guilty or something? Could he tell they'd eloped?

Troy approached the bed. "Gut morgen. Has the doctor released you?" He sounded calm.

Her stomach roiled. She looked around for the trash can, just in case. Spotted a bathroom. Even better.

Daed shook his head. "They said I have to have rotator cuff surgery because the bullet tore my muscle. The doctor was pretty adamant. He says my arm will be worthless if I don't have the surgery. Someone's coming in a few minutes to get me for the operation. I'll need therapy after I recover, but apparently I can do it at home. I'll be stuck here another few days. You'll keep taking care of my farm in the meantime, ain't so?"

Troy nodded. "I'm sorry you have to stay. Really sorry I caused so much damage. But I'll be glad to handle your farm for you."

Daed nodded. "Now then." He glanced at Janna, then looked sharply at Troy. "You married her."

She'd known he'd suspect them. Their guilt must be written all over their faces.

Troy straightened. "Yes sir, I did. Just about an hour ago."

Daed shut his eyes. "I was afraid you wouldn't wait. I shouldn't have said what I did about Missouri's marriage laws." Janna felt Troy's fingers tighten around her hand. "I always imagined you two marrying in our way. With me there, as officiant."

"Mamm suggested we keep it quiet until after Troy joins the church," Janna said quickly. She gave Troy a sidelong glance. She'd never asked whether he intended to join. Mamm had made the assumption, and Janna hadn't the courage to tell her that she didn't know what he would do.

Daed nodded slowly. "I'm not having her live in that haus in town. You move into the dawdi-haus. It's empty. We'll begin a baptismal class as soon as I'm out of the hospital."

Troy smoothed his hand over his jaw but said not a word. If only she could read his thoughts.

"You'll remain clean shaven until you're married in the Amish church." Daed pushed a button, then winced as the top of the bed angled forward with a whirring sound.

Troy leaned forward and helped adjust the pillow, sliding it behind Daed's back.

Daed frowned. "I don't want to lie to the community through a sin of omission. But I see my frau's reasons. It's either that, or Janna will be shunned, and…well, I think that would be hurtful for Meghan."

Troy nodded. "Not to mention everyone else—you, Janna, the rest of the family…as well as her clients who rely on her to do their shopping. And you're right about Meghan. It could be downright destructive for her."

Daed pulled in a breath. "I will talk to the preachers. We will discuss how best to handle this. Until then, jah, we'll keep it quiet."

"Janna is living in the dawdi-haus with me." Troy stated it matter-of-factly.

Janna's cheeks flamed, and she dipped her head, not daring to look at either man.

"I figured you wouldn't have it any other way," Daed said.

Two nurses bustled into the room. "Are you ready for your surgery?" One of them lowered the bed and snapped the side rails up, while the other did something to the IV attached to Daed's hand.

Janna squirmed. If only those nurses had kum a little earlier, so that this entire conversation could have been avoided. But it was a blessing she and Troy would be there for Daed's surgery, since no one else knew about it. Daed must not have wanted to worry them.

Troy touched Daed's hand. "We'll be praying for you."

Daed nodded. "We still need to have that talk." He sighed. "Later."

⁓⌇⁓

Thank God for later. Troy took Janna's hand and started down the hall after the pair of nurses escorting Bishop Dave. He really needed to come up with another name for his father-in-law. It was strange to think that after years of almost fearing the man—because of his position, mostly—

he'd soon be virtually living in his home, since the dawdi-haus was connected to the main building. They'd be taking their meals at the same table. Working side by side in the barn and in the fields. And raising his grandchildren.

That long-overdue conversation would be coming way too soon. Troy still wasn't ready.

Feeling his cell phone vibrate in his pocket, he pulled it out and checked the screen for the caller ID. The police department. His stomach churned as concern flooded over him. He almost pushed the button to answer, but he stopped when he glanced at Janna and read fear and uncertainty in her eyes. She came first. And she needed him right now. He slid the phone back into his pocket. He'd check in with the station later.

One of the nurses wheeled the hospital bed onto the elevator. The other waited with Troy and Janna for the next ride. Once downstairs, she led them into a waiting room.

The room was empty but open to the public. Janna headed straight for a seat in the corner, while Troy fingered his phone. Maybe he should call Kimmy and ask her to let Abbie know about the bishop's surgery. Kimmy could probably find a tactful way of breaking the news in such a way that Abbie wouldn't cancel the canning frolic and rush over here. After all, rotator cuff surgery was pretty routine. His grandfather had undergone the same thing a couple of years ago. Granted, his had been required due to normal wear and tear on the shoulder muscle, not a gunshot wound.

When Janna sent him a curious gaze, he held up his phone, then turned and walked out of the room to call Kimmy.

"Hello?" She sounded chirpy.

"Hey, Kimmy. It's Troy. Bishop Dave has just gone in for surgery. It's for his rotator cuff, and it's a commonplace procedure, so no need to worry. Can you go by his home and tell Abbie? Janna and I will stay here and wait."

"Sure, I can do that," she replied. "I'm helping at my church's vacation Bible school this morning, so I'll go over there as soon as it lets out."

"That's fine. Thanks. I'll call you if anything changes." Troy snapped his phone shut, then returned to the waiting room. He dropped into the chair beside Janna's, wrapped his arm around her shoulders, and drew her closer to him. "Not exactly how I'd envisioned my wedding day."

Janna cast him a fretful glance, then looked down at her apron, wringing it with her hands. "You probably imagined an Englisch wedding, with a fancy bride wearing one of those long, satiny gowns and a lacey veil. A reception, followed by a honeymoon on some remote island...."

He thought he heard trepidation in her voice. "Nein." He fingered one of the strings on her prayer kapp, giving it a playful tug. "I imagined you, and all of our family and friends gathered at your haus. I imagined the wedding feast, the fellowship, and the singing. But, most of all...." He smiled. "I imagined what would happen when we were alone."

Red flooded her forehead and cheeks. "I hope I'm not a disappointment."

He tucked a fingertip under her chin and lifted her head so that he could see into her eyes. "Impossible. But that was the stuff I dreamed of before jumping the fence. After I left, I didn't dare dream of you. Until recently. And then I couldn't stop." He winked and then gave her a kiss on the cheek. "I'm sorry if I ruined your dreams."

She averted her gaze without an answer. His heart deflated. Couldn't she at least find something to say? Something like, she'd always wanted to marry him? Or maybe—pushing the boundaries of propriety—that she couldn't wait until they were alone tonight?

He released a sigh and leaned away. "We need to pray for your daed." *And for ourselves.* What had they done, rushing into marriage like this? Now they had to face the repercussions, come what may.

Chapter 29

*I*t seemed as if hours had crawled by before they heard word about Daed and were able to see him. Daed was awake but groggy. They stayed with him for a little while, then left so that Janna could go home and help put peaches up. She was relieved to see the cluster of buggies parked in the field by the dawdi-haus. The canning was still in progress. When Troy parked the truck, she released her seat belt and sprang out of the vehicle before he'd even turned off the engine.

It'd be gut to do something other than sit in the hospital, a captive audience to her thoughts and doubts. Troy had barely spoken to her since suggesting they pray for her daed. He'd seemed lost in his thoughts, with a demeanor that had silently screamed, "No trespassing!" Or maybe he'd been praying, as she had. It'd been hard to tell.

She hurried up to the haus, anxious to occupy herself with preparing the peaches for jam or preserving them in jars for the winter months. She didn't anticipate any of the other women saying much to her, other than perhaps inquiring where she'd been. If they asked, she would tell them she'd been visiting Daed at the hospital. Better to tell part of the truth than an outright lie.

She hesitated outside the entrance to the dawdi-haus, then decided to enter via the door from the main haus.

Mamm looked up as she came in, her eyebrows raised. Janna nodded, and Mamm exhaled. "How's your daed?"

Kimmy had kum by with the message. Gut. She'd have less to explain. Everyone would have heard the news. No one would question her absence.

"He's settled in his room. He was awake, but groggy, and the nurse said he'll probably sleep a lot today."

"I'll go this afternoon and check on him. I've already arranged a ride with Kimmy." Mamm returned her attention to the peach in her hand.

"What would you like me to do?" Janna looked around the room at all the women working—around the table, at the counter, over the stove, and in the sink.

"Go to the dawdi-haus. You can help with the jam." Mamm nodded toward the connecting door.

Janna washed her hands, then opened the connecting door and stepped inside her new home. Its former occupants had been her paternal großeltern. She looked around the compact kitchen. Grossmammi had never done much cooking there, preferring instead to eat most meals with the family. Janna supposed she and Troy would join her family for most meals, too. It would make sense.

"Nice you could join us, Janna. How's your daed?" someone asked from the direction of the stove.

Janna glanced over at the group of women and saw Rosie Troyer beaming back at her, as if she'd received just the best news of her life. Janna grinned back. "He's all right. He's recovering from rotator cuff surgery."

"Too bad that Hiram Troyer shot him like that," someone else muttered.

"It was an accident." Janna hoped her tone hadn't been too defensive. She pursed her lips.

The smile faded from Rosie's face. She stood, marched over to the sink, and washed her hands, then grasped Janna by the arm and pulled her into the bedroom. One wall was piled high with boxes. Troy had moved in already? No wonder he hadn't said anything about needing to go get his things. That explained all the stuff she'd seen in his truck when he arrived that morgen. He must've assumed she'd say jah.

Rosie Troyer shut the door, then wrapped Janna in a tight hug. "Your mamm told me. I couldn't be happier. I wanted you to know." She stepped back. "After everyone leaves, I'll stay and help get this place cleaned up for you. We're almost finished with the jam, anyway; just another batch or two to go." She sighed. "I do hope the bishop agrees about keeping this quiet. I'd hate to have to shun you." She set her jaw. "You're my dochter now."

"Daed's going to talk to the preachers." Janna looked out the window. Troy paced back and forth in the driveway, his cell phone to his ear. Did this conversation have anything to do with the call he'd gotten when Daed was being wheeled down to surgery? He hadn't said anything to her about that, even though it seemed a frau should be privy to the information. Maybe he planned on sharing later. Her stomach clenched.

Rosie draped an arm over Janna's shoulders and squeezed. "We'll get this room fixed up nice. I think your mamm mentioned something about taking Meghan along to the hospital to give you a little privacy."

Troy shoved his phone back inside his pocket and turned. He was startled to see Meghan standing close by, watching him with burrowed brow, a half-eaten peach in one hand, a sandwich with a peach balanced on top in the other. These she held out to him.

He smiled and accepted her offering. "Thank you."

"So, what's going on?" Meghan tilted her head. "Grandma is like a drill sergeant today, barking orders at everyone in there, but she won't tell me anything. She and your mom keep whispering to each other. But I don't think they're passing along any secrets about canning peaches, even though I've never canned before. I know something's going on. And I want to know what."

"Why aren't you in there helping?"

"I was. I'm taking a lunch break."

"Well, you'll be happy know that your grandpa is fine. He had rotator cuff surgery, but it's a minor operation. Maybe your grandma is worried about that."

A sneer curled Meghan's upper lip. "Uh-huh. And so she'd be whispering a lot to your mamm about that. Makes complete sense to me."

Troy looked away to hide a smile. "Right. You deserve to know more. Take a walk with me?" He took a bite of the sandwich and started toward the road.

Meghan fell into step beside him, quiet for once.

"I...um, did something else today to further disrupt your family."

"What'd you do now?" Meghan finished her peach and tossed the pit to the side of the road.

"I eloped with Janna."

Meghan blinked. "Then, what're you doing here? Shouldn't you be on a plane to Jamaica or someplace? That's where Mom goes with all her new husbands. And boyfriends, for that matter. In fact, she went and married that jerk who—Never mind."

Troy gave her a sharp look.

"So, why isn't everybody talking about you two eloping? And where's the wedding cake? I could sure go for some."

Troy shot her a glance. "Don't think you can change the subject so quickly. You and I are going to talk further about 'that jerk.'" He cleared his throat. "As for Janna and me, we're planning to keep our marriage a secret for now. We're supposed to have a traditional Amish wedding later this year."

"So, you just couldn't wait until then? Afraid Micah Graber would steal her away?" She studied him.

"I...uh...." What was he supposed to say? That he'd let his passion rule his brain? That he loved Janna so much, he'd latched on to some words her daed had muttered—words he now regretted—and run with them? But Janna had agreed. That meant something—just what, he didn't know. Even though he loved her, he'd never told her so. He needed to rectify that. Granted, she'd never spoken those words to him. Either she loved him enough to risk everything to be with him, or desire had colored her thinking, too. He preferred the first one—if not both.

"So, you're my uncle now, but I'm not allowed to call you that yet? This whole situation is messed up." Meghan shook her head. "Hey, did you ever tell Aunt Janna why you freaked out when Grandpa offered you some Amish clothes? Because, if you did, I'm curious about it myself. Admittedly, I'd probably freak out, too, if someone tried to make me wear a dress and a bonnet."

Troy forced a chuckle to mask the painful reminder of what he had yet to tell Janna and her family. Of what he was terrified to tell them, especially since Janna hadn't told him she loved him. Not to mention, they hadn't consummated their marriage, and there was a chance she'd reject him before they did. He could still lose her.

"But I think it's more than that."

He almost choked on his sandwich. He swallowed and turned to Meghan. "Let's just say that I made some terrible mistakes when I was around your age—mistakes I don't want to talk about, other than to say that, once, I was the kid in the buggy trying to flee from the police."

❧◦◦◦❧

At long last, the final batch of peach-filled jars had been lifted out of the canner and now sat on the towel-lined counter for the sealing process. The last of the buggies had left, and Mamm had put Meghan to work scrubbing the floors in both kitchens, while she and Rosie Troyer made the bed in the dawdi-haus and unpacked Troy's belongings.

Janna went up to her room to pack her few things. Her hope chest had already been moved; Troy had hoisted it with his strong arms as if it weighed next to nothing, carried it downstairs, and taken it into the dawdi-haus, where he'd set it in the living room.

Without a single word to her, other than "Where do you want this?"

She blinked back tears as she gathered the bag of her belongings and glanced around the room she'd occupied since early childhood. Troy's teddy bear gazed back at her from the bed. She tucked it under her arm, then headed downstairs and over to the dawdi-haus.

Rosie Troyer gave her another big hug, this time including the bear and her bags. "I'll see you later tonight, Janna. I'm bringing supper over. Already worked it out with your mamm." Smiling, she hurried out the door, just as Kimmy's white van arrived to take Mamm and Meghan to the hospital. If only she could go with them. It'd be better than staying here with Troy. She wasn't sure where they stood, and she was afraid he already regretted his rash decision to marry her.

She followed Mamm and Meghan out to the van, then stood there and watched as they climbed into the backseat and slid the door shut. The tears she held at bay burned her eyes. Troy came out of the barn, where he'd spent the afternoon working—or hiding—and stood by her side as the vehicle receded down the dirt road and disappeared in a cloud of dust.

Then, Troy turned and looked at her, his eyes shining with fear and something else. That something else scared her and excited her at the same time.

"Are you okay?" She wanted to know why he'd avoided her since they'd gotten home, except to carry her hope chest into the dawdi-haus. But the moment she'd asked, she knew the answer. They were married, and yet they weren't.

He nodded. "I got a call from the police chief. They want me to return to work in two days." He whistled a sigh. "And I placed an ad in the paper listing my motorcycle for sale. Somehow it seems wrong having that out here on the farm."

"Are you going back to work?" *Please, say nein. Tell me you're going to join the church and be Plain.*

He touched her hand, then brought it to his mouth and kissed her palm. "Jah. I am. I have a frau to support now." He grinned at her. "But I'll still handle things for your daed, when I'm not on the clock." He kissed each of her fingertips. "In the meantime, we have two days for a honeymoon, of sorts. And nobody else will be here for the next six hours, at least…." He drew her into his arms.

She shivered when his lips brushed hers, then squealed as he swept her off her feet and carried her into the dawdi-haus, kicking the door shut behind them.

Chapter 30

*T*heir two-day "honeymoon" had passed entirely too fast. Today, Troy was to report to the police station at two. While he was excited about returning to work, he knew he'd miss the day-to-day routine of farm life. Not to mention getting to see Janna at all hours. It was almost enough to make him want to resign from his post. But he figured he'd need a job if they kicked him to the curb once they found out the truth.

Troy headed in from the fields when he heard Meghan ring the dinner bell for the noon meal. He washed up as Janna finished arranging the makings of a BLT—homegrown tomatoes, leaf lettuce, and fried bacon—on the table. He caught her eye and noticed the pink blush rising on her cheeks. He didn't want to leave her. In fact, maybe they could skip lunch, and—

Thump. Abbie set down the jar of mayonnaise rather emphatically. Perhaps his mother-in-law was unhappy about his return to work and what it implied.

Meghan brought some pickled eggs and chow-chow from the pantry, then carried over a plate of fresh-baked walnut chocolate chip cookies, still warm from the oven.

After they'd bowed their heads for the silent prayer, the familiar sound of tires on gravel sounded outside. Troy got up to see who'd driven in. As he stepped out onto the porch, Kimmy waved at him from behind the wheel of her van.

She opened the door and climbed out. "They're releasing Bishop Dave from the hospital. I got a call from him this morning, but I couldn't come until now due to my church's vacation Bible school."

"I'll go with you to pick him up," Abbie said, joining Troy on the porch. "We just sat down to eat lunch. Have you eaten yet?"

Kimmy shook her head. "I was planning on grabbing something from McDonald's."

"Kum on in and make a sandwich." Abbie waved her hand. "We can eat them on the road."

Kimmy slammed the door of the van. "Sounds good. My tomatoes aren't ripe yet. But you got yours in a lot earlier than I did."

Troy followed the women inside. Janna was already transferring her mamm's lunch to a paper plate, and then she set out one for Kimmy.

"It's good you can spend so much time here helping out, Troy." Kimmy glanced at him as he slid back into his seat at the table.

"It's the least I can do, since I'm the one who caused the trouble in the first place. Bishop Dave was kind enough to let me move into the dawdi-haus, which is a blessing."

"Has this affected your job any?" Kimmy raised an eyebrow as she spread mayonnaise on a slice of bread.

"I was off a few days while they investigated," Troy acknowledged. "Bishop Dave hasn't said anything to me about it, but I heard that one of the officers visited him in the hospital and verified that it was an accident. I'm just glad his injury wasn't worse."

Kimmy nodded. "Bad enough as it is. A farmer shouldn't be laid up this way." She layered several strips of bacon on her sandwich. "But at least you know what you're doing. I'm sure the bishop appreciates it."

Troy shrugged. "I needed to do this."

Kimmy topped the sandwich with another piece of bread and then picked up the plate. "I'm sure his recovery will take a while. And he may never regain the full use of his arm. My father-in-law didn't. He said it was never the same."

Not encouraging. Troy frowned. "I'll be here as long as he needs me." Of course, that might not be for long, once the truth came out. Or once he could no longer bear having salt rubbed in his emotional wounds on a daily basis. He expelled a sigh. He was certain Bishop Dave would do whatever it took to recover, but he didn't know the odds. Janna caught his eye and gave him a sympathetic smile as she sat back in her seat.

"We'll be back in a couple of hours." Abbie started for the door, then turned. "Meghan, when you finish eating, would you do the lunch dishes and make sure the laundry is folded and brought in?"

"I'll help," Janna offered. "I wanted to do some more baking this afternoon, anyway."

"Bye." Kimmy waved, then followed Abbie outside. A few minutes later, the van rumbled out of the driveway.

Troy finished his lunch, bowed his head for the final silent prayer, and then stood. "I need to go get ready for work."

Janna followed him into the dawdi-haus. "I wish you wouldn't go back to your job. It's so dangerous."

He smiled. "I'm keeping the roads a safer place for you and your family. Besides, I enjoy what I do."

She nodded and looked down.

For a moment, guilt gnawed at him. If he continued down this path, Janna would end up shunned. She had to know that. He didn't want to hurt her, but he didn't see any other option, short of returning. And facing things he didn't want to face.

Lord?

Trust Me.

Right. He could do that.

"Hey, Janna." Troy leaned down to see into her eyes. "Look at me." When she raised her head, he grinned. "It'll be okay. Besides, pretty soon your daed will be home, and you'll be fussing over him so much, you forget all about me."

She moved into his embrace, wrapping her arms around his waist. "That could never happen."

He gave her a quick kiss, then disentangled himself. "I need to get ready. I'll see you tonight." He winked at her.

She nodded, her face coloring, and disappeared through the door to the main haus.

After a quick shower, Troy suited up in his uniform and went out to his truck. Janna followed him, carrying a bagged sandwich and some cookies for his supper break. She handed it off, then backed away from the vehicle, tears welling in her eyes. From the kitchen window, Meghan glared at him, as if he were abandoning them in their hour of need.

He refused to feel guilty. It wasn't like he was doing something unlawful or immoral. He was simply going back to work. An honest means of earning wages.

He parked his truck on the square, clocked in, and went to retrieve his cruiser from its parking space behind the station. Then he drove down Garfield Street, on his way to respond to a call about a bear sighting. At least his first day back on the job promised some excitement.

As he neared the address he'd been given, he came upon a group of people standing in the street, staring up at a tree. Some of them were snapping photos or videotaping. He'd located the bear, all right. He parked on the side of the road, got out of the vehicle, and approached the group for a better look. It was a bear, sure enough, asleep on a thick branch. He returned to his car and radioed in what he'd found. The chief of police told him to stand by while he contacted the state conservation agent.

While Troy hovered by the radio, awaiting further instruction, he kept an eye on the crowd. Everyone was calm, for the most part, and understandably fascinated by the sight of a black bear in a residential area. Black bears were common in southern Missouri, but, to these city dwellers, the sight was rare indeed.

When the radio crackled to life, Troy sprang to attention. "According to the conservation agent, the bear will come down on its own if it's left alone," said the chief. "Maintain crowd control until early evening, then vacate the area of onlookers."

So, the highlight of his day would be watching a bear sleep? He chuckled. He could've gotten a lot of work done on the farm during the hours he sat there.

The conservation agent had been right. Just before Troy's shift ended, the bear climbed down, sniffed around the base of the tree, and then lumbered off into the darkness.

Troy couldn't ignore the parallels in his own life. The words from Michael Jackson's song "Beat It," an old favorite of his, flashed through his thoughts—as did a sense of urgency to escape.

It was the same feeling he'd had six years ago, when he'd stood by the side of the road, miraculously unhurt, staring at the wreck with tears streaming down his face, trying not to see the bodies of his brother and his best friend. Pretty soon, the place had swarmed with police, EMTs, and firefighters.

He'd done what he could. He'd beat it.

❧

Janna awoke, snuggled against Troy, his arm heavy across her chest. How she loved waking up next to him. This part of marriage was better than her wildest dreams. If only she knew his thoughts about the future. Did he plan to stay in the fancy world? Or would he join the church?

She tried to slip away gently, so as not to wake him. She wasn't sure how late it'd been when he'd gotten home. She'd roused at some point and seen he was there, but checking the time had been the last thing on her mind, especially when he'd pulled her into his arms, kissed her, and whispered something that sounded like "Ich liebe dich." Though, in her half-asleep state, she hadn't been entirely certain.

Troy yawned and stretched. "Morgen already?"

As if to answer his question, the rooster crowed.

Janna ran a comb through her hair, then started pinning it up. Troy rolled out of bed and came up behind her, plucking the hairpins out faster than she could get them in. She pretended to glare at him. Chuckling, he caught her mane of hair in one hand, wrapped his other arm around her waist, and nibbled on her neck as he pulled her back into his embrace.

When she finally made it over to the main kitchen to help prepare breakfast, Daed was already there, standing by the window, a blue sling holding his left arm against his body. Mamm had gotten him dressed, somehow. It was gut it'd been his left shoulder, since he was right-handed.

"Gut morgen, Daed." Janna went over and gave him a hug.

Daed patted her on the back with his right hand, then resumed his stance of staring out the window at the barn, as if he'd be over there in a millisecond if Mamm weren't hovering. "I feel so useless," he muttered.

"Aren't there things you can do with only one arm?" asked Meghan. She stood at the counter, her face streaked with flour, and squinted at a faded recipe card, as if it'd been written in gibberish. "One smidgen of soda. Grandma, how much is a smidgen?"

"Don't encourage him, Meghan," Mamm warned. She walked over to look at the recipe.

"Maybe I'll just wander out there to see what Hiram's doing." Daed slid one foot into a laceless shoe.

"It's Troy." Meghan corrected him. "And I'll come too, to make sure he doesn't let you do any work."

"I thought you were helping me make pancakes...."

Meghan was out the door before Mamm had even finished her sentence.

"Ach, that girl," Mamm muttered. "Dave, you tell her to get right back in here because we're not having pancakes for breakfast unless she fixes them."

Daed nodded. "Pancakes sound gut." He slipped his other foot in a shoe, then scooted out the door.

Janna grabbed a basket. "I'll go feed and water the chickens and see how many eggs we have. If I collect enough, I'll make scrambled eggs to go with breakfast."

She loved the new family dynamic with Troy in the picture. If only it could last. At the rate things were going, it was only a matter of time until she was shunned. Troy had gone back to work, despite her wishes. Daed would have no choice but to shun her, depriving her of their daily banter. The preachers wouldn't agree to wait for him to join the church. She blinked back her tears.

If only she could convince Troy to join the church.

His not joining would hurt her beyond measure. Not to mention what it might cost Daed.

"Grandpa isn't supposed to do any work!" Meghan's shout startled Daisy, who stepped back, nearly overturning the milk pail.

Troy raised his head and looked over the cow's shoulder to see Meghan clambering down the cement steps to the cow barn. "Is he coming out here?"

"Yeah. He's, like, right behind me."

Troy's stomach clenched. He was surprised he hadn't formed an ulcer already. He knew what the bishop wanted—not to do work but to have a discussion. The discussion that'd been postponed and avoided time and again, only to loom once more on the near horizon. The discussion that would seal Janna's fate, determining whether she would be shunned. He didn't want that for her. But he needed the security of his job. More than she knew.

Meghan stepped up and peeked inside the bucket.

"You ever milk a cow?" If Meghan were present, then maybe the bishop wouldn't press him to have that talk.

"Nope."

"Well, then." Troy stood, freeing the stool. "Everyone should know how to milk a cow. Have a seat."

She complied without complaint.

"Now, rest your head against her flank."

Meghan gawked up at him. "You want my head touching the cow? I thought that was just what lazy farmers did."

Troy chuckled. "Nope. It's part of the routine. Cows like routine."

"But what if she has lice? Or fleas? Eww."

Troy rolled his eyes. "She doesn't have fleas, okay?"

Wincing, Meghan leaned forward, barely touching Daisy's hide with her hair.

"There you go. Now, take a teat in the palm of your hand, like so." He crouched down and positioned her hand properly. "Okay. Now, squeeze at the top, starting with your index finger. Continue squeezing each finger in succession around the teat, forcing the milk in a stream. Good. You got it. Not so hard, is it?"

This he could get used to. Maybe someday, he'd teach his own kinner how to milk a cow. He sighed. It certainly beat watching a bear asleep in a tree.

"Meghan?" Bishop Dave's voice carried down the stairs. "Where'd you get to? Your grandma would like you to help her with breakfast." He appeared at the bottom of the staircase.

"Can't. I'm milking cows right now."

Chuckling, Troy glanced over his shoulder at his father-in-law. "This is important, ain't so?"

The bishop stroked his beard with his right hand. "Jah, but I don't want to be the one to tell my frau. She wants breakfast served on time."

Meghan huffed. "I'll go, I'll go. Just let me finish this cow. I've always wanted to learn."

"After breakfast, I'll teach you how to muck stalls." Troy winked at the bishop.

"No, thanks. I'd rather wash dishes. Besides, Aunt Janna is going to teach me how to sew today."

"Sounds boring," Troy teased. "Mucking might be more fun."

Meghan sighed. "Extremely boring, but not so stinky."

"Careful, or we'll be putting you to work in the fields," the bishop said. "We could use an extra pair of hands."

"How do I know when the milk's all out?" Meghan looked up at Troy.

He leaned over and pointed to a teat he'd milked. "When it looks like that. Kind of flattened." He checked the one in her hand. "You've got it. Good job. Now go wash up and help your grandma with those pancakes."

Meghan stood slowly, backing away from the cow, then turned and scampered up the stairs.

Bishop Dave opened the barn doors at the back, so the cows could go to pasture. "You're gut with Meghan, Troy. When I see her with you, I think I know why Sharon sent her to us."

Troy still wanted to talk to her about that "jerk" she'd mentioned. Should he confide in the bishop about what Meghan had said? Not yet. He didn't have enough to go on, despite the gravity of his suspicions.

Troy picked up the stool and milk pail, sliding them under the next cow in line. "She just needs a mentor." It sounded like she needed protection, too, from her mother's latest man. That news was sure to make the bishop feel successful as a father. Not.

"Are you working this afternoon?" The bishop's face appeared above the bovine. "The preachers are supposed to kum over after breakfast to discuss your elopement. I would like you there."

So, the day of reckoning had arrived.

Chapter 31

*J*anna unfolded the blue fabric and spread it on the kitchen table. Mamm had bought it yesterday when she'd been out with Kimmy. It was a pretty shade, the color of the sky on a clear summer day. Janna couldn't wait to wear it on her wedding day—the day her marriage to Troy would be recognized as official by the Amish community.

If that day ever came. With Troy going back to work, saying he liked his job.... She sighed. Well, if a miracle happened, she'd be ready.

Mamm entered the room, carrying a large white envelope, a pin cushion, and scissors. She opened the envelope and took out the folded pattern pieces, handing them to Meghan. "Unfold them carefully, and then I'll show you how to lay them out so they match the grain of the material."

Leaving Mamm to supervise, Janna approached the treadle sewing machine to make sure it was threaded and ready to go. She fitted the spool on the bobbin, snapped it back in place, and returned to the table.

A horse and buggy rattled over the driveway. Janna went to the door and peered out. Her stomach took a dive. "It's one of the preachers." She wouldn't have time to try to convince Troy. She needed that miracle now.

Mamm met her gaze. "Jah. They've kum to talk about...." She glanced at Meghan and sighed.

246 Laura V. Hilton

"The elopement, right?" Meghan chirped up. "You didn't think I knew Aunt Janna moved into the dawdi-haus with him? It's kind of obvious."

Mamm gave her a smile, but it quickly faded. "I suppose it is. I don't know what I was thinking. I guess, maybe, that if I kept it quiet, no one would know."

Meghan rolled her eyes and glanced at Janna.

They were here to decide her fate, then. Best to sweeten them up. Maybe it'd work in her favor. Janna went to pile cookies on a plate. "Are they meeting in here or in the barn?"

"Probably in the dawdi-haus," Mamm said, glancing at the table. "Especially since we're working in here. Take over a pitcher of iced tea and some glasses."

Janna nodded, then reached for a large silver serving tray.

Meghan cleared her throat. "What I want to know is, how do you think you're going to keep it a secret if Aunt Janna gets pregnant?"

❧

The roiling in Troy's gut worsened as the last buggy arrived. He hadn't realized he'd be expected to attend the meeting. He'd been a dummchen not to, really, since he and Janna would be the subject of discussion.

His being invited must mean the preachers wanted him to contribute in some way. Like answering the question Meghan had asked on the day of their elopement: "So, you couldn't just wait?"

Troy loved Janna. He wanted to be with her. And it had seemed that the bishop condoned their union. Not to mention, their kissing had gone far beyond what was proper for an unmarried couple.

His face heated. None of his reasons seemed particularly compelling. It had just felt right at the time. And, not to cast blame on the woman, but Janna could've refused. She could've asked him to wait. He would've had no choice but to agree. Even knowing that a wedding would probably never happen because she was Amish and he wasn't.

Unless God intervened, he wouldn't be joining the church, despite Janna's belief—and his in-laws'—that he would. Because, even though he wanted to be a member of the community again, there was no way he would be forgiven. At least, not completely. And he couldn't face that kind of rejection.

Bile rose in his throat. What if he had to confess that?

There was no "What if" about it. Eventually, the truth would come out, and Janna would end up being shunned. The best he could hope for—pray for—would be a delay of the inevitable.

He trudged across the yard after the bishop as if he were walking toward his execution. Would Janna be present at the meeting, too? Pointless question. She was a woman. He was her husband. He'd be the one answering the questions, shouldering the blame, and passing the final judgment on to Janna.

He remained silent as the men greeted one another and filed into the small dawdi-haus he and Janna called home. Without a word, he sat down at the tiny table.

Janna came in carrying a silver tray with glass tumblers, a pitcher of tea, and a plate full of cookies. As she set it in the middle of the table, she glanced at him, her eyes filled with fear. He longed to reassure her somehow, but he didn't know how he could when he was just as scared.

Janna began filling the tumblers with iced tea. Troy caught her eye again and mouthed, "Ich liebe dich." He'd whispered those words last nacht, but he didn't think she'd heard him, already asleep in his arms. Why he hadn't told her he loved her when she was conscious, he didn't know. He should have. Would have, if he'd anticipated the effect: her eyes flooded with joy, and she smiled in a way that made him weak in the knees.

He was still reeling when she left, disappearing through the door.

Bishop Dave eyed the other men seated around the table. "Before we begin our discussion, we need to pray for the Lord's will to be done." The preachers all bowed their heads for a silent prayer. When they'd finished, each one reached for a cookie and a glass of iced tea.

Bishop Dave rose to his feet, struggled to push his chair in, and then stood behind it, as if he couldn't bear to be on the same level as everyone else. He probably needed the impression of control.

Troy's stomach churned at the reminder of one more thing he'd taken away from the bishop—his mobility. As if taking his son and then eloping with his daughter hadn't been enough.

He glanced around the table at the other men. Some of them he didn't know very well, since they were new preachers, ordained after he'd left. Most of them were older. Others... well, Joseph Fisher had been one of Troy's closest childhood friends. They'd gone in different directions, to be sure, but he still might be an ally.

"This news I need to discuss isn't so easy for me." Bishop Dave cleared his throat. "My dochter Janna has eloped with Hiram Troyer." He paused and bowed his head, his good hand tightening around the back of the chair.

Several of the men glanced at Troy. Studying him as if he were Exhibit A.

The bishop raised his head and looked around the table. "I've decided to start baptismal classes right away, since Troy—Hiram—has agreed to join the church."

Actually, he hadn't agreed to anything of the sort. But Troy kept his lips pressed together. He wished it were true.

"My frau has suggested that we keep this elopement quiet, since shunning Janna would hurt so many in the community—all of the clients who rely on her to do their grocery shopping. My granddaughter, Meghan, who was raised in a dysfunctional home. I think it would be truly harmful for her to see everyone turn their backs on Janna. And since Troy will be joining the church, I see no reason why we can't look the other way."

This once, at least. Never mind that the bishop had shunned Janna's best friend when she'd married an Englisch man. That had hurt the community, too, since they'd been down one midwife for a season. Curiously inconsistent. Maybe the difference was because Troy had been raised Amish. Not to mention, the bishop probably couldn't bear losing a third child. Troy reached for a glass of iced tea and took a sip.

"Troy and Janna will marry, in our way, in eight weeks, once Troy has completed the classes."

Troy struggled to show no outward emotion. Hopefully, he was succeeding. At least no one cast him a dubious look.

One of the older preachers pulled on his beard as he scrutinized Troy. "Why couldn't you have waited a few months to marry, if you were planning to join the church anyway?" He narrowed his eyes. "Is Janna in the family way?"

Both questions he'd dreaded. "She's not in the family way." He raked his fingers through his hair. "I love her, and I guess I wasn't thinking too clearly beyond wanting to be with her."

Everyone chuckled. Maybe his answer had been satisfactory. But Troy didn't dare relax. He knew what the next question would be.

"You are having…uh, marital relations, right? What if she gets in the family way?"

Troy's face heated. If they were married in eight weeks' time, wouldn't it be possible to keep it a secret and let everyone think she'd gotten pregnant on her wedding night? He wasn't sure. His mind whirled. "Maybe that won't happen."

Some of the preachers laughed.

He wasn't trying to be funny.

"Will you continue working as a police officer until you join the church?"

A variation of another question he'd dreaded. Worded this way, it was one he could answer honestly. "Jah, I will. Until I'm a church member."

Which would be on the twelfth of Never, unless the Lord intervened.

❦

At the sound of a horse nickering, Janna glanced out the window. It wasn't one of the preachers' horses. She smiled when she recognized her friend Katie and then hurried out to greet her.

"You have company?" Katie looked around at all the other buggies.

"Daed's having a meeting with the preachers. Kum on in. We're teaching Meghan how to sew." *A wedding dress.* Katie would be sure to recognize the sky blue material.

"If you're sure I won't be in the way…." Katie handed the reins to Janna and climbed out of the buggy.

Janna resisted the urge to wrap her friend in a bear hug. If only she could eavesdrop on the meeting next door. It was very possible she would be prohibited from seeing her friend in a few short minutes. That she would no longer be considered a member of the family. Shunned.

It felt as if a bunch of grasshoppers were hopping around in her stomach. She gulped.

"What's wrong?" Katie stared at her. "You look like you just swallowed."

Janna shuddered. "Nothing." She shook her head. "Just borrowing trouble."

Katie touched Janna's arm. "I came by to tell you I got a job! I'll be working at Cheryl's Bed-and-Breakfast. Cheryl has started serving lunch, too—sandwiches and pies, mostly. She hired me this morgen."

"That's wunderbaar, Katie!" Janna smiled.

"Jah. I'm so excited! I get to work in the kitchen, and she said I won't have to wait on customers at all."

Given how shy Katie was, Janna thought it might have been gut for her to be forced out of her comfort zone some. Still, she probably wouldn't have accepted the job without the assurance that she wouldn't be required to interact with the customers.

As they entered the kitchen, Katie gave a slight gasp and grabbed Janna's arm. "Are you—? Who? Micah?" There was a strange little catch in her voice. "I'm happy for you, but rather surprised. It happened really fast, ain't so?"

Meghan looked up. "Not Micah. He's nice enough, but I don't want him for an uncle. She married Troy."

Janna's face heated, and she shook her head at her niece, while Mamm frowned at her.

"I mean, she's *marrying* Troy."

"Troy?" Katie hesitated for a moment. "That…policeman? Ach." Her eyes widened. "Janna…." Her tone was laced with a buggy-load of warning.

Janna looked down. "He was raised Amish. And he'll be going through the baptismal classes." Both true, though she didn't know how long he'd keep up the charade, attending classes he didn't intend to follow through with by getting baptized. He hadn't discussed it with her, but then, she hadn't asked him about it.

All she knew was that unless the gut Lord worked a miracle, she'd end up being shunned at some point.

There was a slight commotion in the dawdi-haus, and then one of the preachers passed by the open door, followed by the rest of them. Janna tried to decipher their facial expressions, to no avail.

A few minutes later, the connecting door opened, and Daed stepped into the kitchen. His look seemed strained. He glanced around, nodding when his gaze landed on Katie. His eyes flickered to Janna, then to Mamm, and he shook his head. Then he turned around, reentered the dawdi-haus, and shut the door.

Mamm looked at Janna and shrugged.

Did Daed's behavior mean what she feared it did? That she was shunned?

Chapter 32

*T*roy stared at his cookie, still untouched on the napkin before him. He couldn't bear the thought of eating. He hated being lied to and tried to always be honest in his dealings. And this whole situation seemed like one big whopper. He looked up as his father-in-law stepped back into the room.

"Janna has company. I'll tell her later." Bishop Dave fingered his beard.

Troy nodded in agreement, keeping his gaze firmly fixed on the older man. He had to tell him the truth or he'd bust. "I'll go to the classes, per your request. But I can't commit to joining the church and becoming Amish. You're just postponing the inevitable."

Bishop Dave nodded. "Your body language communicated as much. I only hope none of the other preachers picked up on it. Because, eventually, you *will* be joining the church. None of this 'can't' business."

"You think?" Troy scooted back in his chair. "It will take an act of God, pure and simple." He hadn't meant to sound disrespectful. But the truth was out at last. Now, to tell Janna. Hopefully, she would take the announcement better than he'd expected, as her daed had.

The bishop sat down across from him, picked up the pitcher of tea, and refilled his glass. "Now, it's time for another overdue conversation. You haven't got a gun on you, do you?"

Troy forced a smile. "Nein. Not today."

"Gut. Troy, there's a saying: 'Those who won't remember the past are doomed to repeat it.' Or something similar." He cleared his throat. "Tell me what happened."

He shut his eyes, praying for the words to say. Or for an interruption, so he wouldn't have to share.

The door clicked, and Troy's eyes popped open. He straightened as Janna entered the room, her expression loaded with uncertainty and trepidation. "What did they decide?"

Troy smiled. "You're safe—for now. Pending my eventual joining the church. Our marriage will be kept secret."

The fear in her eyes didn't fade. "What aren't you saying?" She glanced at her daed, then looked back at Troy.

"I'll go through the classes, Janna. I promised your daed I would. And I don't want to cause problems for either of you. But you need to know, unless God says differently, I won't be joining the church. So, you'll end up being shunned, just not right now." He sighed. "I'm sorry."

"I told him I'm praying for a miracle," the bishop put in.

Janna took a deep breath, then walked over and wrapped her arms around Troy's shoulders from behind, running her palms down his chest. "I'll pray for that miracle, too." She leaned forward and kissed his cheek.

Desire flared. Troy tamped it down, since her daed was watching and she had a friend visiting. "You do that." He stood up, turned around, and wrapped her in a hug. "Just know I never meant to hurt you." He released her, then pulled his cell phone out of his pocket. "I'll need to head in to the station in a few hours. Guess I should get some work done." He gave her a quick kiss, then left, abandoning his tea, cookie, and father-in-law at the table.

Troy headed for the barn, eager to do something, anything. He didn't know just what. Not that there was ever a lack of work to be done. It'd beat sitting in the quietness of the haus while his guilt ate at him. Dredging up the past and reopening old wounds. Even if the bishop deserved to know.

He entered the barn and glanced at the hay pile where he and Janna had landed after swinging down from the loft. Where he'd come so close to kissing her.

Instead of chasing after her, he should've gone straight to the bishop. Or maybe run—past Janna to whatever vehicle he'd driven that fateful day—and driven right out of her life. He should've stayed far away from the too-tempting Janna Kauffman, instead of pursuing her and luring her into his arms, into his heart, into his life. Giving her his name. If he really loved her as much as he professed, he would've kept his distance rather than ruining her life by letting her get involved with his. Hadn't he warned himself about that very thing happening? And yet he'd sought her relentlessly, won her heart, and married her.

He could kick himself.

The worst part was, he couldn't fix this problem by walking away. If he did, Janna would be left in disgrace. *Amish marry for life.* And, to be honest, he didn't want to leave. He wanted to stay with her, to share life with her, to raise a family with her. He wanted the right to love her. Forever. As an Amish man.

Lord….

The words wouldn't come. He didn't know how to pray about this. He wanted the same miracle the bishop prayed for. Freedom from guilt.

"I'm going to go lie down for a spell." Daed stood and glanced out the window. "And then I'm going to wait up for that bu to kum home tonight. He and I are long overdue for a talk."

Janna raised her eyebrows, but Daed didn't elaborate further. He merely shook his head, turned, and headed back into the main haus.

She wiped off the table, then loaded the silver tray with the empty glasses and cookie plate, the contents of which had diminished considerably, and carried it back to the kitchen. Mamm had disappeared. She'd probably followed Daed upstairs to find out the verdict of the meeting.

Katie still sat the table with Meghan, helping her pin the dress pattern to the blue fabric. Janna picked up a cookie and nibbled on it while she watched, feigning interest in the pattern layout. She couldn't keep her thoughts from returning to the brief conversation she'd had with Troy just a few minutes ago. Only now did the truth settle in: *Troy has no intention of joining the church. Never did.* Disappointing, but not surprising. She'd known all along, really. And she'd said so to daed.

Jah, she'd known. And she'd chosen to marry him, anyway. Because she loved him. Always had and always would. She'd chosen to take the risk. And now, she was wasting time making a dress she would never wear.

Maybe she could give it to Katie when she wedded the man who would win her heart. At least Katie would have the gut sense not to fall in love with a man whose feet were firmly planted in the world. She was too devoted to make a mistake like that. She'd probably marry a solid Amish man who had never doubted his faith or calling.

Janna finished the cookie, wiped her hands on her apron, and tried to summon a smidgen of interest as Meghan started cutting the fabric. For a wedding dress she would wear only in her dreams. She blinked back a couple of tears.

One might think that she was bitter. She didn't mean to be. After all, she'd married the man who kissed her senseless and carried all her hopes and dreams.

The man who would cost her everything.

❧〰❧

Troy cruised down the highway, scoping out a new location to monitor traffic from. He finally pulled into a turnaround, positioning the vehicle so that he would have access to either direction.

He'd barely gotten his radar set up when a red convertible sped by at a speed that shook the police cruiser. He didn't need to look at the screen to know the driver had exceeded the speed limit, but he checked anyway. Eighty-eight miles per hour. He whipped the car around, pulled out behind a semi, and sped around it, lights flashing and siren wailing.

Traffic had stopped in both directions at the next intersection, waiting for the lights to turn green. The fast-moving convertible skirted off on the shoulder and zoomed around the line of cars, plowing through the intersection. Troy swerved to follow but slammed on his breaks and watched in horror as the red car collided with a horse and buggy crossing the road up ahead.

Bodies flew as the buggy was crushed. The horse was knocked on its side. The car's front was completely crumpled. An Amish youth ejected from the buggy had landed in the backseat of the convertible. The driver and front-seat passenger battled the air bags, their mouths open wide in screams Troy couldn't hear over the pounding of his pulse. Their mouths opened wide in screams Troy couldn't hear over the pounding of his heart. He reached for the radio, bearing down with all his weight on the brake pedal, and skidded to a stop, tires squealing.

Hopefully his voice didn't wobble as he reported the accident to the dispatcher.

He'd been here before. Another time, different set of actors, same scene. Except he'd landed on a mattress laid out in a pickup bed.

Troy searched for his professional side, slid his sunglasses over his eyes, and opened his door. The red convertible wasn't going anywhere, so the first item of business would be to check to see if by some miracle the other two buwe who'd been in the buggy survived. The one in the backseat of the convertible was alive, wiping the tears from his eyes as he surveyed the remains of his mode of transportation.

In the distance, sirens wailed. Within seconds, it seemed, the scene was crawling with other police officers, first responders, and an ambulance crew, who set to work on the two buwe from the buggy. Within minutes, they pronounced them dead.

Troy's heart sank. He noticed the third bu, the one who'd landed in the back of the car and must have climbed out. He now staggered to the side of the road, retching.

He needed someone to do as Troy's hero had done for him. Reach out.

"What's your name, sohn?" He spoke in Pennsylvania Deitsch.

The bu wiped his mouth and looked up. He had to be about sixteen or seventeen. Dark brown eyes, brown hair. "William Kropf." His voice broke. "I answer to Will."

"Do you know those buwe?"

"My…my brother Walter, and our friend Thomas." Tears dripped off his chin. "They're gone, aren't they? I killed them."

Troy took a deep breath. Same conversation. What was it the bishop had said about being doomed to repeat history? He shook his head. "Nein. The man driving the car did. Vehicular homicide. He'll probably go to prison for this after his release from the hospital."

"Nein. Daed told me not to go on the highway. He told me I wasn't ready. But I didn't listen. We...we were going to have a get-together in a back field, and we...we needed...." He stuttered to a stop. But he didn't need to finish. *Alcohol. Possibly drugs, too.* "I disobeyed. I killed my brother. I can't go home. Can't face the community again."

"Jah, you can. Trust me. I was once the bu who disobeyed his daed. Same story, Will." Troy gestured toward the scene of the accident. "But the similarities stop there. See, me, I ran away and never went home again. I was a coward. But you can be a man and own this mistake. Your family needs your strength. You need their forgiveness. And I can help you work through this.

"I wish I'd had the sense to go home and ask for forgiveness. Instead, I stayed outside the community and forged a new life for myself. As a result, my mamm and daed lost both their sohns that day—one to death, the other to the world."

It dawned on him then that, even though he had a relationship, of sorts, with his family, he still needed to approach them, however belatedly, and ask for forgiveness.

Troy looked back at Will, his eyes brimming, and with wavering voice repeated the words that had haunted him recently: "Might want to start with God. And then forgive yourself."

Chapter 33

Daed stood and resumed pacing in front of the window. Janna wished he'd go to bed. Weariness had colored him gray, and he rubbed his shoulder where he'd been shot, as if it pained him. With Mamm's help, he'd already changed into his pajamas and a robe.

Headlights lit the driveway. *Troy.* Finally. Janna wasn't sure what time it was, but it seemed he was late. Maybe he'd worked overtime. He'd have no way of contacting her to let her know if his schedule changed, unless he called Kimmy to give her a message. And then it'd mean divulging their elopement to a woman who might leak it to the community, resulting in widespread gossip.

Troy parked the truck. Lights briefly illuminated the cab when he opened the door. A few minutes later, his steps sounded on the porch.

Daed turned away from the window. "You're late."

Troy frowned. A muscle jumped in his jaw. "Jah. I took a bu home and sat with his family for a while. There was a bad accident. A speeding car broadsided a buggy." His gaze met Janna's, then slid to Daed. "Walter Kropf and Thomas Fisher...." He shook his head, tears glittering in his eyes. "The accident isn't his fault, but William Kropf was driving the buggy, even though his daed had told him not to take it out on the highway." His voice broke. "I saw the whole thing."

Janna's heart broke that he'd been a witness. The details made it sound similar to the accident that had killed Zach and Henry six years ago.

Troy dropped down beside the table and buried his head in his hands. Janna moved to go to him, but Daed held up his hand to stop her.

"Too familiar, sohn?" Daed said calmly. Quietly. "Tell me about it."

Too familiar?

Troy's shoulders shook. "I was driving that nacht. I'd talked Henry and Zach into going with me. Daed said I was too inexperienced to go out on the highway, but there was a frolic planned, and I wanted alcohol. Because of my disobedience...." He looked up at Daed, his cheeks damp. "I haven't touched the stuff since."

Janna's hand sprang to her mouth. "You...you were there when they died?" She couldn't begin to wrap her mind around this. She felt sick to her stomach.

"I blamed myself for their deaths. And because I wasn't brave enough to go home, I ran away. A police officer was nice enough to help me, to counsel me, or I probably would've ended my own life, as well." Troy wiped his face, but that did nothing to stop the tears. "I'm so sorry."

"I forgive you, sohn." Daed walked over and patted Troy's back. "We forgive you. Your disobedience was a factor, but you weren't to blame. Someone else was responsible. You can see that now."

Janna forced her hand away from her lips. She wanted to echo Daed's forgiveness. But she couldn't believe that the man she loved had been with her brother when he'd died and had never told her. Her vocal chords felt paralyzed. Her feet seemed rooted to the floor.

"I still need to tell my parents, but it was too late to go out there tonight." Troy mopped his tear-streaked face again. "I'll do it tomorrow. And I'll be reaching out to Will Kropf. He needs me. I know what he's going to be working through. The guilt. The despair."

"Jah." Daed pulled in a breath. "You do. And maybe you'll finally be able to heal." He turned and opened the connecting door to the main haus. "Troy, you are accepted in the beloved. Ephesians one—look it up. The whole chapter is gut, but pay close attention to verses six and seven."

Troy nodded.

"The youth in our community need you. You have been called by the Lord. Verse eleven, same chapter."

Left alone with Troy, Janna's mind still whirled, and she couldn't think of anything to say. Other than the words that needed to be said but wouldn't kum.

How had Daed forgiven him so easily?

❧❦

Troy rubbed his jaw and looked up at Janna. His frau. Her eyes were wide with shock, her brow furrowed with pain and hurt. He wouldn't be at all surprised if she told him she was sleeping in her old bedroom tonight.

Still, forgiveness was at the foundation of the Amish faith. It was based on their appreciation that God had forgiven them when they were undeserving. Sent His Son to die on the cross for their salvation.

He could almost read the thoughts running through her mind.

She glanced at the door, then back at him. He steeled himself. Would she be the one who left? Or would she ask him to sleep in the barn? He wouldn't like it, but he'd accept it. This was the reason he couldn't join the church—he'd be rejected. Not only by Janna but also by the whole community. They would forgive him in word only, not in heart.

After a moment, she walked across the room, toward him. He pulled himself to his feet and stood, awaiting the verdict, whatever it would be.

His stomach clenched.

Janna touched his hand, enclosing it with her cold fingers. "I...forgive you."

The tears flowed again. "Danki, Janna." He pulled her against him and held her tight. "I needed to hear that."

She reached around his neck and gently drew his head down to hers, then kissed him with unprecedented emotion. He returned it with everything he had. He didn't know how long they stood there, kissing, before she took his hand and led him back to their bedroom.

The next morgen, Saturday, Troy hurried through his chores, so as to allow himself extra time to set up the church benches in the barn. The Kauffmans were hosting tomorrow's preaching services, and the wagon that delivered the benches would arrive in the afternoon. First, though, he needed to talk to Janna. He went searching for her in the main haus.

Janna looked up when he entered the kitchen, her fists buried in bread dough. He swallowed. What had he done to deserve such a beautiful woman? He brushed a streak of flour from her cheek. She seemed to pull back a little, but maybe it was just his imagination. "As soon as you get that on to rise, will you kum with me to my parents' haus? I want you with me when I tell them, if that's okay."

She nodded. "I'll kum." She pursed her lips.

He studied her. The stiffness in her stance, the chill in her voice.... The truth hit him like a tidal wave. She hadn't forgiven him. Not really. What she'd said last nacht, before loving him, had somehow morphed into something else with the dawn of day. Did the bishop feel the same way? Would his parents?

Meghan glanced over her shoulder at him. "Wow, Troy, that was huge. I heard Grandpa tell Grandma this morning about the accident and about your story. No wonder you didn't want to talk about it."

He mustered a smile. She'd been eavesdropping again. At least it saved him from having to retell the tale. "Jah. No wonder." He still didn't want to talk about it. But at least it was almost over. As soon as he'd told his family. Then, maybe, he could move on. He thought about the verses the bishop had mentioned last nacht, which he'd read that morgen. He was accepted in the beloved. *Danki, Lord.*

As often as that chapter from Ephesians was preached on and taught, how had he never heard that? Maybe he had heard it but hadn't understood.

Better late than never. If only his frau could really forgive him. Accept him. Because, if she didn't, he wasn't sure what to do. Should he resign from the police force and stay here, or keep his job and be ready to go at a moment's notice?

"Can I talk to you after you and Janna get home?" Meghan carried two bread pans over to the table. "I have something I need to tell you."

"Sure. I'll find you when we're back."

Janna greased the pans, then divided the dough and put some in each one. She covered them with a towel before washing up and changing aprons. "I'm ready."

"Gut." Troy grasped her hand.

Even though she allowed his touch, something had changed. He felt it.

Five minutes later, he pulled his truck into his parents' driveway. He took a deep breath. "Pray for me. This won't be easy."

"I will." Janna looked at him. "You can do it. I know it wasn't easy to tell Daed and me. And your family will forgive you."

He noticed that she hadn't tacked on the word *too*. Just as he'd feared, she hadn't forgiven him yet. He opened his mouth to voice his suspicions, but she slid out of the truck and headed for the haus. Mamm stepped out on the porch.

"Morgen, Rosie!" Janna called. "How are you today?"

Troy watched his mamm pull Janna in for a hug. "They didn't shun you?" Her voice was hushed, but he still heard her.

"Not yet. They agreed to keep it quiet for now. It ultimately depends on whether Troy joins the church."

The first baptismal class was tomorrow. He'd keep his word and attend. And he'd pray for the forgiveness that would determine his fate. But he was glad Janna had worded it in such a way that wouldn't get his family's hopes up. He didn't want to disappoint them, too. Bad enough he'd hurt the Kauffman family.

Troy went to the barn to summon Daed, his brother-in-law, and Grossdaedi, if he was around and not visiting one of his other kids. He wanted to tell the entire family together.

Too soon, every member of his family, including his sister, Elisabeth, was gathered around the table. Mamm served some peach pie she'd made. Troy wasn't sure he could keep even one bite down. Bishop Dave and his family had been forgiving. Janna had acted that way, at first. But he was afraid it had been nothing more than that. An act.

What if his own family refused to extend grace? Or what if the pardon they put forth was just as pretend as Janna's?

He swallowed a lump in his throat and glanced at her. She squeezed his hand. At least she was still willing to touch him. Wasn't entirely repulsed by him. Yet.

"Last nacht, there was a fatal accident," he began.

"Ach, we heard. Two buwe. So sad." Mamm shook her head. "A car struck that buggy broadside, just like when Henry and Zach died."

Troy nodded. "Will Kropf survived. The accident wasn't his fault, but his daed had ordered him not to go out on the highway, due to his inexperience. He didn't listen." He paused. "The same way I didn't listen when Henry and Zach were killed." He looked down. "I'm so sorry for my part in the accident."

Mamm sucked in a breath. "Hiram. You were there? That's what took you away from us?"

"I was afraid," Troy whispered, "but it's past time I told you."

Silence stretched on, broken only by his mamm's sniffling. Troy stared at the table, wondering if he should leave.

A moment later, Daed stood, walked around the table to him, and, with tears streaming down his face, pulled Troy into his arms. "We forgive you, sohn. We love you. We never wanted to lose you, too." He pounded Troy on the back and then stepped away.

"Are you going to kum home, then?" Elisabeth asked as tears dripped from her chin. She grasped her husband's hand.

He blinked at the hope in her eyes. His parents had kept his elopement a secret from his sister? Maybe that had been a wise move. If Janna couldn't forgive him, what hope was there for their marriage? "Nein. Bishop Dave needs me. I'll be staying on at the Kauffmans' for now." *And trying to win back the love of my frau.*

"I meant to the community. To the faith."

Troy glanced at Janna and rubbed his chin, then looked back at his sister. "Elisabeth, I'm sorry, but nein." Beside him, Janna sucked in a breath. But how could he go back? He'd lose his source of income—something to fall back on if need be. Plus, he needed to do something significant. Something that mattered. By working to keep the roads safer for the Amish, maybe he could atone for his mistake.

She dabbed her eyes with the back of her hand. "I thought, maybe, since you confessed...." Wincing, she stood up, one hand pressed to her pregnant belly. "Ach, I've been having these contractions all day."

Troy rose to his feet. "Should we call your midwife?"

Elisabeth shook her head. "Kristi was here earlier this morgen, and she's coming back again this afternoon to check on me. She thinks it won't be long now."

Troy smiled. "Well then, I'll look forward to meeting my niece or nephew." He took a step backward. "We should go. I'd like to stop by the Kropfs' and see Will, and then I need to get back to help set up for church tomorrow. Bishop Dave is in no condition to do it."

Elisabeth hugged him. "We forgive you, and we want you to kum home." She grinned at him.

Troy pulled back. "Danki, sis."

Her grin widened. "And marry a gut Amish girl, like Janna, since I've heard rumors you're courting her."

Troy attempted to maintain composure. He managed a wink as he said, "How about we just elope?" That was as close as he could come to telling her, since the marriage was supposed to be kept secret. And also since, for all he knew, it might be ending. *Nein, Lord.* Ignoring his sister's gasp and his mother's chuckle, he grasped Janna's hand and led her outside.

❦

Back at the haus, Janna hastened out of the truck, glad to be out of that crowded vehicle. Troy had invited Will Kropf home with them, and the bu had straddled the console the whole way there. A buggy would have offered more room for three, with its backseat.

Will's eyes were bloodshot. He'd probably spent all nacht crying. Kind of what she felt like doing. She hoped his family had showered him with love, as much as they were able. It was hard to imagine, though, as they'd suffered so much loss—his mamm, several stepmamms, and a sister or two. His daed, Amos Kropf, didn't seem the type to mourn the loss of a loved one long. It was a gut thing Troy had reached out to Will, or he might have been the next loss.

Troy directed Will into the barn, then turned to Janna. "Please tell Meghan if she's free and wants to talk, I'll be out here setting up benches. Otherwise, I'll find her later."

Janna nodded, then started for the haus, her mind already focused on everything she still needed to do today. She'd get a roast going, so they could slice it and serve it cold after church tomorrow.

She opened the door and stepped into the kitchen, where Mamm stood over Meghan, directing her as she guided some blue material through the treadle sewing machine. Pain shot through her.

It was her wedding dress. To wear when she married Troy. The man who'd killed her brother. Accidentally, to be sure, but fact, just the same.

She'd told him she forgave him. She'd even tried to be sincere. But it had been a struggle, one that was yet unresolved. She wondered if Mamm and Daed struggled, too. Maybe it would get easier, eventually.

On the bright side, the accident had made him effective at reaching out to a hurting youth. More than one, really, for Meghan had taken to him as soon as she'd realized he was as wounded as she. And that had worked wonders with her attitude.

Speaking of that…. "Meghan, Troy said he's in the barn whenever you'd like to talk."

Meghan spun around in the chair, leaving the fabric caught by the needle and the foot. "Good. I've been waiting forever. I'll be back."

"Meg—" Mamm began. She stopped as the door slammed shut. "Never mind. You go on." She smiled and shook her head. "That girl never slows down long enough to listen."

Janna got out the roast to prepare for the oven. Mamm came over and held her in a hug. "I never would have dreamed that Troy was there. Everyone wondered why he chose to jump the fence after Zach and Henry passed. In hindsight, it seems obvious. That bu has held a lot inside all these years. Now the healing can begin."

Janna forced a smile. "I told him I forgave him, but saying the words is a lot easier than feeling them inside."

Mamm squeezed her shoulder. "Keep saying it, Janna, and believe it. The feelings will kum. Simply speaking the words out loud is the first step to making it true."

Janna nodded. "I forgive him." She said it out loud, just to test the words. They did kum a little easier this time. Maybe Mamm was right.

"Your daed says the Lord saved Troy for a purpose. He read a few verses this morning, and one of them said something…. Wait a moment." Mamm went into the other room and returned with the family Bible. "In Ephesians one, verse eleven, it says, '*In whom also we have obtained an inheritance, being predestinated according to the purpose of him who worketh all things after the counsel of his own will.*'"

That was one of the verses Daed had mentioned last nacht. Troy had read them out loud earlier that morgen, while Janna had gotten dressed.

"I'm not claiming to understand much," Mamm said, closing the Bible, "but it sounds to me like your daed is right. Troy is destined for something. And maybe it's for working with the troubled youth in our community. After all, he used to be one of them."

Janna nodded, remembering when Daed had said something about God chasing Troy. And her own revelation that followed.

God knew exactly where she was. Had been. Would be.

God knew about this.

Chapter 34

The physical therapist is supposed to kum out on Monday morgen and start working with me on arm exercises," the bishop told Troy and Will as they pushed a wooden pew into place. "It's a little crooked there, buwe. On your end, Troy. Slide it a bit more toward the front."

Troy gave the wooden bench a nudge with his foot. He couldn't blame Bishop Dave for being critical, especially since he was out of commission on account of Troy. But it was going to be a trial if every row had to be perfectly parallel. Hopefully, the bishop would soon return to the easygoing mood Troy was used to. And, hopefully, it was the frustrations of physical therapy that were to blame for the bishop's grumpiness, rather than a struggle similar to Janna's to forgive him.

"There you go." Bishop Dave nodded approvingly.

Will led the way out of the barn for another bench. "Daed would get mad if someone bossed him like that."

Troy smiled. "Bishop Dave wants to be needed. It pains him not to be able to do much right now. We need to keep in mind what the other person is going through." His smile faded as he thought of Janna. He needed to give her time and space to process his confession.

A thoughtful look crossed Will's face, as if he were processing what Troy had said.

Meghan bounced up to them, a peach in each hand. "Hi, William. I brought you a peach." She smiled at him in a kind of flirty way. "One for you, too, Troy. Are you free to talk?"

So, Will was the bu Meghan liked. Troy smiled as he took the peach. "Jah. Will, please tell the bishop I'll be right back. I need to talk with Meghan for a moment."

Troy nodded toward the cornfields, where the stalks were already as high as his waist. "Walk with me?" He took a bite of the peach and waited for her to fall into step beside him. "What's going on?"

She kicked at a clump of dirt. "I have my own confession to make. I lied about something. Tried to make you believe Grandpa was having a…bad relationship with Janna, when I knew it wasn't true."

Troy was proud of her for admitting it. "I've known it wasn't true. Your grandpa told me about this. And he was greatly bothered, Meghan. Do you want to tell me why you came up with a lie like that?"

"I guess I thought maybe Grandpa would send me home to my mom. And that, if I went home, I could talk her out of marrying that jerk." She shrugged. "She never listens to me, though. I don't know why I thought she would this time."

"Tell me about the jerk she married." Troy pretended to keep his attention on the peach.

She shrugged again. "Her boyfriends have all been terrible. None of them has kept a job for long. When I was little, one of them locked me up in the closet while Mom was at work. All of them were mean, and some of them hurt me. Mom never believed me when I told her what they did. I know what they did to her, and she just took it."

Meghan bent over and picked up a rock, tossing it in her hand. "The last one, the one she just married…he forced me to do some gross stuff I didn't want to do. I told Mom, but she still wouldn't believe me. She said I lied. So, I started drinking and hanging around kids she didn't approve of. I came home drunk so many times, trying to block it out, and then Mom said that *I* was the problem." She huffed.

"Meghan, what your mom's boyfriends did is against the law. And if your mom allowed it, that's wrong, too." He would report this. As a police officer, it was his responsibility to bring abuse to light. With Bishop Dave and Janna already named as guardians, they wouldn't have to put Meghan in foster care. He finished the peach and flung the pit out in the field. "I need you to tell me how to reach your mom. I need to talk to her."

Meghan frowned. "She's on her honeymoon in Jamaica. And they were moving someplace. I'll have to wait until the next time she writes me. I have her phone number, but my cell phone is worthless out here. Once the battery died, I had no way to charge it." She flung the rock into the distance.

"I can charge it at the station, or even in my truck."

Meghan nodded. "I need to go to town for my final exams. The school says I have to come in on Monday to take them, and I'm not allowed to talk to anyone, and I have to leave the building right way. And if I don't show up, I'll fail."

"We don't want that. I'll take you to the school on Monday."

"Thanks, Uncle Troy. You're the best." Meghan grinned at him, then went running back through the field toward the barn—and Will.

❧

The following week, Daed's therapist, who'd introduced herself as Lisa Davids, hooked up a strange-looking contraption to the door connecting the main haus to the dawdi-haus. "This works like a pulley," she explained. She positioned a wooden chair under the contraption and demonstrated how to grab ahold of the hooks with the hands and use the good arm to raise and lower the other. "I want you to practice until you're able to do ten repetitions, holding your left arm up for a count of ten each time." She stood. "Let me see you try."

"That kind of looks like fun," Meghan observed.

Lisa smiled. "Maybe for a healthy teenager. It'll be torture for your grandfather for a time."

Daed sat in the chair. The therapist helped him get his hands in the hooks, then directed him as he slowly pulled his left arm up. He grimaced.

"Good. Now, hold it for a count of ten." Lisa counted for him. "Slowly lower it. Now, rest a few seconds and try it again."

"My arm is worse than I thought it would be, ain't so?"

Lisa smiled. "It will take some work to get it back to where it should be. But each time will get easier, and I know you're determined to have a full recovery."

Janna was determined to have a full recovery of her marriage. Hopefully, that would get easier with time, too.

"Jah. I feel pretty worthless now." Daed pulled his arm up again, this time counting for himself.

"I'll be back in a couple of days to see how you're progressing," Lisa said. "I'll let myself out." Lisa gathered her things and bid them good-bye.

Janna glanced out the window and watched Lisa stride toward her car. Troy and Will stood by the pickup, talking. Troy wore his police uniform. He must be scheduled to work today. She hadn't kept track of his hours. Instead, she'd been avoiding him as much as possible. Had he noticed? He must have, because he no longer snuggled with her in bed. Last nacht, he hadn't so much as touched her.

That had hurt. She'd quickly learned to love that part of their relationship.

Well, to be honest, she loved him, but she'd made a mistake marrying him. She was working toward forgiving him for killing her brother, but, even though he'd been through two baptism classes, he showed no sign of warming to the idea of joining the church. He was just keeping the promise he'd made to Daed.

Janna sighed. The only miracle that might occur would be her learning to survive as a shunned woman. What kind of fancy church did Troy attend? Would they welcome her as a Plain woman? Because she didn't think she could bring herself to dress as immodestly as some of the Englisch women she saw in town.

Maybe the miracle would kum in the form of them somehow salvaging the remnants of their marriage. Of her forgiving him completely. If only she didn't struggle so.

Meghan dashed out of the haus, slamming the door behind her, and ran up to Troy and Will. She said something to Will, who smiled.

Troy winked at Meghan, then glanced at the haus. When his gaze met Janna's, he froze. She didn't move, either, though she wanted to. Wanted to run outside and tell him she forgave him. To tell him she loved him. To beg him to stay. But she didn't move.

He didn't smile. Didn't make a move toward her. Instead, he reached for his sunglasses, climbed in his pickup, and followed the therapist's car down the driveway. Dust rose behind the truck as it disappeared out of sight. Janna turned away.

Daed caught her eye. "Everything okay, dochter?"

Janna lifted a shoulder. "I'm coping." That was about all she could say.

Ach, Troy. Pain knifed through her again. *Lord, whatever it takes, help me move past this.*

Daed let the pulley raise his arm, wincing as he held the position for the requisite ten seconds. "We have a lot to adjust to, for sure."

"Jah."

Daed lowered his arm and rested a moment. He looked ten years older. Had the shooting taken so much out of him? Maybe Troy's confession had.

Daed cleared his throat. "You need to know something. Your sister Sharon's in jail, along with her new husband, for sexually abusing Meghan. Troy took me aside and told me this morgen. Not sure how long they'll be there, but it will be at least until there's a trial. And I'm not sure when that is yet. Meghan will be staying with us indefinitely."

"Sharon abused her own dochter?" Janna's eyes widened in shock. How could her sister do such a thing? No wonder Meghan was such a mess.

"She didn't abuse her, but she knew it was going on and did nothing about it. Troy says they confessed when they were confronted by the local police. She hasn't communicated with me." Daed slumped in the chair. "I cannot believe that a child of mine would land in jail. I dread telling the other preachers. They might ask me to forfeit my position. A man called of God is supposed to be above reproach in every area, including the lives of his children. This reflects on how I raised all of you."

"Daed...." Janna wanted to encourage him, but she didn't know what to say. After all, she was hardly above reproach. She had eloped with Troy—and would be shunned in the not-too-distant future. That had to reflect badly on Daed, as well. And if their marriage ended, even more shame. She couldn't allow that to happen. *Lord, help me to learn to forgive* him. *Help him to kum to love me again.* She pulled in a breath. "I'm sorry for all the ways I've hurt you, Daed."

He released the pulley, stood, and pushed the chair back under the table. "Enough of that. Troy is a blessing. And he needed to be here as much as I've needed him here. I really feel the Lord is working this out, in His mysterious way. Now I just have to wait on Him to work out the rest of the details. Troy was an answer to prayer with Meghan. He was an answer to prayer for Will, as well, even though we knew nothing of the circumstances beforehand."

"But…." Janna blinked back tears.

Daed crossed the room and hugged her. "The Lord works in mysterious ways, Janna. We might not have chosen to lose Zach, but the Lord is using it for gut. We need to accept this. I know you're struggling. I see it. I know Troy does, as well. Forgiveness is for the benefit of the forgiver, not the forgiven. For your sake, you have to do this." He backed away. "Have you told him you love him?"

Janna shook her head. "Nein." Not once. Not ever. Shame rattled her.

"Tell him, Janna. He needs to know this."

"I don't know if I can." She did love him. She always had. But the words seemed to get lodged in her throat. Even Troy seemed to have trouble with those three words, having mouthed them to her just that once. And maybe whispering them in her dreams.

❧

Troy adjusted his e-reader so that the sun no longer glinted off of it, then settled back in his seat to read. But he couldn't concentrate. He sighed. How could he fix his relationship with Janna? He loved her. Maybe he needed to say those words. Would that be enough? Everything had changed between them since he'd confessed about the accident. He'd pulled away from her, emotionally and physically, as a result. He wished he knew how to mend the problem.

He exited out of the book he'd been reading and clicked on a Bible program, instead. Maybe God's Word would offer some answers.

He would search for instructions on how men should love their wives. He was so new at this marriage thing, he didn't have a clue where to begin when it came to showing his love. Maybe it wouldn't hurt to pick up a red rose—make that a dozen—and bring them home to her tonight. Just as a beginning. Maybe he could beg for forgiveness again.

Should he resign from his job? Would that help? He shut his eyes. *Lord, show me what to do. Save our marriage. Help Janna to really forgive me somehow.*

He knew he shouldn't expect that from her, when he hadn't been able to forgive himself until he'd seen a recreation of the accident. He was asking for the impossible.

His radar beeped. Troy looked up as a white Taurus drove past, going five miles over the speed limit. He merged into the traffic lane and followed the car, his siren blaring. When the Taurus pulled over, he parked behind it and called the plate in, then walked up to the window. He'd lost count of how many times he'd caught housewives speeding. Police work was no longer the fulfilling job it had once been. If only he found true forgiveness, he'd turn in his badge in a heartbeat. "May I see your license and registration?"

The elderly woman opened her wallet and handed it to him. "Sorry, Officer. It's wedged in there and I can't get it out." She shrugged. "I'm eighty-three, and my fingers aren't as strong as they used to be. I don't know what I did with my registration. I looked in the glove box, but maybe it's in the door beside me. Am I allowed to open the door and look?"

"Keep your hands where I can see them and move slowly." Not that she was much of a risk. Troy glanced at the license as Betty Sue pawed through the mess of papers in the door. Finally she unearthed the necessary slip and waved it at him with a flourish. Troy tried to keep his grin at bay. "Do you know how fast you were going?"

"Yes, but I had to get there before I forgot where I was going." She frowned. "And now I forgot where that is. Oh, dear."

Troy chuckled. "I'm letting you go with a warning this time. But please slow down so you arrive alive, wherever you're going. Besides, the next officer might not be so nice."

"Thank you, Officer." Betty Sue took back her wallet and registration. "I'll drive slower, I promise. Maybe I'll remember where I'm going before I give up and go home."

Troy nodded. He scanned the road as the woman closed her door and buckled up her seatbelt. As he started back to his vehicle, a beat-up pickup flew by, almost hitting him. It looked like a paint store had exploded on the sides. Loud music blared from the open windows. The passengers looked back and laughed. His anger flaring, Troy ran back to his car, yanked the seatbelt across his chest, and pulled out again, lights flashing, siren wailing.

There were three or four people crammed inside the cab of the truck. He really couldn't tell for sure by the way they jostled around. The driver pulled to the side of the road sooner than Troy would have expected. As he called in the license plate, the truck shook as the occupants—men or boys, he couldn't tell—scuffled in the front seat. Troy got out of his vehicle, shut the door, and approached the truck.

A loud crack broke the silence. Troy jerked the door open, crouched behind it, and called for backup, then pulled out his gun and returned fire.

Chapter 35

*J*anna escaped into the quietness of the dawdi-haus. She took a few steps into the bedroom and glanced down at the bed, covered in a log cabin quilt she'd made as a teenager. It was beautiful, with rich, vibrant colors of black, turquoise, and purple. She reached for the pillow closest to her. Troy's. She hugged it against her, remembering the time she'd done this at his rental haus. His piney scent filled the pillow. Filled her senses. *Ach, Troy.*

Her eyes burned. She fell to her knees beside the bed as the tears fell. Troy was still the same person she'd fallen in love with as a child. The same person she'd married. Nothing had changed, except for her perception of him.

He was human. He sinned. So did she. And if the Almighty could forgive him, and if Daed could, how could she do anything less?

Lord, I'm so sorry. Forgive me for being so judgmental of Troy. Help me to do what I must to restore our relationship.

She didn't know how long she knelt there beside the bed, praying. But when she finally stood to her feet, a sense of peace washed over her.

Troy fired another two shots and ducked back behind the door as a bullet whistled past his ear. He hoped someone was praying for him. Janna, maybe. Did she care for him enough to think to pray? Janna might be a widow before he had the chance to tell her he loved her. Pain jolted him, but not from a bullet. Hearing sirens, he glanced behind him and saw a police cruiser squeal to a stop. Another came toward them, swerving across oncoming traffic. Out spilled several officers to end the dangerous confrontation. The paint-splattered truck had both the highway side front and rear tires blown out, and one of the men's arms dangled, useless, by his side. Troy didn't want to shoot to kill unless he had to, and, so far, he hadn't been hit. There had been some close calls, though, and his police car had taken several dings.

Traffic squealed to a stop as an officer skidded sideways across the lane behind Troy, and then others converged on them from the front. The four men in the truck surrendered and were handcuffed and patted down. Several officers searched the vehicle and confiscated ten pounds of illegal drugs. When most of the dirty work was done, an officer opened one of the lanes and started directing traffic through.

A car pulled up behind Troy's cruiser as he shoved one of the shooters into the backseat. He glanced over and saw it was a white Taurus.

It appeared to be the same elderly woman he'd pulled over just before the shoot-out. She sat there, not opening the door or moving, just watching him. It made him nervous. Another police officer approached her car, then returned a few moments later. "She wants to talk to you."

"I'll be over as soon as I can." Troy expelled a breath and tried to imagine what she might have to say to him. He couldn't think of anything, unless she wanted to share that she'd finally remembered her destination. A couple of minutes later, he walked back to her.

She rolled down her window.

He peered into the car. "Is something wrong, ma'am?"

"I just wanted you to know that God told me I needed to pray for you. And I am. Have been, since that pickup almost ran you over."

Troy blinked. Some of those bullets had come awfully close. "Thank you, ma'am." Wow. God had provided prayer backup. *Danki, Lord.*

"And something else. This is unusual, I know, but I feel I need to tell you something. I don't know if you're familiar with the Bible or not, but there's a story in there about the prodigal son. It's in Luke, I think."

Troy nodded. His heart raced. "I'm familiar with it."

She smiled. "The son returned home to the father and was gathered back into the fold. I have no idea why you need to know this, but I'll keep praying for you."

Troy managed a nod even as his heart flooded with hope. He remembered the words he'd felt earlier: *Trust Me.* An amazing peace washed over him.

❧

Janna was putting supper on the table when she heard tires crunch over the gravel. Too early for Troy to return home. She wished he were home, so she could make things right between them. So she could say the words he needed to hear.

Daed pushed away from the table and walked over to the door. "I hope it isn't that physical therapist kum back because she forgot to give me some exercises." He flung the door open. "Troy?"

Janna hurried to the door. She stepped out on the porch as Troy emerged from the truck carrying a vase of red roses and a small white teddy bear. Her heart lodged in her throat.

"Janna, I'm sorry." Troy closed the truck door with his hip and approached. "I don't know how to begin to make things right between us, but I want to try. Whatever it takes."

She caught her breath as the door clicked shut behind her. She glanced around. Daed had disappeared. Giving them privacy. She looked back at Troy.

He held out the roses.

Tears blurred her vision. "I forgive you, Troy. I really do." This time, she felt the freedom behind the words. "I'm so sorry I—"

"I resigned from work. Handed in my gun and badge." Troy moved another step closer and expelled a breath. "I will join the church. You can marry me—as planned—after I do, if you'll still have me. And I hope you will, Janna." He pressed the teddy bear into her hands. A red ribbon was tied around its neck with two hearts, each bearing the words "I love you," dangling from each end. "I'll do whatever it takes to win you. Ich liebe dich."

Tears brimmed in Janna's eyes. "Ich liebe dich." She pressed her fingers against her lips, then touched them to his to keep him from speaking. "I always will. I'm so sorry I was unforgiving. But you don't need to join the church for me. I'll still love you, whether you do or not."

Troy set the vase on the porch step. "I want to. I've always wanted to return, but only as a forgiven man. I don't need to run from my past anymore. I'm accepted in the beloved."

Janna wrapped her arms around his neck and pressed against him. "Ich liebe dich." She kissed his cheek. His ear. His eye. The corner of his mouth. And then whispered the words again.

His lips met hers. Brushed against them. He pulled away, hesitated, and glanced toward the haus. She giggled when he scooped her up into his arms. With another quick kiss, he carried her into the dawdi-haus, kicking the door shut behind him. "Ich liebe dich. Forever and ever."

About the Author

Laura V. Hilton graduated with a business degree from Ozarka Technical College in Melbourne, Arkansas. A member of the American Christian Fiction Writers, she is a professional book reviewer for the Christian market, with more than a thousand reviews published on the Web.

Her first series with Whitaker House, The Amish of Seymour, comprises *Patchwork Dreams*, *A Harvest of Hearts*, and *Promised to Another*. In 2012, *A Harvest of Hearts* received a Laurel Award, placing first in the Amish Genre Clash. *Surrendered Love* follows *Healing Love* in her latest series, The Amish of Webster County.

Previously, Laura published two novels with Treble Heart Books, *Hot Chocolate* and *Shadows of the Past*, as well as several devotionals. Laura and her husband, Steve, have five children, whom Laura homeschools. The family makes their home in Arkansas. To learn more about Laura, read her reviews, and find out about her upcoming releases, readers may visit her blog at http://lighthouse-academy.blogspot.com/.